on the streets of New York only one color matters...

# HARDWHITE

NOVEL BY
## ANTHONY WHYTE

BASED ON THE SCREEENPLAY BY
## SHANNON HOLMES

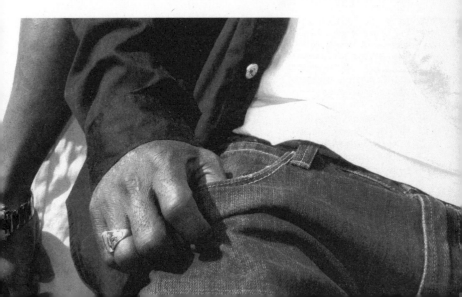

# HARDWHITE
SHANNON HOLMES

WHERE
**HIP HOP
LITERATURE**
BEGINS...

AUGUSTUS
PUBLISHING

© 2010 Augustus Publishing, Inc.
ISBN: 9780982541531

Novel by Anthony Whyte
Story By Shonnon Holmes
Edited by Juliet White
Creative Direction & Photography
by Jason Claiborne

Augustus Publishing paperback JUNE 2010
www.augustuspublishing.com

**No man of woman born, coward or brave, can shun his destiny.**
-Homer, Iliad, VI

# Acknowledgements

REST IN PEACE
Mrs. Diane Lewis
Jeanne Lee Moultrie
Stanley Rice AKA Stan Strong
Gloria Jean Harrison

FREETODDWILLIAM@AOL.COM
Facebook/FreeToddWilliams
YouTube/FreeToddWilliams Campaign
Write to: The free Todd Williams Campaign
P.O. Box 690066 Bronx, New York 10469

I would like to thank Gerard Emptage AKA Shakim, and Angelo Barretto.

To all the readers, thank you for supporting, and keep on reading. Special thanks to Augustus Manuscript Team, Shannon Holmes, Jason Claiborne, Jasmine Clemente, Tamiko Maldonado, Juliet White, and Anthony Whyte.

**Shannon Holmes wishes to thank the Cast & Crew of Hard White for all your help in making my dream come true.**

Roberta James
Freida Hickson
Richard Samalot/ RTS Films
Filmmaking Shaun
Luwana Arthur
Brandon Munroe
Keenan Perkins
Damion Omar Lee
Charles Murray
Craig Jihad Scott
Ian J. Findlay
Shana A. Solomon

Miriam Morales
Edgar Ribon
Kim Knotts
Torre' Reigns
Carlos Hendricks
Nikko Nin
Nickalette Nin
Rich Rivera Julie
Nelson Nin
Floyd Cromwell

E D E N W A L D

# prologue

In New York City's most northern borough of the Bronx, lies the second biggest Housing project in the city, the infamous Edenwald Houses. Its brownish-red brick buildings stand out ominously like an eyesore against the urban landscape. The enormous project buildings can be seen from near and far. Just like its high visibility, Edenwald project's reputation, for murder and mayhem, exceeds itself. Edenwald's dark side lives in infamy. The mere mention of the name, Edenwald projects seems to threaten the tranquility of the surrounding neighborhoods. Some residents from the criminal element are fond of saying, "Edenwald is loved by few, hated by many, but respected by all." That statement is by no means a stretch of the imagination.

The Edenwald housing area is a city within a city, an occupied territory, a breeding ground for lawlessness, and is impossible to police for extended periods of time. Since construction was complete, the projects have been a thorn in the side of the 47th police precinct. It's a place where outsiders dare to venture, due to Edenwald's penchant for violence. Inside this urban maze is a place where poverty, hopelessness and ignorance, could set in at any moment to create a murderous climate. Edenwald is a place that seldom offers happy endings, success stories are rare. There is a black cloud that seems to hang over Edenwald project and it's called negativity. Here everyday young lives are up for

HOUSES

grabs and any given day could be your last.

Inside the confines of Edenwald projects there lies an inescapable hunger, an unquenchable thirst of the have-nots, for the finer things in life. Some residents are willing to risk it all, life and liberty, in an all out pursuit of the American Dream. The drug game offers residents their only viable option and gives them a glimmer of hope. Selling it, however misleading it might be, there's always a slim chance for overnight success. The ever-present allure of fast money is, in most cases, way too easy to resist.

In this day and age the drug game may be played out for many, resulting in stiff penalties handed out by the law. The drug game is alive and well twenty-four-seven in the Edenwald projects. It's a never ending cycle that only changes with faces and names. Here a drug profit is willingly exchanged for a lifetime of despair. In Edenwald projects this process repeats itself hundreds of times, from dealer to fiend.

Despite the drug raids and sweeps by local and federal law enforcement agencies that have been deemed successful. Temporarily put an end to the drug crews that once ruled the projects with iron fists. Nowadays, younger, brazen and even more dangerous criminals seemed to have sprouted up overnight. For all intents and purposes the end of the crack era marked the birth of a new generation of thugs, killers, stickup kids and would-be drug kingpins…

Welcome to Edenwald… Come in peace or leave in pieces.

# My Projects
Chapter One

Melquan's nostrils flared, entering the project building. A pungent odor suddenly assaulted his senses. A sour expression donned his face immediately. With his nose squinted in disgust, Melaquan quickly scanned the building's lobby for the source of the foul smell. Instantly his eyes revealed the puddle of fresh urine sighted dormant in a corner. He paused staring in disbelief at the golden cesspool of bodily fluid waste.

"Nasty muthafuckas…!"

His mind was distracted when he cursed aloud. Melquan could not, for the life of him, understand the ignorance of people who pissed inside the building. A lifetime of living in Edenwald projects had numbed him to the stupidities and atrocities of its residents, nothing really surprised him anymore. Whoever did this was doing one of two things, either going upstairs to an apartment, or headed outside. Wherever the destination was, that place would be better equipped to handle urine. It seemed like the projects halls, elevators where portable potties to people, even if the staircases and hallways amplified foul odors.

Down right nasty in his book, Melquan thoughts turned to his mother, who still lived in these projects. She had taught him a long time ago about not violating the place where you lived. Probably some stupid kid or a fiend Melquan reasoned.

Shaking his head, Melquan quickly distanced himself from the foul smell. Taking stairs two at a time in rapid succession, Melquan leapt and bounded. Without so much as breaking a sweat or wrinkling his expensive True Religion jeans, he vaulted up the steps from one floor to another. The sight and smell of the puddle of piss was soon a distant memory.

Running up a few flights of stairs was a small feat for twenty-four year old, Melquan. He was an athlete in every sense of the word. Six feet tall and a chiseled two hundred and ten pounds, the dark skinned, bald headed young man had rugged good looks, and a strong bone structure.

Melquan grew up playing every sport and project game imaginable. There were a few shorts stints at Riker's Island jail, which didn't do anything but helped build his physique. Melquan, unlike most young men his age, didn't smoke weed, and had no bad habits that would hurt his athletic prowess.

There was another added incentive for staying in tip-top shape. Dealing with the police was an occupational hazard. In his profession as a drug dealer, to be out of shape meant the difference between going to prison for an alleged criminal charge or evading the police. He was a soldier in the war going on outside his project window, and the chance of him engaging with the enemy on any given day was highly likely.

Right now, keeping in shape was the last thing on Melquan's mind. Pussy was the motivating factor in his venture into the project night. He was on his way to Precious' apartment. She was his ride or die, side-chick, catering to all his needs, business and otherwise. Precious was a down-ass-bitch and always had his back. Funny thing about Melquan and Precious' relationship, other than mixing business with pleasure, he already had a PC, India. When they were on good terms, Melquan was the Mack, living from time to time with India.

Melquan reached Precious' third floor apartment in no time. Before he could even use the doorknocker on apartment 3A, Precious quietly and quickly opened the door. Precious placed a finger to her lips in an effort to silence him before he could utter a word. It was already too late.

"Hey yo…" Melquan mumbled, caught off guard.

"You gotta hold it down and chill. My grandma's sleepin'," Precious whispered. "And I ain't tryin' to wake her up."

"Oh shit, my bad. I forgot 'bout dat," he whispered, admiring her curves.

Precious didn't have the luxury of sharing bed or body with anyone else. Melquan wouldn't tolerate that. Precious belonged to him alone. The fact that she had to settle for being his sidekick didn't bother her. It was a minor inconvenience that did nothing to stop her from thinking that she could replace India. Someday she could be girlfriend number one. In her mind Melquan was her man just as much as he was India's. How true that was, only Melquan knew. Each visit for sex reinforced Precious' belief.

"Come in Mel," she whispered, grabbing his arm.

Precious was a wild child. Her home situation was in shambles. Her father remained unknown, and her mother, Julie, was strung-out on dope. Precious would see Julie on daily drug treks around the projects. She treated her mother as if she was a stranger. This was the same way her mother had treated her when she was a baby. Precious would give her mother the most despicable stare. Feeling ashamed of herself and condition, her mother would drop her head and walked on. This routine occurred on the occasions when they crossed path.

Precious' grandmother had custody of her at an early age. The arrangement was supposed to be only until Julie completed rehab. Despite bold promises made, Julie never went to rehab. She never came back for her daughter.

The thought of seeing her granddaughter with the child welfare agency never crossed her grandmother's mind. She adopted Precious, loving and raising her as her own. Precious was spoiled rotten by the old woman, and did whatever she wanted. Her grandmother felt Precious never caught the same break that other kids did and gave her a lot of freedom. It was an excuse that Precious used constantly as a crutch to have her way.

Precious pushed her freedom well past the limit. Her grandmother repeatedly caught her having sex with Melquan inside the apartment and gave up trying to prevent it. Precious now had permission to have Melquan over anytime she wanted. He walked inside the darkened apartment with enough illumination on her five foot three, olive toned complexion.

The oversized white wife-beater she wore did nothing to hide her voluptuous breast. Her sexy ass cheeks playing peek-a-boo underneath Victoria Secret boy shorts left little to his imagination. The twinkling of her light brown eyes confirmed what time it was. She was in the mood. Pausing at the doorway she waved her long bleached blonde hair off her shoulder.

Licking his suddenly parched lips, Melquan gazed licentious at his Puerto Rican Princess. Enticing him her flawless 36-26-38 frame had Melquan sizzling with sexual anticipation. Hot sex on the platter was sure to be on tonight's menu.

A devilish smile of approval spread like hot butter across Precious' succulent lips. She loved the fact that Melquan wanted her sexually. Precious wanted him just as bad, in every way possible.

She always wanted him as far back as she could remember. Melquan was that dude for her. Everything about him, the way he walked, talked even his clothes and his style. Melquan's swagger made her bananas. Precious had eyes for him since she was a freshman in John Philip Sousa Junior High School. The guys in her class were too childish and immature for her.

Melquan was a perfect fit. He walked the school hallways with his boys like he owned it. School safety officers, teachers acknowledged him, often calling to the Dean's office to squash beefs that the adults couldn't even handle.

Her infatuation for Melquan grew the older she did. Precious had to love him from a distant until they crossed paths. The fateful event was the sweet sixteen birthday party of a mutual friend. That evening in Edenwald projects recreation center they were formally introduced.

From the jump Precious claimed Melquan and he rewarded her

by taking Precious' virginity. This one fact of her existence was never lost on her. She was peeved to learn how quickly Melquan forget the whole thing as soon as the intercourse was over. It was as if she was one of many to him, but to her Melquan was the one.

Over time, Melquan recognized Precious' true value, especially later when he entered the drug game. Melquan fooled around with other girls from the projects, and were a source of constant strife in her life. Precious understood that when your label was 'That Nigga' in the projects, chicks tend to flock. She was up for the challenge and was ready, willing, and able to fight for her man. There were plenty of battles because rivals for Melquan's affection sprung up left and right. One way or another Precious seemed to always chase them off, except for India.

Precious was known for knocking on chicks' door and challenging them to a fight. She was a drama queen and couldn't wait to do it India. She knew sooner or later, Melquan's spot would be blown.

The duo moved in silence through the darkness, feeling their way down the narrow hallway. On the left and all the way to the back was Precious' small room. Inside the dimly lit room, Melquan was rock hard. Precious could see the imprint of his well endowed member poking through his jeans. Finally here, the moment they had both been waiting all day for. On cue, Precious dropped to her knees and assumed her role.

"Damn mami! Ya head game's official. Ah yeah, I can't even lie. You da truth!"

His whispers came harsh against Precious' ears, her mouth was full, and she didn't bother to reply. Pleasing her man by any means necessary was the only thing on her mind. Precious was going to make it hard for Melquan to stay away from her bed for long periods of time.

Melquan reached down and pulled Precious' hair aside to get a better view of the fellatio being performing.

"Ah yes," he moaned.

Nothing like a bad bitch that could and would give head, Melquan thought. He was relishing the biggest sexual turn-on of his life. This was just the thing Melquan needed to forget all about the problems he was having at home with his girl, India. This was a wonderful way to relieve a little stress. Leaving Precious' warm loving tonight wasn't an option Melquan wanted to exercise. Tomorrow would come and he would deal with India. He was quite skilled at making up excuses about his activities. Melquan used his drug operation as an excuse, or get his mother to cover for him. Either option felt real comfortable. Melquan's eyes closed when the tip of her tongue tickled his balls.

# Everyday Struggle
Chapter Two

A beautiful baby blue sky ushered in the dawn of a new day. The serenity that seemed to exist in the heavens didn't exist on God's green earth. At least not in Edenwald projects where Melquan and Precious were deep asleep. Almost noon and they were awaken by the them loud sounds of New York City's Housing Authority's dump truck mixed in with workers' voices, brooms and rakes performing the daily janitorial duties.

Still half asleep, Melquan awoke to discover Precious sound asleep in his arms. From the feel of the sheets against his skin, Melquan could tell that he was butt-ass naked. The sticky clammy taste of his mouth let him know that he wasn't the only one that engaged in oral sex last night. Melquan always gave as well as he got with Precious.

Drained and in a daze, Melquan glanced at the clock on the cable box. Nine a.m., Melquan had no reason to get up and quickly fell back asleep. He lived the life of a drug dealer. His day didn't start till late afternoon, and spilled into the wee hours of the morning.

Melquan was aware that Precious' grandmother was working a double shift at her job downtown, where she worked in a hotel as a maid. His girlfriend, India was already at work in the Bronx Lebanon Hospital. His burgeoning crack business was being handled capably by his man, Mike Copeland. Melquan was in no rush to leave.

Besides all of that, he wanted to go another round with the luscious body of Precious. There was no better sex than when one had to leave. That alone was worth the wait. Armed with that knowledge, Melquan smiled and drifted to sleep. He enjoyed sleeping. Melquan always said that if death was anything like sleeping, he'd love that too.

Later in the afternoon Precious was the first to wake up. She opened her eyes and gathered her bearing. Pausing, she watched Melquan sleeping for a minute. His muscular chest rose and fell as he inhaled and exhaled. All the while Precious enjoyed the ride, listening to the sound of his heartbeat, staring deeply into Melquan's face and fantasizing.

Melquan awoke. Precious was staring at him, her eyes stained red. He recognized the look and it scared him. Melquan had seen it all too often. It was the look of love.

"Good Morning Mel," she said.

Her lips hugged the words seductively. Melquan glanced back over at the clock on the cable box. It was two-thirty p.m.

"You mean good afternoon, don't you?" he remarked. "Damn, I didn't know it was that late. I didn't mean to sleep that long. Musta been real tired."

"Hmm, hmm, you must've been," Precious said. "Plus I did put it on your ass last night."

"Oh yeah…? Well, I don't remember that too well. You can show me better than you can tell me."

A devilish smirk immediately spread across Precious' pretty face. She glimpsed down at Melquan's manhood showing clear through the white sheet. Precious grabbed as much of it as her hands could hold. She squeezed it so hard that Melquan's dick suddenly rose from overnight slumber and stood at attention. Repositioning her body, Precious began to slither down to Melquan's lower body, pausing when she reached the region around his groin.

"Is this what you want?" She asked.

Her tongue flickering at the tip of his exposed dick. It was hard with the head pointing directly at the ceiling.

"Umm honey… Do you, ma."

Slurps and moans from sexual ecstasy flooded the room. Melquan looked down at Precious' angelic like face while her tongue twirled around the glistening head of his erection. His eyes were soon closed. Unable to take anymore stimulation, he prayed not to cum too soon. His head rolled back and his body became lost in the moment. Precious' tongue coiled around his dick and Melquan moaned from the pleasure. She was on top of her head-game all the while fingering her exposed pussy.

His throbbing member was in her mouth and this brought Melquan to dizzying heights. Precious repositioned herself in a sixty-nine position. Her vagina was warm and when Melquan sucked and fingered Precious' love box it got so hot, sticky cum juice oozed into his mouth.

Upstairs in the apartment, sex was already bubbling over. While outside Precious' room window, the project world below was beginning to heat up.

"Yo, that's my custy, son!" One dealer shouted. "C'mon Macho, don't even play yerself like that!"

In the Edenwald projects there was no such thing as a drug free zone. Wherever there was money to be made, drugs was sold. Regardless of whose child or parent was around. Dealers would grind all day and night. Hard white was the product primary pushed.

The 227th street drive known as the horseshoe, also referred to as the shoe, was currently the officially the largest open-air drug market in Edenwald. The shoe was comprised of seven short, three-story brick buildings. This was the prime destination for drug addicts seeking the best crack cocaine. In Edenwald drug money was known to shift from one side of the projects to another. It could go from strip-to-strip, or even building-to-building. There were two factors that dictated this shift, police presence and better product. Right now the horseshoe had both things in its favor.

School was already out on this unseasonably warm fall day. Temperature of was high, and crowds of kids scattered about the projects' grounds. Drug dealers, drug addicts, and older residents were outside doing whatever it was that they did to enjoy what was left of the Indian summer day. Because of the warm temperature, there were more people out than usual.

In midst of all this madness, a cat and mouse game was being waged by a single addict against the dealers. He was frail, and shabbily dressed. Everyone knew the African American crack-head named, George, moving almost undetected from dealer to dealer. George seemed like he was on legitimate business to cop crack, just like he had done a couple other times that day. He would closely examine each glassine bag handed to him, tasting the product each time.

"Nah, I'm good," George stated and walked away shaking his head. "That shit don't even taste right. I'll pass. Know-wha-I'm-sayin'…?"

After rejecting that dealer's product, he proceeded to another, and repeated the same act.

"Who got that good shit?" he'd asked.

"Right here, fam," another unsuspecting dealer hollered. "These other niggas out here got garbage. Fam, you know me. You've copped from me before. Just tell me how many you want?"

"Slow your roll," George hastily suggested. "I copped from a lot niggas out here. Know-wha-I'm-sayin'…? What makes you so special?"

The young dealer immediately began to show George a hand full crack rock he removed from a large ziplock bag. The conversation would be momentarily ceased. Silently salivating over each individual bag, the crackhead carefully selected the largest rock he could find. Greed mingled with the sickness of getting high raced through George's mind.

"Somebody beat me last night," he complained. "I bought some shit and the shit didn't even burn. You believe that? Sonofabitch sold me some synthetic coke! So I hope you don't mind if I taste this shit. I need to know if this is the real deal before I spend my paper with you. Know-wha-I'm-sayin'…?"

The young hustler gave the man a funny look. There was just something about him that he couldn't quite put his finger on it. He remembered something an old-timer once told him, 'usually when people talk a lot they're lying'. Despite his better judgment, he let the man do as he had asked.

Scrutinizing his every move, the dealer eyed George carefully opening one of the packets. George removed the rock, nibbled on it, and handed it back to the dealer. He was awaiting any signs of approval from George.

"That was good money, right?" the dealer asked.

George firmly shook his head and continued on about his business as if nothing had ever happened. Unbeknownst to him he was now under the suspicious glare of a young, wild, irate drug dealer. The dealer made a signal to other dealers from his crew.

Not far away, a group of youths gathered round to witness the current rage of a freestyle battle rap contest. Two of the hottest rappers from the projects who also peddle drugs faceoff in a rhyme fest. The contest was more interesting because they were from different drug set. There was a genuine dislike between the two MC's and this fact was sure to spill over into their lyrics.

"Yo, I'm a spit sumthin light fa y'all. Check— check it out, huh…" Young Feddi began.

Wish a nigga try it, that nigga won't be eatin' put 'em on a diet. I been told niggaz I was on my shit, fuck all these haters man they just on my dick….

I'm da liviest. I let da nina spit, break 'em like Kit-Kat, flip 'em like a Sidekick….

I'm cheddar getter AKA cheddar flipper, that Bitch you lovin' ain't wifey she just lettin' you lick her…

"Whoa who-who …" a roar went up from the crowd that had gathered.

They were still buzzing when Sylk Smooth confidently stepped up. Sylk Smooth spat, clearing his throat.

Hear my bars prove I'm fire, sickest nigga ballin since Magic retired… When its beef he known to take the track route, threw the car in reverse the only time he backed out……

Fiends say my dope is Ipod music, once you hear it you gone be noddin' to it. They like Sylk got that Brett Favre gene. No matter the damn team I stay with green….

Bars murder shit call it disaster rap, gotta lotta so called

MC's taking casket naps…

This is sleep you won't see him wake, tryin' to put a square in a round hole you outta shape…

My rhymes piff like haze and jars, this year I'm goin' Cinglar, I'm raisin' my bars…

"Whoa-a-a- whoa…" The crowd really went wild.

Each of rappers had supporters and they were cheering for their man. The approval from the crowd ignited the rappers passion to outperform the man in front of him. The competition was mild at first, a disrespect word here, and there. Finger pointing, yelling, and offensive body language suggested that the battle could get ugly in a New York minute. For twenty minutes straight Young Feddi and Sylk Smooth went bar for bar, with no clear-cut winner.

Word spread like virus spread through the projects about the rap battle. The infectious performance caused the crowd to grow, attracting the attention of grown-ups as well as the brother and sister tandem of Jose and Maria Torres. Dressed in catholic uniforms, they were on their way home from school.

"Oh, shit!" Jose cursed. "What the fuck is goin' on here? I know these niggas ain't battling?"

Maria heard the change in her brother's language and stared at him in disbelief. His attitude changed immediately and she shook her head as if she never heard a curse word in her life. Unlike her brother, Maria was not as adapt to the ways of project living. In her mind she didn't live in the projects. She pretended to only go there to sleep. Her innocent act always irked Jose. He simply ignored her.

Jose was curious and excited to see the battle taking place. Glad handing with all around, he seemed to know everybody including the two participants. His Catholic schooling seemed to be the only thing that separated, Jose and his childhood peers. Every free moment he got, he ran the projects with them.

A latchkey child who preferred to sit in the house and watch

TV, Maria, was the opposite of her brother. She was never outside playing with other girls her age. She was Jose's lil sister to those who knew her.

Suddenly Jose broke away from his sister and rushed closer to the battle.

"Jose, what do you think you are doing?" Maria yelled. "You know daddy said we have to come straight home after school. No stopping for nothing! I'm telling!"

"Maria fallback," Jose quickly responded. "Stop bein' a lil' tattletale… I'm just goin' to see what's goin' on. So chill out, I'll be right back."

Maria defiantly crossed her arms. Infuriated she stood on the sidewalk staring at her brother. He moved closer to where the crowd of teens was hanging. Wading through the crowd, Jose shouted out an abundance of greetings and daps to whomever he knew. He managed to make his way directly into the sea of bodies that were waving with the rappers.

Meanwhile inside the horseshoe, George was still running his game to perfection. He found no shortage of dealers to hustle. George continued perpetrating his fraudulent game on many unsuspecting dealers. Tasting the crack to test the potency of it, he kept right on turning down product.

"Rodney," a dealer called out. "Lemme git dat… I got a custy waitin' on me."

The look on the crowd's face suggested they were upset that this kid had bust through and straight up interrupted a good rap battle.

"My dude, dis shit can't wait?" He barked. "Can't you see what the fuck I'm doin'?"

The dealer gazed coldly at the rapper before speaking.

"Yo, my man, fuck this battle shit right now. This shit ain't gonna feed you when you broke, nigga… You better snap outta it and make this paper. I'm tryin' to help you out. I already knocked off my PK."

"Aw-aw-aw-aw man, that's that bullshit!" Someone in the crowd shouted. Rodney abruptly exited the crowd.

"Just say no nigga! C'mon back and finished what you started."

"Loser…! Loser!" The crowd chanted.

"I got bizness to handle," the rapper shouted back. "I'll be right back. Don't go nowhere gimme a minute. Ya heard?"

Rodney was clearly bothered by the crowd's lack of understanding. He couldn't just go on rapping and not go to take care of his hustle, making drug transaction. The further away he got from them the more furious he became. He began looking for anything to spark an argument with his co-worker. He had to take out his frustrations on someone.

"And yo, what the fuck is wrong wit you calling out my government like that? Huh?" Rodney roared. "Nigga, out here I told you my name is Feedi. F-E-E-D-I," he said, spelling his moniker. "Man, save that other shit for school. How many times I gotta tell you that?"

"Why you spazin' like that fam?" The other dealer responded. "It ain't even that serious."

"Speak fa delf, nigga! I don't like niggas callin' me out my government… Now where da fuck is da custy at? He better be copin' more than just one joint too… The way I'm feelin' right now—"

"Be easy, nigga. He right over there, nigga…!"

In a rush, Rodney removed a black pouch filled with tiny crack vials from his crotch as if he had just wiped his ass.

"How many you want?" He barked.

"Lemme see what you got first?" George impatiently replied.

"Nigga it's da same shit you always cop! I ain't got time for no bullshit, man."

Rodney stared intently at the fiend before opening up his black bag and removing a few samples. George studied the vials closely looking for the fattest rock. Once he spotted it, he opened the vial putting the crack to his taste test.

"This shit ain't all that, George said, voice his disapproval. "This shit got too much baking soda in it. All you niggas must got the same batch of shit or the same muthafucka cooking up for y'all. I don't know if you niggas sellin' cake mix or drugs? I can't do nothing with that there, man... Here take this shit back."

"What?"

With his teeth tightly clenched, Rodney glared angrily at George who was attempting to hand him back the vial of crack. George shoved it at the dealer repeatedly trying to return the product. The dealer fiercely stared at George, eyeing closely. Something seemed to click. Rodney recognized the fiend from around the area.

His peoples from Grenada Place, on the North side of the projects, had beaten down a fiend for trying to buy crack with fake money. Now Rodney had come face to face with the same conniving crackhead. Still he didn't let on to the man's true identity. He knew the man had a bad habit of burning dealers out of crack, but he wasn't about to take an L to feed this fiend's crack habit. Finally he announced, "You ain't about to play me out. Dat's yours, money. I don't even want that back. You bit it-you bought it!"

The commotions attracted the attention of other drug dealers. A few quickly moved in closer. George felt nervous from all the eyes on him. His speech slurred, and his tongue now moved uncontrollably inside his mouth. Crack cocaine was slowly disintegrating in his mouth and he was trying to reposition it under his tongue.

"Yo, why da fuck you sound like dat? Fuck is wrong with your mouth?" Another dealer asked.

"Son, dis nigga on some ol' bullshit!" Someone else said.

Unsure of what to do next, the fiend began to take unnoticeable baby steps backwards. He was copping a plea, imploring the dealer to take back his vial of crack.

"I don't want no trouble. It's not like that. And you know me?" George said, pleading.

"Money, you got about two seconds to produce my bread. I ain't tryin' a hear dat other shit!" Rodney interrupted.

"I think this nigga got something in his mouth. Yo, my man, open up ya mouth for a sec," another dealer chimed.

George felt his luck running out. From the screws on the dealer faces, he knew he was in deep trouble. He started looking for another avenue to escape. Rodney struck George with a straight right hand and those thoughts vanished from his mind. The blow landed on George's jaw, but it lacked enough power to put him on the seat of his pants. He tried to run, but all thoughts of escape came to a crashing halt when several drug dealers pounced on him.

"Get him!"

The battle cry rang out and everyone seemed to respond to it. Kicks and punches was George's reward for his dishonesty and trickery. The drug dealers rained down each blow on him with bad intentions. George's body exploded with pain as he absorbed the punishment. Soon more and more kids joined the fray. The beating had snowballed to unprecedented proportions in a matter of seconds. Everyone wanted a piece of the action it turned into a feeding frenzy.

George had no choice but to take his medicine. Finally the fiend fell to the ground and the angry mob stomped him. Still the man took his beating and refused to open his mouth. The ruckus drew lots of attention.

Melquan was in the bathroom taking a leak and heard the faint sounds of the scuffle outside the window. He finished letting nature take its course then went to investigate. He heard what sounded like a cry for help from Precious.

"Melquan! Melquan!" Precious yelled. "C'mere! Hurry up!"

Shaking off any excess urine, Melquan put away his penis and hurriedly rushed toward the room.

"Look, they gonna kill that man," she said, looking out the window.

"What? Who?" He replied.

"Come on over here and see for yourself," she said, inviting him. "Look! Oh God!" Precious said.

Melquan looked out the window and saw a mob pummeling someone with their feet and fists. He couldn't identify who was on the receiving end of the beating, but the sight of the mob against one person was a disturbing thing. This would draw unwanted attention. Melquan thoughts turned to business. It wasn't good for his drug business. He saw his money going down the drain.

"Mel are you gonna just let shit go down like that?" Precious questioned. "Them niggas about to catch a body out there."

"My team ain't involved, so I really don't give a fuck what they do?" He deadpanned.

"That's beside the point, Mel. You better care. If they kill him then it'll be too hot out here for God knows how long. Nobody will be able to walk outside much less sell some fuckin' drugs," Precious said. "Mel, you do need to look a little bit closer. There's a few heads out there that's slinging for y'all and they involved in it too. Shit's gonna get outta hand and someone gonna call the cops."

Precious' words resonated in his ear. Everything she had said was true. Melquan had to rethink his course of action. He quickly made a decision. Melquan threw open one of Precious' drawers and took out a fully loaded semi-automatic nine-millimeter. Gun in hand, he dashed out the apartment.

He had moved so fast that she had no time to protest. Precious ran to the door, hoping that Melquan wouldn't do something he might regret. She was nervous about what Melquan might do next. She went back to the window and continued to watch the beat down. At any second she was expecting Melquan to appear with his gun blazing.

The unmistakable sound of gunfire suddenly caused all activities to standstill. Having heard it so much, most residents of the projects were immune to the loud clap. The guilty parties began to scatter like roaches when lights were turned on. Their eyes were desperately trying to locate the shooter.

Even the fiend, who was bloodied and beaten, curled up on the ground in a fetal position, looked around from his defensive position to see who was shooting. The residents of Edenwald projects scanned their urban terrain. They saw Melquan looking down on them from the roof with the nine raised high over his head.

"Git da fuck off a him!" He barked. "Don't nobody else touch him. Dat's my word, if anyone of y'all lay another hand on him, the next shot I let off won't be in the air! Y'all niggas about ta make it real hot out here over some ol' bullshit."

The power of the gun was an intoxicating high for most of the youths. Some openly stared at Melquan with envy. With the potential for tragedy in the air, cooler heads prevail. Melquan had restored order. The fiend sprung to his feet, quickly seizing the opportunity to make his escape. Before anyone realized it, he was hauling ass in the opposite direction.

When Maria heard the warning shot, terror gripped her like never before. She stood frozen to the spot. Even before she heard Melquan issue his threat, she knew it was time to go. This wasn't the place for her or her bother to be. They had overstayed their welcome.

"Jose! Jose! C'mon let's go," Maria pleaded, her voice crackling with fear.

Jose rushed over to his sister and placed a protective arm around her shoulder, ushering her out of the area. They left the bustling horseshoe just as all the other spectators began to disperse.

"Jose, you're crazy to hang with those people—"

"Maria, calm down. I'm right here. Stop being a lil' scaredy cat," he chided her.

Maria shook her head, thinking how amazing it was that her brother had recklessly risked their lives for what a rap battle. She walked, staring straight ahead, wanting to admonish him, but knowing that would only lead to an argument, she let it drop. The incident had left Jose excited.

"Dat was crazy right the way they was beating that crazy head up. Then that guy just starts shooting off the roof," Jose chuckled.

She was no longer able to control the angry raging in her.

"No it wasn't crazy. It was stupid. Why were those boys beating up the poor man? And why does that guy even have a gun? He's not a cop! Things like that give the projects a bad name. You just wait till I tell daddy!" Maria said, interrupting her brother.

Jose removed his arm from around Maria's shoulders. He heard what he deemed to be reckless talk and no longer wanted to comfort her. The same event had affected each sibling differently. The violence action that had excited Jose had disgusted Maria. They walked the rest of the way home to their project building in silence. Each of them intensely contemplated what had just transpired.

Melquan returned to Precious' apartment after leaving the rooftop. He stashed the gun until he needed it again.

"I'll see you later," he said then went downstairs.

All eyes were on Melquan, including the leader of his chief

opposition for drug money, Nashawn operated on the other side of the horseshoe. He was the projects' resident bad guy, and walked around with a chip on his shoulder. Nashwan, who stood five feet, eleven inches tall with dark skinned and closely cropped wavy hair, always had something to say about anything and everything. His mouth was the only physically imposing thing about him. His small, beady, black eyes made him appear sneaky.

Oblivious to everyone around him, even those who greeted him, Melquan waved and nodded in response to the outpour of greetings he received. Even with all the love that was showering him, Melquan could feel the hatred too. Overcome by a strong sense of someone's intense stare, he did a quick survey of his surroundings and found the source of the ill feelings, right across the drive. Nashawn was sitting on the benches with a few of his soldiers, mean mugging him. Flaunting hostility in Melquan's direction caused a light laugh to escape Melquan's lips. It was pointless for him to acknowledge Nashawn's presence in any other way.

Melquan saw Nashawn but their eyes didn't lock long enough to make Melquan uneasy. Nashawn felt slighted by Melquan's cool reaction. To save face he deliberately started loud talking about Melquan.

"Nigga's fuckin' clowns," Nashawn spat. "What da fuck did that do? Huh? Niggas got a few guns and start thinkin' they gangsta for lettin' off a few shots. Now all of a sudden they wanna regulate the block and shit. Who died and left that clown the keys to the kingdom, huh? I ain't havin' it. I wish a muthafucka would say sumthin to the kid or any of my people. Word…!"

Nashawn's verbal assessment of the situation had more bark than bite. Still he came away with the notion that something like this wasn't happening again without repercussions.

From across the drive, Melquan could not hear exactly what Nashawn was saying. Melquan saw their nonthreatening stares. He knew that whatever the tough talk being made, Nashawn wasn't prepared to back it up. It was all just talk. If Nashawn truly had a beef all he had to do was bring his ass across the drive and approach him. They could get it popping right then and there. Melquan tired get back to the business at hand, but couldn't dodge the thought.

The drive was divided, and if a war popped off between them, the general consensus was that more people disliked Nashawn. In a popularity contest, however, the tide could turn at any given moment. Melquan was a good dude who never gave anyone the business that didn't have it coming. Nashawn on the other hand, was a snake, the grimy type who would turn on his friends if he felt he could get away with it.

Melquan walked up to the guilty parties and admonished them for their senseless use of violence.

"Y'all niggas know y'all dead wrong," he announced. "What da fuck is on y'all's minds? We tryin' a open this shit back up and keep it that way."

The young boys looked up at Melquan nodding. They took their medicine in silence none of them dared objecting. They knew they were at fault.

As soon as Melquan was done, a motorized wheelchair, rapidly approached, guided by a middle aged, African American male. He was well dressed in the latest athletic apparel. Despite his physical handicap, the man appeared to be in an upbeat mood.

"What up, Charlie Rock?" Melquan said.

"Hey Melquan, what's good nephew?" Charlie Rock answered, reaching out with a handshake.

Charlie Rock used nephew as an affectionate term on younger dudes he liked. There were no family ties between him and Melquan.

"Ain't a damn thing, Unk. What's really good wit you?" Melquan greeted, shaking Charlie Rock's manicured hand.

He bent over and warmly embraced the man in the customized

wheelchair, a sign of respect.

"Nada, but what's up with all that shooting I heard when I was up on the Ave, nephew? These niggas wilding out again?"

"Nah Unk, that was me… These lil' niggas out here were about to beat a crack-head to death over nothing. Wilding out, you know how they do? I tried to tell them niggas to stop. But they wouldn't listen. So I had to pull out the hammer just to get their attention."

"Man didn't I teach you better than that. We only pull out guns for a reason, not for the season. A true hustla only uses gunplay as a last resort. Life or death…"

"Yeah, I know that, Unk. I was kinda wrong there. But—"

"But, but nothing. There are no excuses, nephew. You keep that shit up and you'll be the hottest thing around here. Much too much snitches around for all that. These lil' niggas ain't worth the shells you spent to break that shit up. Next time fuck 'em! Most of 'em don't belong out here anyway. They ain't doin' nothin' 'cept gettin' in a true playa's way."

"Unk, you right," Melquan conceded, taking a deep breathe. "Lately, I've been thinking about locking this whole thing down. It's like every man for himself right now. And that ain't gettin' us nowhere. If everybody come together we could get some real money out here. We can bring the flow back instead of letting fiends go to White Plains or Boston road. We can bring it back to where it used to be."

"That sounds all good. But nephew, you know these niggas. They love disorganized crime. Niggas wouldn't come together to save their own damn lives. Let alone to get some damn money…"

"You ain't neva lied. But I still think it's worth a shot, though. There's too much money out here not to try."

"If you believe that in your heart then you should go for it by all means. Don't let anyone stop you from reaching for the stars. Never let it be said that your ol' Unk is a hater. Nephew, nothin' beats a failure, 'cept a try."

The loud ring tone from a cellphone interrupted the conversation. Melquan checked the caller ID before speaking.

"What's up, Mike…? You back? A'ight, I'm on my way up there right now. You need anything? Razors, sumthin to eat, drink? What? You good…? I'll be right there."

"Where you headed, nephew?"

"I gotta go see my man, Mike Copeland. He waitin' at the spot for me. We gotta handle some BI real quick."

"That's what I like about you Mel, you about your business. You like that shit Tupac use to shout, M-O-P, Money Over Pussy. Lemme tell you sumthin, pussy is like snow, it's fun to play in, you never know when it's gonna cum and only some of it is clean enough to eat. Feel me?"

Melquan let out a hardy laugh. It was vintage Charlie Rock, he was good for that old school advices.

"That's a good one, Unk. I'll remember that. That's all good, but lemme let you in on a lil' secret, Tupac used to say M-O-B… Money ova Bitches… That's just for the record. Now look, Unk, I gotta go."

"Don't lemme hold you up, nephew," Charlie Rock laughed. He moved closer to Melquan. "Listen, before you go, let a nigga hold a couple dollars."

"How much you need? Twenty… Fitty… A hundred dollars…?"

"Twenty dollars is good, nephew. That's all I need."

Melquan reached into his pocket and pulled out a knot. He peeled off a crispy twenty dollar bill and handed it to Charlie Rock.

"And nephew, please do me a favor and go put that money away. The police would love to run up on you and find all that cash. That money would keep 'em supplied with a lifetime of coffee and donuts."

"I feel you. I'm about to bounce up right now."

"A'ight nephew, watch yourself. Be careful coming in and out of these buildings.  Ask me, I know that shit."

"No question.  Good looking out, Unk."

Charlie Rock gave Melquan dap and watched him walking away.  He waited until Melquan was out of sight.  Then he signaled a dealer.

"Hurry, lemme get four nickels.  And keep it on the DL," Charlie Rock said.

# No Place Like Home
Chapter Three

The Torres family lived in building 1159 East 229th St Drive, on the Southside. The brown buicks was nothing special, it was an exact replica of the rest of the other buildings in the projects. Marie and Jose had a hardworking father, Jose Torres Sr. to thank for their modest apartment and any luxuries provided. The furniture was adequate but not extravagant. Most importantly the three bedroom apartment was always clean. Jose Torres Sr. may have been raising his kids in the projects by himself. Mr. Torres did his best to keep the projects, and all the foul mannerisms associated with it, outside his door.

Maria sat on the sofa in the living room. She was quietly doing her homework in front of the television. Down the hall, Jose sat on his single bed. His laptop computer on the Internet, he was multi-tasking, watching music videos on BET's 106 & Park and texting a girl on his Sidekick cellular phone.

The loud jingling of keys and the sound of the lock's cylinder turning caught Maria's attention. She greeted her exhausted dad, Jose Sr. as soon as he entered the apartment. The fortyish, single father smiled when his daughter raced down the narrow hallway and leapt into his arms. Maria kissed him on his cheek as her father beamed.

"Papi, papi, you're home," Maria said, hugging him tightly.

"Hey my princess, you make me feel so good after a hard day at the job. You make me wanna walk through that door again and again. How was your day? Huh?"

Jose Torres Sr. was strikingly handsome with dark piercing eyes. His black curly hair showed a few strands of grey. The bags under his eyes and calloused hands betrayed his otherwise youthful appearance. Jose was a father and a hardworking man in every sense of the word. There was nothing average about him.

"Okay Papi. That's so sweet. You made my day. How was your day, huh?"

"Oh, you know the usual. I gotta do this and fix that. Ah I don't complain, work will always be work. It always leaves you tired. Anyway, sweetheart how was school? You learn anything new today?"

"Of course, I did. We learned how to solve new algebra problems in math class today. I like math. Miss Henderson makes math fun."

"That's good to hear. I pay good money so you and your brother can go to Catholic school. I want the best for the both of yous' future. I don't want you's to turn out to be working at manual labor like myself. I would rather you work for yourself versus working for someone else. I really want you's to go college and become lawyers or doctors. Whatever your hearts desires… I want you's to have a career, not a job. Anytime the city is in a finical pinch, they always talk about cutting jobs. I'm always worrying about being laid-off."

Maria hugged her father and they walked back into the living room. Jose Sr. instantly became aware of his son's absence. This raised some concerns. He paused and glanced around the well-kept place. His home was a source of pride and the things he provided for his children made Jose Sr. feel proud. After a bad start he made a decent man of himself by making a honest living.

"Where's your brother?" he asked after a beat.

"Jose, daddy's home... He wants to see you," Maria shouted down the hall.

She turned to her father with a wide eyed expression then asked, "Guess what happened today, papi?"

"Tell me what happened, princess?"

"On the way home from school today, we saw these boys beating up a crack-head."

"Wha...?"

"And then they started shooting and—"

"Oh yeah...? Where did this happen at?"

"In the horseshoe, papi," Maria said frankly.

"What...? Jose get ya ass out here. Right now, mister...!"

Maria heard the anger resonating in her father's voice. She saw the grimace on his face and felt pleased. She wanted to laugh, Maria knew what her father was about to do next.

"I'll be right there, dad," Jose shouted from the bathroom.

"Get out here now!"

"Yes dad," Jose said, coming into the living room.

"Now, what I told your ass about walking through that damn horseshoe?"

"You told us not to go through there," Jose robotically answered.

"Alrighty then...! Why the hell did you choose to walk through there on your way home from school today? Huh? Tell me why, Jose!"

"I didn't mean to do it. I wasn't thinking I was real tired and, you know… That's the shortest way home."

Jose Sr. took a deep breath before speaking. He was trying hard not to scream in front of his daughter. His stare alternated between both of them. There was complete silence before he passionately started his explanation.

"Look I don't give a damn if it's shorter. I want you to go the extra distance to walk around trouble. I'm not concerned with how quickly you's home. I'm concerned with yous' safety… Both of yous' making it home safely, period… For instance your sister just told me about the shooting and fighting in the horseshoe today. What if something happened to yous? Bullets have no name on them. I've told you over and over, think safety first. Don't go through that damn horseshoe. God forbid if something was to have happened to either one of yous… I'll kill or die for the both of you's. Either way, please don't make me prove it, alright?"

Jose Sr. was feared throughout Edenwald projects in his time. Having run with some of the most notorious thugs and murders that the projects had to offer, he had a rep. The younger Jose was not aware, but his father was no slouch with his hands or a pistol. His English was bad, but in the language of violence, Jose Sr. was very fluent.

He cleared his throat and there was a long pause. Both Jose and Maria listened carefully to their father. They knew he was right in every way possible. Jose was the first to respond.

"Okay dad, I hear you. We won't go through the horseshoe no more."

"That's all I ask. Stay from over there and keep both you's out of harm's way. Jose, you getting older now you gonna have to be more responsible… Do the right thing, and I'll give you the world. Do the wrong thing, and I'll be on your ass…"

Jose glanced up at the vexed expression on his father's face and knew he what was coming next. He would be given an extended list of things to do and there would be no videogames, no Internet until his father was over it.

"Okay dad, I hear you," Jose nodded.

Feeling justified in what she had done, Maria sat smug on the sofa. Her father's talk was what she thought it would be, chastising her brother. She tried to warn Jose, but he wouldn't listen. Maybe now he would. She sat quietly watching as the two males in her life bumped heads.

"You're on punishment for a week. Don't even think about going outside. No more video games until I say so. Put that playstation in my bedroom," Jose Sr. angrily ordered.

Jose stood speechless. He was addicted to videogames in fact he would rather give up his laptop than that. He dragged his feet too long, moving too slow for his father.

"You better put some pep in 'em step! Boy, I'm tellin' you, you ain't gonna like it if I have to go get it."

## A Drug Dealer's Dream
Chapter Four

    Mike Copeland was Melquan's right hand man. He was holed up inside a small, decrepit, two-bedroom apartment on the project's North side. In this despicable working condition, Mike was cooking up crack cocaine on the stove. The sink was filled with dirty dishes that smelled like they hadn't been washed in weeks. Cockroaches were in plain view, from the walls to the floor. Every so often, Mike would see a mice or two darting around the kitchen. None of this mattered to him. Mike's sole focus was on the transparent, nonstick, light brown Pirex pot that was slowly simmering. He watched his product intently, stirring every so often to help the transformation of cocaine into crack.

"Hey, Mike is that thing ready yet?"

He heard the voice and without even glancing around, Mike Copeland knew who it belonged to. Slowly he lifted his eyes from the pot and stared maliciously at Tess. She was dark skin, tall with short nappy hair and the resident crack-head. The apartment belonged to her.

Tess was known to have a foul smell and a nasty attitude. Her poor hygiene and bad habits had contributed to the poor living conditions inside her home. Tess didn't care about much of nothing accept getting high off crack.

"Bitch, do it look like it's ready yet!" Mike spat. "Stop sweatin' me. Fuck outta here!"

Tess gave Mike a dirty stare, not liking his tone of voice. It burned her up to think that somebody was disrespecting her in her own house. She opened her mouth to say something, but thought better. Now was not the time. She didn't want to blow the get high she had coming by arguing with the help. Tess ignored Mike and walked back to her bedroom.

She didn't want to tangle with Mike Copeland and his bad boy swagger. Not only did he talk tough he was about his business. At five-seven, the muscular Mike weighed about one-hundred and sixty pounds. His heart and not his physical attributes were his strong suit. Although he wasn't physically imposing, Mike Copeland was menacing just the same.

Tess was banished to her room and Mike concentrated on the task at hand. Seeing that the cocaine was beginning to take that gel-like form, he picked up the pot with one hand and turned the cold-water faucet on with the other. The scalding hot and ice cold water mixed causing steam to rise.

Mike Copeland administered liberal doses of cold water until the gel started hardening. Two hundred and fifty grams of powder cocaine had been successfully transformed to crack.

"Oh, baby! You still got it." Mike Copeland said, admiring his handiwork. "Chef Boyardi ain't got nothin' on me!"

Mike Copeland was about to drain the remaining water from the pot and dry the work. He heard the knock at the door. Mike Copeland reached for the government issued nickel-plated .45 automatic, from his waistband and went to the door. He clutched the gun in one hand and the pot in another. Mike Copeland didn't trust Tess as far as he could throw her. He wasn't about to leave his prized possession unprotected.

"Who dat...?" He barked.

"Melquan..."

Mike Copeland immediately put away the gun and turned the lock cylinders. Melquan walked inside the place. Once Melquan crossed the apartment's threshold, he turned and locked the door securing the apartment.

"What's good, Mel?" Mike Copeland greeted, giving Melquan a pound.

"Ain't nothing, Mike. Another day another dollar," Melquan fired back. "So let's get it."

He entered the kitchen and watched Mike Copeland continued the process of preparing crack for packaging.

"Look, my dude. Ain't that shit pretty? And I ain't loss a gram."

"Yeah, Mike that shit look like a buttery beige. Heads gonna be lovin' this."

"Mel, pass me that fan behind you."

Melquan handed Mike Copeland the fan. He placed the mound of crack on a stack of paper towels and turned the fan on high to accelerate drying process. Melquan and Mike Copeland were about to engage in conversation, there was a sudden knock on the door.

"It better be Precious, Mel. Shop's closed. I'm not letting none of Tess crack-head friends up in this joint. Not while we doin' this. I don't give a fuck if it is her house or not," Mike Copeland warned.

Armed, Mike Copeland exited the kitchen and entered the hallway. Tess suddenly appeared in at her bedroom doorway. She glared evilly at him, watching closely to see who was at the door. Satisfied that the person at the door wasn't for her Tess retreated back into her room.

"It sure took you long enough," Mike Copeland said. "Fuck was you doing? Huh? Washing that nasty, stinkin' ass…?"

"Shut da fuck up, Mike!" Precious replied. "Where's Melquan?"

"That's all you fuckin' worry about. Melquan this, Melquan that, Melquan! Melquan! Gimme a fuckin' break…! Why don't you let dat nigger's balls hang? The nigga's in da fuckin' kitchen. Goddamn!"

"Fuck you, Mike! You just mad cause ain't no bitches on your lil' dick."

"Bitch, ha, ha, ya muthafuckin' liar! A'ight! I got soo many ho's in all area codes. Cause ya bird-ass don't see 'em, don't mean they ain't around. I don't be lettin' people in my BI… Ain't you ever heard this from the old folks, 'You keep tellin' yo bizness you ain't gone have no bizness.'"

Mike Copeland and Precious had a friendly rivalry between them. There was no harm meant and all gloves were off in this friendly bickering. At the end of the day it was all love, crew love. They had each other's back one hundred and ten percent. Still they traded insults wherever and whenever possible.

"A yo, Precious, can you get the fuck in here and close that muthafuckin' door?" Melquan shouted.

Precious did as she was told, pushing past Mike Copeland to enter the apartment. She walked into the kitchen to find Melquan seated at the small wooden raggedy kitchen table. Three badly soiled dinner plates were placed in front of the three chair, along with dozens of tiny packages of clear glassine bags and Gem star razorblades. Every inch of the kitchen table was covered with crack cocaine and drug paraphernalia.

"Hey Melquan…"

"Yeah, what up…?" He coolly replied.

Precious knew there would no affectionate response coming from Melquan. It was as if last night never happened and their relationship didn't exist. Melquan had a tendency to downplay the depth of there relationship all the time, especially in front of Mike. He wanted to maintain the respect of his lieutenant, first and foremost. Melquan had an image to uphold.

"Wow," Precious smiled sarcastically. "How soon we forget."

"Forget about what?" Melquan sternly asked.

"Nothin' Melquan… Whatever!"

"Mike check on that work. Maybe it's all dry by now. We really need to bag it up and put it on the streets."

Mike Copeland went over to the mound of crack and lifting it up and breaking it into two, he inspected it. After the careful examination, he gave Melquan the go ahead to start bagging it up. Precious, Melquan and Mike Copeland tackled the task. Mike Copeland precisely weighed the crack before doing anything. They quickly formed an assembly line with each person performing a specific task. Mike busted the boulder of crack into dimes. Precious opened all the glassine bags, and Melquan stuff the bags full with crack. Silently they went about bagging up the crack for street distribution.

"Oh, I almost forgot, Mel what the fuck is this I hear about you bussin' ya gun? You know I feel some kinda way about that. That's my specialty," Mike Copeland said, interrupting the flow.

"Yeah, some niggas in the shoe jumped on a crackhead. They was about ta body him. I had to do sumthin before shit got out of hand."

"Yeah, I heard you handled ya biz though. I heard a couple niggas salty behind that too."

"Fuck all 'em niggas!"

"Yeah, that's what I've been sayin.'"

"Anyway, who told you that…? Precious…?"

Precious rolled her eyes and sucked her teeth at the mention of her name. She stared at the other two before speaking.

"Why my name gotta be mentioned in everything? Huh? You makin' me sound like some kinda snitch or something. And I feel some kinda way about that shit, Melquan."

"You'll get over it. That's why they call 'em feelings, cause they come and go," Melquan replied.

"Mel, you got it twisted. Precious ain't tell me shit!" Mike Copeland added. "You know the streets watching. Plus you already know where we at. This da fuckin' projects… Somebody always seeing or hearing sumthin and nigga's was blowin' up my phone before the shell even hit the ground."

"Wow!" Melquan replied. "Fuck it! I did what I had to do. I don't even wanna talk about that shit no more. That ain't about nothing. Not to change the subject, I do wanna speak to y'all about something else."

"What Mel?" Mike interrupted. "Speak on it, my dude."

Suddenly the incessant sound of razor blades slicing through crack rock and hitting ceramic plates halted. Melquan had everyone's undivided attention.

"Member a while back, on the way home from City Island, when I was chopping it up with you about taking over the projects?"

"Yeah," Mike Copeland answered.

"Mike, you said then the time wasn't right. And I went with that."

"That was then this is now, big homie. It's time to do the damn thing."

Mike Copeland couldn't contain his excitement. He leaped out of his chair, damn- near spilling the contents of the table on the floor.

"Mike be easy!" Precious rudely suggested. "Nigga you almost knocked all this shit over. You and your crazy-ass self..."

"Now, this is what the fuck I been waiting for! You know me I'm into disciplin' muthafuckers by any means necessary. With the hands, knife work or the gunplay, it don't matter."

"Slow ya roll, Mike. We gon' do this my way, a'ight?" Melquan warned.

"Are you kidding me? There's only one way you can do this and that's by force. You think niggas just gon' lay down, and let you have shit. We gotta straight smash these niggas and take all this fuckin' money. You think big, you get big!"

"A yo, Mike, be easy. I still got my doubts about whether we can pull this shit off.

"What?" Mike Copeland uttered in disbelief. "Mel, we can do anything we fuckin' want! Who gonna stop us? Tell me, who? Once we put our thing down niggas gon' fall the fuck in line. You feel me?"

"I hear you," Melquan began. "But it ain't that easy. We can't take on the world and win. We gon' need more people… We gonna need an army to pull this shit off."

"My dude, we ain't gon' need no fuckin' army," Mike Copeland assured him. "All we need is me!"

Melquan paused and looked over at his longtime friend, Mike Copeland. He studied his face for any signs of insincerity, and saw none. Melquan saw the same bold, brash guy that he had known since they were kids. Mike's bravado and his heart was what always endeared him to Melquan. Mike had a one track mind when it came to handling beef. He always went through the problem, never around it. Mike didn't back down to no one.

"Mel, I never doubted you on this coke shit. When you tell me we gonna flip these oz's to a certain amount. I believe you. So, why you doubting me…? Lemme do what I do best, and that's put in that work," Mike said, placing his gun on the table.

"Melquan, Mike is right," Precious said, interjecting on Mike's behalf. Melquan stared at her as she continued. "He's a shooter. The only reason he's not wildin' out is because of you.  But if you just give him the word then these niggas will be history.  Let Mike clear the lane so we all can eat."

The idea for a takeover belonged to Melquan.   He took a minute reflecting on everything that had been said.  All the while he kept packaging the crack.  In his mind, Melquan weighed the pros and cons of their course of action.  It didn't take long for him to render his decision.  Melquan knew that their window of opportunity would not be open forever.  If they didn't make their move now, someone else would.  That was for certain.

"Okay, let's do it," he exclaimed, rubbing his chin. "But let's talk this thing out thoroughly.  Because if we fail to plan, we just planning to fail… So dig this, Mike.  Here's what I want you to do for me…"

Melquan singlehandedly put the plan together.  They knew it would take all hands on deck to pull this off, and roles had to be rehearsed until everyone knew exactly what was expected of them.  New people had to be recruited.  Melquan would have to strengthen some of his old ties, and get trusted people to buy into the grand scheme.  It was a bold and ambitious plan.  Edenwald projects never experienced the likes of in a very long time.  If the plan was successfully executed, the dynamics of the drug game in the projects would be change for the foreseeable future.

The trio was in the midst of their discussion when Tess reappeared from her bedroom.  Clad in a raggedy robe, rundown Nike slippers and a black scarf tied around her head, she looked a mess.  The dark rings around her eyes were evidence of her lack of sleep.  Melquan spotted her and signaled for silence.  He knew what she came for.  Tess' insatiable crack habit demanded to be fed.

For years Tess had been having difficulties breaking free of the stranglehold crack had on her.  Her task was impossible when she got fed a steady diet of crack from hustlers who bagged up in her apartment on any given day.

"Melquan, can I get paid now?" Tess asked, skipping the formalities.

Mike Copeland smirked when he heard her request. He thought Tess was trying to go over his head and perceived this to be disrespectful.

"Why don't you go somewhere and sit the fuck down? You drivin' us crazy! All that walkin' ain't gonna get you no crack any faster, bitch," Mike said.

"Nigga, this my muthafuckin' apartment," Tess snapped back at him. "I do as I please in my muthafuckin crib, nigga. I'll be damned if I let any muthafuckin' nigga tell me what the fuck to do up in here!"

"Bitch, you ain't paid no bill since you been livin' up in here," Mike Copeland laughed. "Who da fuck you think you kiddin'? Welfare pay all these bills round here."

"Look muthafucka, I don't care who pay these fuckin' bills. They gets paid one way or another. I don't care if I gotta suck a thousand dicks, me and my baby boy ain't gonna be homeless… You know what Mike? I liked you a whole lot better when you were younger. This drug game be changing young, simple-ass niggas like you. Nigga you startin' to think you all that… I got news for you, you ain't no Scarface! Nigga you ain't nobody!"

Tess was a tall, frail woman who talked tough but who wasn't. Mike Copeland had offended her time and time again. She wanted to draw a line and defend herself.

Mike Copeland quickly stood up. Tess verbal barrage hit him in a weak spot. Clearly heated, he was ready to explode on her.

"Bitch, I don't know who da fuck you think you talkin' to, but one more word out your mouth, and I will seriously hurt you up in here. I don't give a damn if this your crib or not. You'll die up in this piece… Tess, your fuckin mouth is gonna get you in trouble one day… I'm tellin' you. This the last time I'm saying this. No more muthafuckin' warnings! You hear me, bitch?"

Tess wasn't the least bit scared of Mike Copeland. She knew that nothing was going to happen to her, as long as Melquan was around. There was an intense but brief staredown between the two. Tess took another shot at Mike Copeland.

"Whateva nigga," she said rolling her eyes. "Fuck you!"

Mike Copeland was infuriated by Tess' smart mouth response, and jumped at her. Melquan quickly intervened before the situation became a physical altercation. Anger boiled his blood and Mike Copeland struggled to free himself from Melquan's firm grip. A brief tussle ensured, causing some of the product and material to spill on the floor.

"C'mon Mike, chill, man. It's not even that serious. Don't be feedin' into that bullshit. Let's finish handling our BI and bounce," Melquan said, holding his man back from getting at Tess.

Unable to free himself from Melquan's grip, Mike Copeland glared angrily at him. If this had been a stranger surely Mike Copeland would had attacked him with all his might. It was his man and cooler heads prevailed.

"Mike, you're overreacting, fall back," Melquan advised.

"A'ight, I'm good," Mike Copeland said, sitting down. "Mel, you better give da bitch some coke so she can get da fuck outta my face. I don't wanna see da bitch no more today. And that's my word."

"Precious, handle that for me. Hit Tess off," Melquan ordered.

"Why…?" Precious asked, perplexed by Melquan's kindness.

"Cuz I asked you that's why," Melquan said, sounding agitated.

"She's out of control. Let Tess wait. She's just trying to extort y'all just because we here bagging up in her crib. We could do this shit in my crib. Fuck her! She's not doing us no favor," Precious sighed.

"Precious, please not now. Let that shit go. We here to do what we do, and bounce. A'ight…?"

"But that bitch is—"

"Just do as I fuckin' say, Precious!" Melquan said.

"Fuck that Bitch why you bein' so nice to her."

"Yeah, you call it bein' nice. I call it playin' fair. So just hit her off, and we can get on 'bout our bizness."

"Whateva Melquan, it's your shit."

"Thanks for the reminder. Now go do what I ask you to do, a'ight?"

Precious made no attempt whatsoever to hide her great dislike of Tess. She walked over to Tess and slammed the large pieces of crack cocaine into her dirty outstretched palm.

Tess licked her lips when she spotted the sizable piece of crack cocaine Precious gave to her. She roughly calculated it be the weight of an eight ball. Tess' eyes lit up and she raced out of the kitchen.

"Bitch, don't even got no manners. You could at least say thanks," Precious said.

"Oh yeah, my bad, thanks… Fa nuttin…!" Tess laughed from down the hall.

"I hope you have a fucking heart attack smoking that shit, bitch!" Precious said.

"I heard that. You another one… And I'll surely try," Tess laughed, locking the bathroom door.

Minutes later, a thick cloud of smoke enveloped the area around the bathroom door. Tess was in the bathroom blazing the crack rock in a pipe made from a soda can. She quickly replaces the burnt out rock with another piece. She sparked the lighter on high, and inhaled very deeply. A feeling of exhilaration washed over her body as the drug took effect immediately.

Tess' pupils became dilated, darting all over the small bathroom. Paranoia crept up on her and her heartbeat quickened. Suddenly the walls felt like they were closing in. A loud knock on the bathroom door startled her causing her to drop the makeshift crack pipe.

The sudden noise seemed to push Tess into a state of confusion and fear. She flushed the toilet and turned the shower on. Then she stood around staring at herself in a mirror, over the sink, checking to see if she looked high.

"Who is it?" she answered, cleaning ashes off an already dirty floor.

"It's me, mom, Sheron," the boy responded.

Sheron was the mature twelve-year-old son of Tess. Unlike most boys his age, Sheron was not concerned with videogames or T.V. He had more pressing needs like taking care of himself. He rarely indulged in the childhood games.

"Mom…?" Sheron said almost inaudibly.

Quietly Melquan, Precious and Mike Copeland got up from their seats to watch the exchange. Melquan was most touched by the boy's timid behavior. Wearing a puzzled look, Melquan glanced first at Precious then Mike Copeland. He was completely appalled by what he was witnessing. Mike Copelan and Precious both had snide expressions on their faces. It was as if they were enjoying themselves.

Melquan looked back at the bagged up drugs that were on the table. A powerful overdose of shame shot through his veins. Melquan wanted to leave but stayed riveted watching this scene play out. Even though the youngster wasn't in the same room, the thought of bagging up drugs with a kid around dogged Melquan's conscience. He went off on a guilt trip.

"Yo, where shorty come from? I ain't even know that someone else was here," he said.

"Me either. But what's da big deal? He's just a lil' fuckin kid," Mike Copeland said, shrugging his shoulder.

"Man, I ain't tryin' to corrupt nobody who ain't already corrupted, especially no lil' kid. God don't like ugly. Precious, go find sumthin to cover that shit up with real quick," Melquan said, pointing at the table.

Sheron was still standing at the bathroom door waiting on his mother to respond. He leaned against the door, trying to hear her reply.

"Ma, ma," Sheron whispered.

"Boy, if you don't get the hell away from this door, and leave me the fuck alone, I'm gonna come out there and hurt you. Now leave me alone!"

Sheron turned dejectedly and walked away from the bathroom door. Moping around the apartment, Sheron stopped when he reached the kitchen. He stared in wide-eyed surprise at three unfamiliar faces. Mike Copeland and Precious gave the boy a look of indifference.

"Hey shorty, c'mere... What's your name?" Melquan asked, attempting to stir a conversation.

The kid walked a few feet up the hall toward Melquan. Although he didn't know Melquan, he still didn't fear him.

"Sheron," the boy responded.

"What's good, Sheron? My name is Melquan. Yo, you hungry, Sheron? Cause I was just about to send my girl to the chicken spot to get some eats."

"Oh no, I didn't know I was about to go to no chicken spot. Melquan, I'm ya girl only when you want sumthin. I gotta hair appointment today and I just ain't got no time to get no chicken."

"Wow," Melquan smiled, shaking his head. "I know you frontin' but that's cool. What comes around goes around."

"I'm dead-ass, Melquan. I do too have a hair appointment."

"Look, I ain't tryin' to hear all that rah-rah. You ain't right, shorty ain't got nothin' to do with nothin'... And you here just shittin' on him for no reason," Melquan said staring down Precious.

"I ain't shittin on shorty. I just gotta go get my hair did, wash and set. The Dominican's got a special on Wednesday."

"Oh you just realized that... Or is that is just an excuse, because of who his mother is, right?" Melquan asked Precious.

He turned to look at Mike Copeland. His lieutenant vigorously shook his head, rebuffing Melquan's non-verbal request.

"Don't, even look at me dog. I'm grown ass man. What I look like lettin' you son me like that. You know what they say if you want sumthin done, do it yourself."

"A'ight, a'ight, fuck both y'all! I'm a take shorty to the chicken spot my damn self. Y'all got the game fucked up doin' shit like that. Both y'all ain't gonna have no luck. Y'all can't keep takin' from the game and don't give nothin' back. Have a heart sometimes muthafuckas," Melquan said, walking out with Sheron.

"Havin' a heart will only get a nigga knocked. Precious what da fuck is up with your man?"

"I don't know what he on. That nigga only calls me his girl when he wants some ass or wants me to do sump'n. Any other time, I'm just his down-low bitch," Precious sarcastically said.

Mike Copeland and Precious stayed with the task at hand. When the process of cooking and packaging the crack was done, it was now time for the product to hit the streets.

# True 2 Da Game
## Chapter Five

Out on Laconia Avenue, blue and white police cars raced through the street with sirens blaring, rushing from the 47th Precinct on 229th Street to God knows where. A block up the street, and what seemed like a world away, Melquan and Sheron sat in the Kennedy Fried Chicken spot eating the house special, chicken wings and French fries. They kicked it for a minute about everything from school to sports. Melquan soon realized that Sheron loved sports but hadn't participated because of his mother.

"She'd be showing up to the games all drunk and high talking shit. So I quit."

"Shorty, you gotta forgive her, cause no matter what she's still ya mother," Melquan said between bites of chicken. "She knows not what she does."

They continued chatting and hit it off, laughing and playing. Melquan stole food off Sheron's plate and Sheron did the same to Melquan. Both of them quickly became real familiar with each other.

"You still hungry, Sheron? You want sumthin else? Or maybe you wanna take sumthinupstairs with you for later on? Maybe another soda, ice cream, or whateva…?"

Melquan's voice trailed off as he watched Sheron's reaction. The kid seemed caught between shyness and neediness. There was a hesitation before Sheron gave an answer.

"Thanks, but I guess I'll be alright. We can head back by my building. I got some homework to do."

"But how can you do your homework if you hungry? You know you can't even concentrate when you stomach's makin' funny noises, shorty."

"I know, but really Melquan, I'm good. Thanks anyway."

"You sure…? Never let your pride get in the way of asking for sumthinthat you need. Closed mouths don't get fed. Shorty, think about it. You working, and you get hungry later, and you ain't got nothing in the house to eat…Hmm, hmm?"

Melquan saw shyness in Sheron but asked anyway. There was something about Sheron that made Melquan recognize that he was a good kid. He had not been tarnished by the ways of the world, or the projects. It seemed as if he wanted to really accept the offer but was too bashful to do so. Still Melquan had to make an offer that Sheron couldn't refuse. It was the drug dealer in him.

"Look, I don't care what you say. I'm get you sumthin anyway. How about that…?"

"I guess, alright," Sheron said, giving in. "But my mother gets her welfare check tomorrow. So we'll have whole lotta food to eat. Tomorrow, we'll be good."

"Okay, but you gotta make it through the night to get to tomorrow, feel me?" Melquan said.

Melquan got up from his seat and walked over to the counter and bought another order of chicken wings and French fries to go. After the order was processed and paid for he returned to Sheron and handed him the bag of food.

"Here, you go, shorty."

"Good lookin'out, Melquan."

Together they exited the restaurant and walked the short distance back to the projects. They made small talk the entire way, but deeper things were on Melquan's mind. He couldn't believe how Sheron had initially resisted the meal but was anticipating his mother's welfare check. To him there was a strange irony in that. Melquan had equal feelings of both pity, and respect.

Back in her apartment, Sheron's mother was geeking. High as she had ever been, Tess was feeling herself. She walked out the bathroom glancing around the apartment like her head was on a swivel. The slightest sound got her complete attention. Tess meticulously surveyed every inch from the entrance through to the kitchen. She entered the kitchen on her hands and knees, crawling. Tess was looking for lost crack rocks or anything resembling one. Real or not, they would be smoked on sight.

Tess didn't bother to hide just how high she was. Being discreet wouldn't make the crack monster go away. Tess found it damn near impossible to come down once she was got this high. Anyone coming inside her apartment at this very moment would have to bear witness to her desperation. Tess was on her knees searching the floor for more get high. The crack was urgently calling her.

Back in the projects, Melquan and Sheron navigated the concrete walkways. Everyone they passed seemed to know and acknowledge Melquan. The outpouring of love captured Sheron's attention. There were enough handshakes and embraces for Sheron to see that Melquan was very popular. He watched carefully as Melquan showed love back, kissing females on their cheeks and hugs for the dudes. It was like he was walking with a famous person, a ghetto superstar.

"Wow Melquan, who don't you know?" Sheron smiled as another group stopped gave daps, and moved on.

Continuing down the block, they walked past Melquan's building, number 1132. Close to home, they showed him lots of love. Melquan's ghetto pass was on full display. The projects area was really his stomping grounds. It was the place where he was born and raised.

They entered Melquan's building on the South side. Melquan and Sheron got on the elevator and rode it to the sixth floor.

"This is where I rest, shorty," Melquan said, reaching for his keys.

He opened the door to the two-bedroom apartment occupied by his mother. She was up, walking around the living room, dressed in a fluffy pink bathrobe. Miss Tina was honey-brown complexioned, five foot six inches tall and big boned. A curvaceous fortyish woman, Miss Tina was still hanging on strong to her youthful appearance. Her makeup was already in place and her hair perfectly wrapped up in a scarf.

Sleeping all day and pampering herself, was her daily routine. She could afford to do so because of the hefty disability check she received for hurting her hand at her post office job, some years ago. Her life was akin to that of a drug dealer, except she slept all day and partied all night. Miss Tina was a barfly; she loved to frequent the upscale bars and lounges through out the Bronx and Harlem, where moneymakers, mover and shakers of the underworld were known to gather.

"Come on in, shorty. Now you know where I live, if you ever need anything, for real, call me or come by."

Miss Tina stood in background posturing. She halfheartedly glanced at Melquan, eavesdropping on the conversation.

"Melquan, who is that kid you got with you? Is he one of your workers, or something…?"

"Ma'…" Melquan sighed. "C'mon now… What I look like, huh?"

"Boy, you better watch your mouth and save your teeth. I don't care how big you get I'm still your damn mother. Don't you get too smart. I ain't one of your lil' friends out there in the streets. Get that! I was asking a simple question. Anyway, I'm glad you're here. I need some money. I'm going out tonight."

"Round how much do you need?"

"I don't know… Lemme see, I'm gonna need money for a cab to get back home… Hmm um, just give me two hundred. Yeah, that should be enough. What you think…?"

"Damn ma, where you going…? Two hundred dollars…? You killin' me." Melquan said.

Despite his objections, Melquan would never say no to his mother. She had him wrapped around her pinkie. Miss Tina took good care of him growing up and now that he was making money, it was his turn to return the favor. Melquan couldn't believe how avaricious her appetite for money had grown, and how selfish she had become. It was like the more he gave his mother, the more money she asked for.

Melquan reached into his pocket, and pinched off a few bills. He didn't dare remove the money from his pocket because his mother would get greedy and ask for more. Unfortunately for Melquan, the amount of money he pinched off was more than the amount requested. He stood in front of mother attempting to count it.

"Thanks." Miss Tina sardonically said. "No need in counting it. That looks like enough."

Melquan shook his head in disgust and watched Miss Tina strolled back down the hall back into her bedroom. He couldn't help but think just how much his mom was involved in the drug game, however indirectly it might have been. Most of his friends' mothers would never take this blood money, as they called it. Miss Tina wasn't like most mothers. She was money hungry.

Back in the days, Ms Tina would use her good looks to get whatever her heart desired. She was the pick of the litter in the projects, a hustler's wet dream and his worst nightmare rolled into one. Her heart was equally dark, and she was corrupted like anyone in the streets. Miss Tina would chase a dollar just as hard as any crack-head chase get high.

"Melquan…!" Miss Tina shouted from her bedroom.

"Yeah," Melquan answered.

"What did you say boy? You're a no manners having somebody. You know that…?"

"Huh? What you say?" Melquan laughed.

"Anyway, that lil' heifer, India keep calling my phone… She left about five messages on my damn answering machine. I started to pick up the phone and tell her about her a thing or two. Don't you give her your cell number? What she keep calling here for? That girl worst than any damn bill collector, you hear? You better talk to her 'fore I do."

Melquan removed his cellphone from his pocket and realized that his phone had been on silent mode. When he checked, there were more than a dozen missed calls. All were from India.

"Ma, what you got against India? She ain't done nothing to you."

"Lemme tell you a thing or two. For one, I just don't like her. Sumthin 'bout her attitude don't 'gree with my spirit… India's a little too bourgeoisie for me… Talking all proper and shit… She act like her shit don't stink," Miss Tina said, re-emerging from her room. She marched up the hall to where Melquan sat checking his cellphone.

"Melquan are you staying at that heifer's house tonight?" Miss Tina abruptly asked in her best caring mother's voice.

"Most likely…But why…?" Melquan asked, sounding perplexed.

"Hold up, wait right here. I got something for you," Miss Tina said, walking back to her bedroom.

She returned with a handful of condoms and unceremoniously dumped them in Melquan's unsuspecting hand.

"Here take these. And make sure you wear them. Lemme tell you a thing or two. Don't let that heifer trick you into getting her pregnant. India's just looking for a father for her other child and it ain't going to be you. The only already made family you going to support is this one," Miss Tina said, index finger pointing at herself.

Melquan was dumbfounded as his mother strutted her away, mocking him with a sinister laugh. India wasn't even on it like that, though his mother wouldn't believe that. She had an extreme dislike for India and it blinded her to everything good about his girlfriend. He was through trying to convert a non-believer into a believer. Melquan had tried and that attempt failed miserably. The outcome remained the same. He was trapped between two strong-willed women and they would never see eye to eye. Suddenly the house phone rang. Melquan jumped out of his thoughts when he heard his mother's voice.

"Melquan!" she shouted.

Melquan could hear the irritation in his mother's voice, and knew the call was for him. He also knew who was calling.

"It's that heifer, India! Answer the goddamn phone, please!"

"Hello…"

It was not the sweet voice Melquan had grown accustomed to hearing. India's voice dripped with a venomous hiss. As soon as Melquan answered the phone, she immediately went on the attack.

Rattling off question after question, she was on a never-ending quest for the truth. Melquan unsure how she would react or what she would say, just listened. He decided to play possum and say as little as possible.

"Melquan…?" India exploded. "I've been calling all day and night. Where were you? Where have you been? What's going on?"

"Right here… I'm at my mother's house. Don't you know where you callin', girl?"

"Why didn't you answer your phone? I've called before and left you messages on your cellphone. I've goteen no answer. For all I know you could be in jail, or God forbid the morgue."

"Oh, I accidentally put my phone on silent while doing my hustle, and after I came up here I fell asleep. Me and Mike had a lot of business to take care of."

There was no guilt to the lies he was telling his girlfriend. If lying was a class Melquan would have aced it. True to fun and not to one, Melquan was very promiscuous. Melquan was presently feeling India. He was almost was in love with her. Almost didn't count.

"Damn, so you just forgot all about me huh?" she asked after an extended pause. She had to process his excuse. "You mean to tell me that you didn't wake up in the middle of the night to even go to the bathroom?"

"Nope, I was dead tired. All that rippin' and runnin', you know…? Finally all that kinda caught up to me."

"Uh, huh…"

"What's that suppose ta mean?"

"Not a thing, Mel. Not a thing."

His thoughts caused an increase in Melquan's heartbeat. No way in hell India was going to believe a lie like that. She was a seasoned veteran when it came to men and relationship. She had seen it all and heard damn near everything. Still she had no proof of his infidelity. India had her suspicions, but what she knew, and what she could prove were two different things. Melquan quietly listened.

"Anyway, I missed you. You should've been with me," she said with that sad, sweet ring in her voice.

It was mushy stuff and made him thought of love. He shivered then he heard her voice ringing through the phone. "Melquan, did you hear me? I said what you been up to, baby? How was your day?"

"I'm good thanks for askin'… Anyway, I had a real busy day," Melquan said quickly.

"Doing what?"

"C'mon you know… Takin' care of some business…"

"Doing what…?" India repeated.

"Doin' me," Melquan answered. He could hear the suspicion on the voice and quickly added, "C'mon India, don't start with me."

"And exactly what's that supposed to mean, Mel?"

Melquan took a deep breath and exhaled. He felt that the conversation had taken a wrong turn somewhere and attempted to correct the course.

"India, c'mon now, we both know where this is headed."

"And…"

"So, let's not take it there. Not now. I can't deal with it. At least not right now…"

Melquan sensed doubt, and tried to put them to bed. He knew that would be better done person to person. India was sneaky and had resorted to unusual methods to gain information about him. She had got his password on both his Facebook and Myspace accounts. With her current line of questioning, India was fishing for more info.

"Don't act like you're any type of saint, Melquan. We both know otherwise. If I'm acting a certain way, it's because of your past behavior. You made me this way."

By watching his mother, Melquan had learned how to be a whore. In the mid to late eighties, when Melquan was still a youngster coming up, Miss Tina began bedding a succession of hustlers. Charlie Rock was amongst the most prominent. Different men came in and out her bedroom at all hours. Melquan was there to witness all their exploits until the streets called him. Melquan's perception of right and wrong was distorted, after having being shaped by these different men. Family values were quickly replaced by street principles.

There was a long pause on the other end. India wasn't sure if the call was somehow disconnected and she shouted into the receiver.

"Melquan, are you still there...?"

"Yeah, I'm here..." Melquan released another heavy sigh of total exasperation. "But lemme ask you a question why you yellin', huh?"

"Oh, I'm sorry. I thought I dropped the call because I'm driving, that's why. But to get back to what we were discussing..."

"You call that a discussion? It sounded more like an interrogation on my end. The police have been a whole lot friendlier to me."

"Melquan, your behavior hasn't been all that great. You bought this on yourself. You go M-I-A, missing in action and you just expect me to accept any old excuse like that. Sometimes you're so full of it, Melquan. You know what I mean?"

"How could I forget...? You remind me of it almost every day. How we gonna ever move pass that if you keep remindin' me of da past? We'll never move forward cuz all you do is keep bringin' up the ol' shit. And I thought you forgave me already? Remember...?"

"I did. But it seems like as soon as we get over one thing, here comes another. You're always trying to be so secretive and elusive whenever I ask a question concerning your whereabouts. If you're going to be around me then you've got to make choices. And one is you've got to be open with me or—"

Melquan heard it in her tone. India was trying hard not to spaz. Being lied to she was finding it harder and harder not to go off.

"If you really must know what I was doin' all day, I was baggin' up. Okay, are you happy now? If I ever get indicted, you'll know why. You got me talking all reckless on my cellphone...!"

Melquan turned around to see that his mother was

eavesdropping on the conversation. He stared at her, shaking his head in disgust. Miss Tina had that I-told-you-so look on her face. Melquan could tell that she had heard the entire conversation. She shifted her body weight from one hip to the next as if growing impatient. Finally she crossed her arms across ample buxom, and glared at him with an evil smirk. Melquan stared at her for a quick second. Seeking any little bit of privacy he could get, Melquan turned his back.

"I'm so sorry for making you say that, Melquan. I really am sorry and apologize for it. I don't know what's gotten into me lately."

"Yeah, a'ight…" Melquan tone suggested that he was still upset by India's informal questioning.

"Ever since I had that bad dream about you, a couple weeks ago, I've been thinking that you've been cheating on me. Anyway, are you coming over, boo? I need to see you. I'll make it up to you when you get here. I promise…"

"A'ight, I'm gonna catch a cab over there in a minute. I just gotta go get sumthin from Mike Copeland, and then I'm on my way there."

"Okay, see you soon, boo," India said and pulled into the parking lot space of her Co-op City apartment.

She parked her Honda Civic and removed her eight-year-old son, Zach from his seat belt. They walked up to the elevator and got on. Both entered the apartment and India put away her bags and set off to prepare Zach something to eat. The boy was fascinated by cartoons on the television and quickly indulged. His mother was soon finished with the meal and called him to the kitchen.

"Come on and eat this before it gets too cold," India said.

The light skinned boy sat at the table and ate heartily while his mother went through a stack of mail.

"Look at all these bills…" she quietly said under breath.

"Mom, I'm finished eating. Can I go to my room and play my Playstation for a little while before I get ready for bed?"

"I didn't know you were finished eating. Zack, please eat all your vegetables. You're all worked up over the videogames. Did you do your homework yet?"

"Yes mom. I did it while you were making dinner."

"You're not lying to me, are you boy?"

"No mom, I swear, I'm telling you the truth," Zach said.

"Zach, what did I tell you about all this swearing? It's not that serious, boy."

His mother's tone of voice caused Zach to feel sorry and his facial expression changed to one of discomfort. He slowly picked at the vegetables remaining on his plate under the watchful eyes of his mother. The look of sadness enveloping her son's face made her feel bad.

"You okay, Zach?" she asked, mussing his curly hair.

The boy smiled and nodded. He was already feeling better, knowing that his mother was not really angry at him. India smiled and spoke.

"Okay, I'll make a deal with you. Finish eating all your vegetables then put the empty plate in the sink, and you can play your game for one hour. Oh yeah, and take a bath before you start all that videogame. I want you in bed and asleep after that."

"Thanks mom," Zach said and excitedly ate the rest of the vegetables.

Couple minutes later, he bolted from the dining table and raced to his room. India watched him moving too quickly before shaking her head.

"Boy, you better stop running through this house like that before you break something. You hear me?"

"Yes mom," Zach responded, disappearing into his room.

"And take a bath first," India said, clearing the table and going to the sink.

She had hardly touched her meal. She was caught up cleaning

the dishes with a look of concern adorning her pretty face. India did not hear when Melquan entered the apartment. He quietly sneaked up behind her and affectionately hugged her. India was at first startled then she became lost in his embrace.

"Baby, I'm so happy you're home. It feels really good to be in your arms," India said, kissing Melquan.

"Sounds like you had a bad day," Melquan said.

"Not really. It's just the same old BS. You know how it is, day in and day out. It's the same old stuff. I got to put up with BS from the patients and also get it from the doctors with their nasty attitudes."

"Yeah, I hear you, ma."

"Please, and if that's not bad enough, I used up almost all of my sick days going back and forth to the family court with Zach's father. If it ain't one thing it's another. Plus, I've got to get back to school. I'm so tired of dreading to go to work. It's like I sit there and watch the clock all day. I can't wait for three p.m. I hate my job. The only thing it's good for is paying my bills. That's it… And right now it's not even doing that."

"What, you need some money, India?"

"Melquan, you know I don't like asking you for money. You do enough already for me and Zach as it is... I made this mess, and I've got to clean it up by myself."

"India, come on now. Don't let your pride get in the way of accepting some money from me when you need it. Everybody needs a little help here and there."

"Yeah, but my here and there are starting to become more frequent with each month… Each week… I feel like I'm taking a handout from you," India said, sounding sad.

Melquan hugged her tightly. She was definitely wifey material. India was twenty-six years old, light skin complexioned, hard working, mature woman. She was beautiful, her features richly Native American and African American quality. Her sexy hourglass figure showed in anything that she wore. He couldn't just walk all over her like he did with all the other women he had. This was the thing that really attracted Melquan to India. Being in a relationship with India was a challenge. She dared him to want more out of life. She wanted him to see life outside of the projects. India was more of a woman than he ever had.

Despite the big front she had put up on the phone, and no matter how mad she was, India was always approachable. All their problems were momentarily forgotten, now that she had deeper concerns about other things. At this point India was vulnerable and Melquan was just the person to console her.

"Yeah, I hear you, but stop looking at it like that. I'm not giving you a handout… I'm giving you a hand up," Melquan said, holding her tighter.

India turned around and caressed his face and planted a juicy, wet kiss on his lips. With her head was on his chest, he rocked back and forth silently with her in his arms. Melquan's thoughts melted into two years ago. It took him back to the evening when they first saw each other in PathMark supermarket in Co-op.

He was just becoming a successful hustler and had all the trappings of street success. When their eyes first set on each other, he thought she was a Puerto Rican chick from the hood. She looked like some young girl he could bag. Initially India wasn't interested in him at all.

Melquan had spotted India up and down the supermarket aisles. By chance they ended up in the same checkout line. Seizing the opportunity, Melquan turned around and spoke to her.

"What's up Mami?" Melquan greeted her.

India had given him the meanest mug he'd ever seen from a woman and pulled her blackberry out her purse, fiddling with it, without responding. Melquan wasn't used to getting dissed in this manner. He had to think fast to save face.

"I'm good! Thanks for asking," he said in good humor.

Despite not wanting to laugh, India had to. The comment caught her off guard. She loved a person with a sense of humor. Melquan had plenty of that.

"Oh, you like that huh?" Melquan said, capitalizing on his good fortune. "You know you look a whole lot prettier with that smile on ya face. Yeah, I could get used ta that smile."

Melquan continued to heave compliment after compliment on India. She quickly began to blush. Now Melquan had the green light to push up on her.

"What's your name?" Melquan had asked while eyeballing her sexy frame.

"It's India, not mami," she announced. "I'm not Hispanic."

"Oh, my bad, India," he apologized. "You look…"

"Looks can be deceiving, now can't they?"

"Say no more. One thing I do know I wouldn't care if you was blue. Girl, you fine. You look good. Word..."

"Boy, you're killing me right now. You probably say that to all the females you meet. What did you say your name was?"

"Melquan," he stated confidently. "Before me there was none and after me there shall be no more."

"Okay, Clever aren't we? What're you, some type of rapper."

"Amongst other things I've been told. But enough about me let's talk about you. I wanna know everything about you. First, I need your number though."

"Oh, you think it's that easy, huh?" she had said smiling. "You kick a few lines and you get want you want? Listen, I don't even give my name to strange men."

"I'm Melquan, a nice guy from Edenwald. You're India from…?"

"Co-op," she answered. "I don't even know why I just said that."

"See, now we're no longer strangers," he smiled.

"If I'm not mistaken you said you're from Edenwald? I've heard stories about that place."

"Like the ol' sayin' goes, 'believe none of what you hear and half of what you see'. It's not as bad as they say. It has its ups and downs just like everywhere else. From what I hear they got Bloods & Crips in Co-op City. So, there that go… Now back to that number."

"Melquan, I would feel more comfortable taking yours," she told him.

"Why? You gotta man or sumthin?"

"No, I have a child though. Beside, that's just my rule of thumb. I don't just give out my number. It's unlady like. I know we're not stranger any more but it just a rule I have."

"Well rules are made to be broken," he suggested.

"According to the law, they're also made to be enforced."

"Oh, you got jokes, huh?"

"Sure do…"

"A'ight, I give. You ready? Here goes my number."

Melquan gave her his digits and made sure she got them by repeating them slowly and writing them down.

"Got it," India exclaimed. "And don't worry I will call you."

"Yeah, you do that."

Meeting a female of India caliber was a dream for Melquan. The demeanor of this smart, sexy, sophisticated woman easily impressed him. Melquan had enough around the way girls, hood chicks and ghetto girls, he was seeking to upgrade. He felt their personalities meshed. Melquan was not about to let this opportunity slip through his fingers.

They chatted and the long line progressed. Soon it was their turn to pay for their groceries. First Melquan went and waited on India when he was done. Together they walked out the store and toward the parking lot.

"What you cookin' dinner or what?" Melquan asked.

"Why…?" India replied.

"You need ta let me take you out ta dinner. That's why."

India suddenly went silent. She turned and looked at him strange. Soon she broke out into a smile. His rugged good looks gave her a moment to pause.

"My bad," Melquan said. "I shoulda known betta."

"Yep!"

When India's voice trailed off Melquan heard no satisfaction in it. Instead he saw the regret in her almond shaped eyes. They continued the short distance to her car. Melquan helped place her grocery bags in the trunk of the modest grey Honda Civic.

"I guess this is goodbye," she said.

"Don't say goodbye. You'll definitely see me again. And soon."

"Okay, never let it be said that you lack confidence."

"Nah, it ain't confidence. I'm just convinced, you're feelin' me like I'm feelin' you. I'm convinced that this is not some chance meeting. This is destiny—yours and mine."

During the ride to her apartment on Dreiser Loop in Co-Op City, India couldn't keep Melquan out of her mind. She hadn't quite felt like this since she had met her son's father, Shamel. They had broken up and she had run into a lot of imposters, but not any real suitors. India was in need of a man in her life. She secretly hoped that Melquan would fill that void.

Here in the living room of India's apartment, Melquan had managed to ease most of India's fears. His presence had a calming effect on her. They sat on the couch, cuddling, watching a television show called Real Housewives of Atlanta. Although Melquan didn't much care for the show itself, whenever and wherever he found the time to spend quality time with India, he did. He wanted to take advantage of this situation and score some points in the process.

Holding India close made Melquan's nature rise. In between the commercials the two would fondle each other. By time the show went off things got really hot and heavy. The couple lost awareness of time and place. A touch turned into a feel and a light peck on the lips turned into a wet, passionate tongue kiss.

Melquan's hands slowly roamed all over her body, and India's senses were awakened. They were about to disrobe and let their passion drive them to ecstacy. Suddenly India stopped him.

"No, we can't do this," she whispered.

"Why not…?"

"Zach!" she calmly hissed. "He might come out here at any moment. And I don't want my son seeing us like this."

Melquan thought about it for couple beats. His heart was heaving in his chest. He glanced down at his rock hard dick then looked at India. Her facial expression said it all. India didn't have to say anything else. She got up from off the couch, her cleavage showing, and her clothing was in disarray. India began straightening her clothes. He knew better too.

"I'm gonna take a shower," Melquan said, sounding disappointed.

In the shower, Melquan scrubbed the grime off his body but couldn't remove the guilt on his mind. Like he was new to it, he had took it too far, got carried away and he knew it. Melquan realized he had played himself, pointblank. He hoped their relationship didn't suffer because of it.

Melquan showered and picked up his dirty clothes, a pair of jeans and the sweatshirt he was wearing. Unbeknownst to him, a large wad of money fell out along with a bag of drugs.

Clad in wife-beater and boxer shorts, Melquan entered the bedroom. India immediately exited it. They avoided making eye contact as they passed each other. A call suddenly came through on his cellphone. Melquan answered it and was still on the call when India walked back into bedroom. She unexpectedly went ballistic.

"Whoever you're talking with on the phone, please tell them you'll call them back," India said, staring angrily at him. "Melquan, we have to talk right now."

Melquan's mind suddenly started racing. He paused looking at the cellphone and wondering what was up with India. While his heart did laps, his first thought was about his romp with Precious the night before. Melquan stared at India with curiousity locked in his eyes.

"Look, I gotta call you back," Melquan said, holding India's stare. "What's up, baby?" he asked in as soft a voice as was possible.

"I told you, how many times, not to bring drugs, drug paraphernalia or drug money, to my place. It might not be much to you, but this Co-op apartment and my child is all I have. This is everything I hold dear in this whole wide world. I'm not gonna let you F it up, okay Melquan?"

"What are you talkin' about, baby? Why even you trippin'? You're not makin' sense right now. This some random sh…"

"I'm trippin' huh? I'm not making sense, right?"

"This is totally random spaz… I don't know what the hell you talkin' bout?"

"You don't, huh? Alright, maybe this will refresh your memory?" she asked.

India out of nowhere threw a bag of cocaine at Melquan. It smacked him dead center of his surprised face. Melquan watched her as the coke fell at his feet. She quickly tossed Melquan the roll of money with rubber band wrapped around it. He caught it easily.

"I'm sorry… I didn't mean to bring that here. I forgot I had it on me…" his voice trailed when he bent over to pick up the drugs.

"You forgot…? I went into the bathroom and found all that just sitting right there on the floor. Melquan what would I have told my son if he had walked in there and seen that. All I need is for him to go and tell his father what he saw and there goes my custody case.

Melquan, I'm not going to lose Zach over your silly bullshit."

"You're right. My bad, India, I was dead wrong. I was supposed to drop that off before I left the projects. What else do you want me to say…?"

She stared at Melquan with fire in her eyes. Her veins seemed to pump rage into her pores. She was livid when she spoke.

"Yes, it's your bad, Melquan. That goes without saying. Now, please put on your clothes and get out. I can't deal with this shit, at least not tonight! My mind is not right. I'll only act like a bitch for the rest of the night. And I'd rather not let you see that side of me."

Melquan glanced at her in disbelief before he began putting his clothes on. He was now feeling anger and was happy to be leaving. His thoughts raced as he thought of Precious. Fully dressed, he was stomping out the apartment and was met at the door by India. Tears were in her eyes.

"Could you give me back my keys, please Melquan?"

Melquan stared at her and realized this could be the end. And he wasn't ready to bow out gracefully. He felt love for India and wanted her in his life. His anger spilled over in his words.

"I ain't giving you nothing… Nah, you gave me these keys in good faith and I'll return them in good faith," he said, brushing past India.

"I don't believe you, Melquan. And you call yourself keeping it real? Let me have my keys …" her voice trailed as the door slammed shut. India stared blankly at the door with tears in her eyes. "How did I get myself in this situation…?"

She walked to the door and put the night lock on. Then went to her bed where she saw a stack of bills on the nightstand. She paused for a minute, staring at the money. Licking her lips, India said, "Un-fucking-believable!"

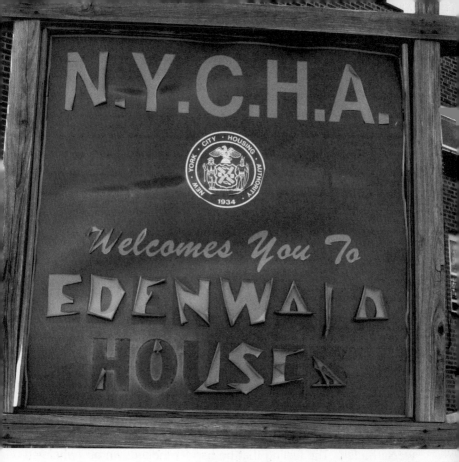

## Love Me Or Leave Me

Chapter Six

Melquan stared up and down the relatively quiet streets of Co-op city. It was minutes after the witching hour. At this time of the night the working class neighborhood was preparing for tomorrow's work and school day. With the exception of an occasional empty MTA bus, a passing car going by from time to time, nothing else seemed to move. Finally after thirty minutes of waiting and thinking, Melquan waved down a passing gypsy cab. He hopped into the backseat and slammed the door shut.

Before the cab driver could get the destination, he had already put the car in motion. It's unlikely he would have done so if he knew his passengers destination.

"Edenwald Projects," Melquan said.

"Huh, where...?" the cabbie asked.

"I said Edenwald!" Melquan shouted.

"I'll take you to east 229$^{th}$ street only. I no going up inside the projects this time of night..."

It sounded like the cab driver was asking Melquan a question. Melquan stared at the cabbie's face in disbelief.

"What...?"

"They crazy up there man. You have a lot of shootin' and robbin' going on in there. I don't want no parts of it. You know.... So that's as far as I go. Take it or leave it."

"You a scary dude... A'ight whateva, man, fuck it... Drop me at 229$^{th}$ street then... "

Staring aimlessly out the cab window, Melquan thoughts drifted silently with the ride. The incident resulting into the argument was fresh on his mind. The more it replayed over and over again the worse he felt. The feeling that he had let India down overwhelmed him. He tried to take stock of it and realize what exactly went wrong. This only served to frustrate him even further. He needed something to ease his mind. Melquan ordered the cabdriver to drop him off on the Ave.

When he reached his destination, Melquan paid the cabdriver and walked a few feet to the liquor store at 226$^{th}$ Street. He purchased two bottles of Hennessy. He walked across the street to the projects and knocked on Precious' door. He immediately knew that her grandmother wasn't home from the way she grinned when she flung the door open.

"To what do I owe this pleasure?" she smiled, greeting him at the door.

"Please, not now," Melquan said in protest. "I ain't in da mood fa no smart ass mouth."

"Okay, well please excuse the shit outta me."

Melquan didn't say much of anything about his reasons for this unannounced visit. He just drank, shot after shot of Hennessy, under the suspicious eye of Precious. Soon she joined in a game of who can drink the fastest and the most.

Each shot of liquor seemed to fade Melquan's ill-feelings. It was time for some good fuck. Melquan wanted to get busy with some raw sex. There would be no gentleness or tenderness in his strokes tonight. He felt like bringing the pain.

Precious didn't know Melquan reasons for coming to her apartment that night. It really didn't matter. Who was she to care? Ideas floated in her. She never expressed them and they stayed there. Before Melquan even touched her breast, Precious was sure what would come next. This episode would lead to the same place where dozens of others had led, her bed. In a flash they were panting, naked and cuddling in her queen sized.

Precious' excited body was receptive to Melquan's every touch. Her flesh tingling, she fervently went along with the program. Precious attempted to do what she did best. Roughly grabbing his dick and sucking the tip until he squealed. She covered his lips with her hot mouth, quieting him. She was about to continue her head game, but Melquan pulled her blonde mane back.

"Nah, uh, huh… I want some pussy now," he demanded. "I wanna blow ya back out, mami."

Her legs went rubbery with excitement and her body collapsed when he peeled her panties off. Melquan smiled and turned her over doggy style. Precious' ass cheek jiggled when she assumed the position. Melquan smacked Precious' ass cheeks hard twice. She wiggled her reddened round butt cheeks in the air, and begged for more. Melquan couldn't resist. This was a prelude for what was to come.

Melquan shoved his dick deep inside her, fucking her vigorously. Hennessy ran through his veins and his rod had no concscience. He hammered into her gushy pussy.

"Oh yes!" Precious screamed. "Fuck me!"

Melquan didn't care if Precious' grandmother was home. He was driving his dick hard into her.

"Oh yes, Mel. It's all yours. Take it, take it," she begged. "Oh, oh… oh yeah…!"

Precious was screaming loud enough to wake up the dead. Melquan kept on rapidly beating down the walls of her pussy, digging her back out. In between changing position, Melquans thoughts flipped to India. He plunged his Henny charged dick into Precious moist pussy. His thoughts were jarred by how loud she screamed.

India never ever screamed like this Melquan thought pumping his dick in and out of her. Melquan's thoughts cleared, he focused on what was in front of him. Tracing his fingers around the circumference of Precious' round ass, Melquan licked his lips. He spat on the shiny cheeks and rubbed his saliva into the crack of her ass. India would never let him spit on her, she would freak. Precious wiggled her ass and bucked her hips. She wanted him to fuck her harder. This turned him on even more and he fucked harder until he had worked himself into a fucking frenzy.

"Give it to me, gimme all that dick, Mel," she chanted in wild abandon.

With a hardened Henney dick, Melquan kept stroking until he felt sore. It was near dawn when he was through beating the pussy. They curled up against each other and went to sleep. Melquan was knocked out, sleeping and his cellphone vibrated. Precious undid his leg wrapped over her and went to check the caller ID. W-i-f-e-y, popped up on the screen. Precious jotted down the number real quick and went back to bed.

The cellphone vibrated again. Precious put her head down and watched it. She was tempted to answer it, but held herself in check. She was playing with Melquan's balls and the cellphone went off again.

Precious kept stroking Melquan's dick with her hand.

"Go to bed, bitch. No need to blow up his cellie. Tonight and forever, this dick be's mine."

Back in her Co-Op City apartment, India sat alone in front of her television playing low. Repeatedly, she dialed on her cellphone. India placed the phone to her ear, listening to Melquan's outgoing message on his voicemail.

You know who you called. Now you know what to do! One!

India had been the woman in Melquan's life for sometime now, but failed to understand his hood mentality. She tried to work with him, bending her on own strong morals and accepting his street lifestyle, his drug dealing ways. India had opened up her heart and home to Melquan. She hoped that he would change for the better, go back to school. Hopes of changing Melquan and turning him into a workingman was fading fast. She didn't know how much more time she was willing to invest in him. India had other responsibilities. There was her son Zach, her home and her job.

Melquan came with too much baggage. He was a thug, and a cheater. There was no physical proof of this, just her woman's intuition. India was building her case against Melquan. She had caught him in several lies already. Soon she would indict him with his own words. She loved him, but was in a no-win situation with Melquan. It seemed like the streets captured his attention more than she ever could.

India's mind was in a swimming in deep confusion. All the risk she was taking on dealing with Melquan seemed to outweigh the potential reward. Her heart craved what she wanted. There was anger fueling her obsession. Even distorted, love still coursed through her veins. India hit the redialed again.

# Who Shot Ya?
Chapter Seven

Around mid-day the following day, Charlie Rock was out and about, dapper like he was heading to an award show. If there was ever prize for best dressed wheelchair person, Charlie Rock would win that award, hands down. His unsoiled Jordan's were well coordinated with his black Champion sweat suit. Although he traveled in a wheelchair, Charlie Rock wasn't a homebody. He refused to be a prisoner inside his project apartment.

A work truck filled with Housing Authority workers passed by and came to a stop nearby. Charlie Rock recognized the familiar face of a longtime friend.

"Jose, what up? It's been a minute now, huh man," Charlie Rock hollered.

"Oh, what's going on, Charlie?"

"I can't call it. Ya hand better than mine, Jose."

"I hear that. I'm just workin'. Out here punching the clock, tryin' to make ends meet. I got my family to feed."

"I'm hip! I'm hip!" Charlie Rock humorously chided.

"Time's hard. I need every dollar, and all the overtime I can get."

"I hear that shit… By the way, how's the kids doin'?"

"Oh, they good… Growing up fast… It's cheaper to clothe 'em than feed 'em. Yeah man…. You know, my boy, is goin' through that rebellious stage. He tryin' to test me. I gotta put my foot in his ass from time to time. But my daughter, she's an angel, man. You know girls, they less trouble than boys."

"Yeah, until she meet some snotty nose boy… Man it's only a matter of time before she give you the blues too," Charlie Rock warned. "It happens to every parent."

"Yeah, I know I got my eye on it though… Oh, by the way, "How's your mother doing, she still down south?" Jose asked.

"Yeah, man she loving that there downsouth thing. She comes up every now and then. She said New York ain't for her no more. The city will make you happy twice… Happy to come and happy to go," Charlie Rock chuckled.

"You tell her hi next time you talk to her. I hope she remembers me."

"Yeah, she remembers you. C'mon now, as much time as many times you came to my house to eat, how could she forget? Anyway, Jose, you a good dude and even a better father… The way you raising your two kids like that. We need more fathers like you around. Ask me, I know that shit. I'm proud of you, Jose. It's rare that you see a dude like you make the transition from the hustle to working-man… Everybody can't do that. Some just get stuck in the game… They can't seem to make that transition."

"Thanks, Charlie Rock. I really appreciate that coming from you. Cause I know you been around me and watched me grown up. We even did some dirt together. We seen a lot of our peoples come and go. Generation after generation these projects been swallowing dudes up whole, chewing them up and spitting them out like garbage. We seen dudes get washed up before they got a chance to shine. But me and you, we still here… Must be doin' sumthin right…"

"No doubt…"

Charlie Rock and Jose Torres were project lifers. Both were born and raised in Edenwald projects and seemed, for different reasons, destined to stay to their dying day. Reminiscing about back in the days made Charlie Rock fall into a reflective mood. It was as if he could see his life flash before his eyes.

"Yeah, I've just about seen it all and just heard it all!" he said, becoming emotional. "I ain't got no regrets. Oh, well one… That bitch ass nigga who put three in my back… Put me in this chair… But I'm still here. Look what happened to him behind that…. He got his!"

"He sure did. You know God don't like ugly… You know the game. We both do."

"I guess that's why they call it a game…" Charlie Rock's voice trailed. He looked to the blue skies before continuing. "Anything can happen at anytime. Who would've thunk it? This shit that happened to me…? And in my own hood, at that…?"

"Yeah, but never mind that now, Charlie Rock. We's got to be thankful that we breathing. Any day above ground is really a good day."

"No doubt," Charlie Rock said, nodding in agreement.

"Charlie Rock, let me get back to my work. You take it easy. Be safe."

"Yeah, you do that. I'll definitely see you around, Jose," Charlie said, waving. "Come by and holla at me sometimes. We'll watch the Knicks game or sumthin. They got some new players, look like they might be about sumthin this year… Drink a few brewski's… You know my moms ain't the only one that can burn. I do my thing too."

"Ok, that sounds good. We'll hook up real soon. Later, Charlie Rock…"

"A'ight, good seeing you Jose…"

They exchanged pounds and went in different directions. Rolling down the Ave., Charlie Rock enviously glanced back at his friend and his wish list grew longer. Long after the conversation ended, thoughts of the night he lost the ability to walk haunted Charlie Rock. Although the physical scars from the gunshots to his back had long since healed. He remained emotionally scarred for life.

Back in the days Charlie Rock was a jack-of-all-trades. He was always in the mix of illegal activities. If the item had a price tag on it, he sold it. His gift of gab granted him entrance to many criminal circles. He knew the dope boys, the thieves, the stick-up kids, and the prostitutes.

He threw enough stones at the penitentiary to assure himself a permanent residence, but the jail cell was not his destiny. Some may get away with a lifetime of doing dirty, while with others their sins will comeback to haunt them in different ways. Charlie Rock was the latter.

It was just another afternoon, Charlie could hear the a loud clattering sound a pair of green dice made, rattling furiously against each other in the hand of a hustler. Holding them ear high, the cubes suddenly exploded out of his hand banging against the wall without warning. The dice bounced a few times on the floor before rolling and coming to a rest. The echo from the crashing sound was music to the player's ears. A wave of excitement swept through the project's hallway then momentarily things lowered to a hum. All eyes were on the dice. One seemed to spin for a lifetime. The friendly dice game had swollen to close to a dozen hustlers strong.

He watched the young kids shoot dice across the way in the lobby of the building and Charlie Rock remembered the day.

There were large bills littered the floor. Two parallel lines of hustlers formed the parameters of the dice game. A crush of bodies inadvertently blocked the buildings entrance.

"Hmm, hmm, head-crack!" someone shouted.

"Hot damn…!" another player cursed.

"What's the bank, what's the bank?" someone else asked.

The man picking up money from off the ground looked up to see who was inquiring about his hard earned money.

"My main man, Charlie Rock… What's good? You want some o' this, fly-guy?"

"You what's up, Ace… That's as far as I can see," Charlie Rock replied in an upbeat tone. "I want in," he said, puliing out a couple bills.

Ace let Charlie Rock know what the bank was amongst other things. The two laughed and dicussed events like old friends shooting the breeze. Then it was back to business.

"Whatcha got? Whatcha got…?" Ace suddenly asked, surveying the crowd while shaking the dice in his right hand. Quickly he pointed to each player with his left hand.

"I'm takin' all bets. Put your money on the ground. If it's a bet lay it down. Whatever's down is a bet.

Ace threw the dice down and rolled a point. His eyes lit up and Charlie Rock watched intensely like everyone else. He saw that the bank had blossomed into a nice amount of money, but refrained from going in large on the first roll. The feeling that Ace was going to have a hot hand crept in. His gut told him to bet with Ace, and not against. Gambling provided an adrenaline rush for Charlie Rock. This was one of Charlie Rock's vices. He was in his zone and enjoyed the way the game was going on.

"Umm, plenty niggers fell to the deuce," Ace said. "You push, you pay."

Two players simultaneously reached down to grab the dice that lay harmlessly on the ground. Their over anxiousness caused their heads to collide. Ripples of laughter broke out.

"Niggas too eager," Charlie Rock chuckled. "You know what happens when you rush the dice. You ain't gonna have no luck but bad."

One gambler took heed to the warning. Another young gambler, Edgar, shot Charlie Rock a cold stare. He wasn't about to adhere to some foolish superstition.

Charlie Rock was too cool to even feed into the youngsters foolish. He had a notion to leave the game at that very moment, but he didn't. His pride prevented him from doing so. He wasn't about to let some young punk spook him with a hard stare.
Everybody knew if it came to a fistfight that Charlie Rock would wipe the floor with this kid.

Charlie Rock wouldn't normally be within fifty feet of these young dudes. He disliked the younger generation with a passion. Getting money wasn't enough for them, they had to be violent too. All the gunplay was making it hard for everyone to eat. Charlie Rock did his best to stay out of these young kids way and hoped like hell that they stayed out of his. Charlie Rock felt it was his generation didn't get the respect due for laying the groundwork so these kids to eat.

Edgar picked up the dice, shook them in his closed palm for a few seconds. Then he let them fly, snapping his fingers when the dice left his hand. Much to the astonishment of the crowd, the dice settled and Edgar had rolled an ace.

"Feel that! Stupid ass niggas don't know shit! Watch his face when I ace this again!" Edgar shouted, pointing in Charlie Rock's direction.

"Young boy, you best watch your mouth and save your

muthafuckin' teeth," Charlie Rock shouted, firing back.

Laughter echoed through the building lobby. The other gamblers may have found the statement amusing but Charlie Rock wasn't laughing. He didn't take too kindly to disrespect in any form or from anyone.

The dice luck suddenly changed on Edgar. On his very next roll of the dice, he rolled one-two- three, an ace in the worst way.

"Alright, you know what it is, pass the dice," Charlie Rock confidently said, taking a shot at Edgar. "Let a real gambler roll!"

The losing hand left Edgar feeling frustrated. He got so mad he didn't bother to pass Charlie Rock the dice, but left them on the floor. Another player passed the dice to Charlie Rock. Edgar glared angrily when Charlie Rock took possession of the bones.

Charlie Rock's face lit up with an arrogant smile. He loved the fact that Edgar was pissed off.

"What you got young boy?"

"Nigga, I'm out!" Edgar confessed.

"Move out the way then. Let a player who got some real money occupy that spot," Charlie Rock's body shook with laughter.

"Fuck You!" Edgar announced.

Charlie Rock landed an open hand, flushed on Edgar's right cheek, smacking him in the face and flooring him. It left him dizzy and Edgar didn't know what to do. He shook his head like a knocked down boxer, trying to regain composure and never responded.

Charlie Rock leaned over him, his fists balled up, ready to strike. The fight was already taken out of Edgar. It was clear that he wanted no parts of a fight.

"Who is this lil' nigga? I don't even know him and he be talkin' all reckless like that to me. If y'all like this nigga, y'all better get 'em 'fore his lil ass get hurt…"

A couple of the gamblers helped Edgar off the floor. He wore a mask of shame when he scrambled to his feet. Edgar hurriedly exited the building. They played on as if nothing happened. Charlie Rock didn't expect any retaliation. He was after all, the legendary Charlie Rock. This was his project was and he had been holding it down before a lot of these kids were born.

After the altercation, Charlie Rock immediately caught fire with the dice. He had the hot hand, rolling winner after winner. Taking all the other gamblers money was Charlie Rock's only thought. Edgar wasn't even an afterthought.

No one noticed Edgar slipping back inside the lobby, blending in with gamblers, but staying in the background. Having changed clothes and donning an oversized baseball cap, Edgar effectively hid his facial features.

Charlie Rock was talking that talk at the other gamblers while taking all their dough.

"You lil' niggs sweet like young deer meat…! This shit too easy… I swear you lil' niggas call yourself gamblers, huh? I can't tell!"

The crowd roared, laughing and not watching Edgar inching his way ever so close. He discreetly made his way through the crowd. Finally, he was within arm's reach, but just out of Charlie Rock's eyesight. Most of the gamblers who had witnessed the altercation had left. Their luck had run out long before their money. The ones who remained were wrapped up in the dice game and paid no attention to Edgar.

"Git 'em girls…!" Charlie Rock shouted, after intensely blowing on the dice.

The dice rolled from his fingers and Charlie Rock, along with all around him, followed the bounce of the bones with their eyes.

"Yeah, I done bust the bank open with that!" Charlie Rock said, leaning in closer to get a better view.

Caught up with awaiting the result, put Charlie Rock in a vulnerable position than ever. Edgar seized the opportunity to strike. He drew a nine-millimeter from his waistband and fired three shots in rapid succession.

"You ain't so bad now, huh Charlie Rock," Edgar said, holding the smoking gun.

Charlie Rock felt three sharp pains exploded in his back. A burning sensation unlike anything Charlie Rock had ever known engulfed him. His paranoia spread, when his body shook uncontrollably. He was going into shock and gamblers rushed to the elevators, staircase and the building's exit. They were running out of fear that they might get shot also.

Edgar used this moment of temporary bedlam to flee the building. He brandished his weapon at anyone who dared to get close to him. When a few brave friends of Charlie Rock tried to give chase, Edgar turned and let off two shots in their direction. They ducked and gave up the chase. And that was the end of that.

Charlie Rock meanwhile, lay, in a semi-conscious state, motionless on the floor. His clothing was soaked in blood. Residents quickly placed frantic calls to the authorities. Help was on the way, but Charlie Rock didn't look too good. Miraculously the man known as Charlie Rock survived.

A short time later, Edgar's bullet riddled body was found in one of the projects dumpster. Members of the Edenwald's underworld reportedly settled the score for Charlie Rock.

Rumors still continue to swirl about who made the hit. No one was ever charged with Edgar's murder. The incident shattered two lives. Edgar was confined to a coffin for eternity. Charlie Rock left to live in a wheelchair, pondering the thought of walking again for the rest of his life.

Over the course of his street life, Charlie Rock had been shot, stabbed and cut. He perpetrated these same criminal acts against others. Nothing can compare to the pain he now felt, the anguishing depression of knowing that he was a cripple. It was like his soul had died. Charlie Rock turned his body over to heavy drug abuse.

Melquan and Mike Copeland began to implement their plan the next day. Early the night before they started rallying the troops who were necessary. From trusted soldiers who had worked for them in the drug trade mixed in with some neighborhood tough guys, the recruit drive was successful. In a matter of hours, a dangerous team made up of a dozen dudes, were assembled. Those who didn't have a gun of their own gun were immediately issued a handgun. With the required soldiers behind them, Melquan and Mike Copeland began spreading the word. This was a movement. Move with it or get moved on.

First they tracked down every major dealer that they knew. Those capable of posing a threat and offering resistance, from the North side to the South side of the projects, were the first to be hit.

Unless you push our product as of today you are no longer allowed to sell drugs in Edenwald.

Their message hit each person with the same clarity. Drug dealers who balked at the idea were pistol-whipped and or shot on the spot. Others whose cooperation was doubtful or those with unknown allegiance, were pressed constantly, roughed up, harassed and robbed.

The team's objective, primarily Mike Copeland, was to make the opposition feel like they should have never left their apartment that day, let alone sell some drugs.

A harsh message was sent using brutal violence, extreme at times. Dealers quickly realized that this was not some rag tag takeover attempt, and they quickly began falling in line, one after another. Melquan and his team were for real, applying a suffocating full court press on the projects. There proved to be no drug dealer immune to this form of pressure.

Having stepped to everyone they targeted, Melquan and Mike

Copeland turned their attention to the drug dealers in the horseshoe, the most lucrative open-air drug market in the projects at the time. It was time to pay them a visit.

From every possible entrance, Melquan, Mike Copeland and their small army of black hooded goons entered the horseshoe. They descended on the horseshoe, guns drawn. They pushed their prey, drug dealers, into a mini-playground enclosure, while letting children and innocent by-standers escape. Guns were produced to get everyone's undivided attention and assure everyone's co-operation.

"Yo, pat these niggers down," Mike Copeland ordered. "Make sure none these niggas got gun on 'em."

One by one, from their waistline to their ankles, persons in question received a thorough frisk. From the look on their faces, no one liked what was happening. With weapons trained on them, they were in no position to object.

"Mike, I found a ratchet on dis nigga," a soldier shouted.

Mike Copeland calmly walked over to the dealer in question. His worker handed him the gun, and he quickly examined it then stuffed it in his waistband.

"So what was you gon' do with that?" Mike asked the dealer.

There was no response. The dealer defiantly stared at him, triggering raw emotion. Mike Copeland viciously bitch-slapped the guy's face.

"Nigga, you ass…!" Mike Copeland spat. "You couldn't bust a grape in a fruit fight. That's my gun now."

Two things were achieved by Mike Copeland's public humiliation of this dealer. One, they confiscated a firearm, gun were becoming increasing harder and harder to come by in New York City. Now there was one less gun in the projects and one less weapon in the enemy's hand. Two, now let them worry about getting shot with their own gun. This negatively affected their mental and gave them a defeated attitude. They were now less capable of defending themselves.

After everyone was searched, a sweep of the vicinity was conducted. This was to ensure that no one had stashed a gun nearby that they could have accessed. It could mean more than just the end of a meeting. Melquan, Mike Copeland and any of their soldiers, this could mean lost of life.

When the search was over, everyone was forced to sit down. Melquan, Mike Copeland and their crew were the only ones standing up.

"Ga 'head, homie," Mike Copeland announced. "It's on you."

Melquan waited for the rumble to subside. Then he addressed his captive audience.

"Lemme first of all say, ain't nothing personal 'bout this. Dis bizness! I know all y'all, and y'all know me… I'm a keep it brief. This is what this is, y'all who heard, maybe didn't hear… We takin' over da projects! So from this day forth until we say so, this is what it is…"

Back talking and rumblings were heard coming from amongst dissenters. The noise grew, drowning the speaker's address. Mike Copeland quickly dispatched himself to put a cease to it.

"A yo, money," he said, stepping up to the biggest dude. "Don't you hear my man talkin'? So why is you fuckin' talkin' huh?"

Before anyone knew Mike Copeland had quickly sucker-punched dude in the face. Embarrassed, the dude placed his face inside his palms and fell back. Mike Copeland momentarily, glared with evil intentions at him.

"Melquan, go ahead and continue," Mike Copeland said. "You won't have any more interruptions outta none of these niggas. That's my word!"

Melquan paused, and invitingly staring down at a few of them, he waited but no one dared utter another word. If they had a problem with what was being said, then they kept it like a deadly secret.

"Yeah, so like I was sayin'," Melquan continued. "Things getting outta control out here in da shoe. Niggas wildin' but ain't gotta single dollar to show for it. It's only a matter of time 'fore po-po come shut this shit down. So before they do, I will… Y'all goin' ta buy all y'all weight from me. No more goin' ta Broadway, Amsterdam or wherever ta cop. You git it from us or you don't git it at all… I got it all, eight balls, quarters, halves and ounces of that Hard White. It's a slightly higher price than you use to… But the good thing is y'all don't have ta hop in no cab and take a risk of gettin' knocked… We've already done it fa you. Da work's already here in the projects."

"So how we know that shit is official?" someone asked.

"Cause I said so. You got my word that the work is flavor. You won't git no complaints from the heads. We got samples for anyone interested."

There was a rumbling amongst the crowd. Dudes sighed while others sucked their teeth to express disinterest. Mike Copeland and the rest of the goons were ready to crack their heads if necessary. Melquan waved them off. He waited for the voices in the crowd to be silenced before he continued.

"Yo, like it or not, this is what it's goin' ta be. If any of you nigger's not down ta kill or die over this shit then shut the fuck up…" Melquan barked. "Fa' all y'all who can't afford no weight we'll front y'all sumthin reasonable… Start y'all out with packs before movin' y'all to some weight… Y'all won't be workin' fa me… Rather with me."

Melquan let his words resonate amongst his distinguished guest. He watched the stares of disbelief registered on their faces. Loving or hating his idea didn't matter to Melquan, they would respect it.

Warning was issued to all of them. There was nothing else for him to say. The meeting came to an adjournment. The ball was now in their court. The next move was theirs to make, if they had the balls to do it.

"I ain't rockin' wit dat!" someone said in the distance. "Those niggas got to be fuckin' crazy. Ain't nothing in dat shit fa nobody but them."

Melquan heard the accusation and immediately he heard his lieutenant's response.

"Pussy-ass niggas…!" Mike Copeland shouted. "Tell ya fuckin' story walkin'. I see you out here pushin' that shit I'm tax dat ass!"

Nashawn was conspicuously absent from the meeting. It bothered Melquan. He wanted to see the look on his rivals face when he flexed his muscle. That wasn't to be so he sent him a message.

"Hey yo," he said. "One a y'all tell Nashawn we wanna holla at him. And it's in his best interest if he sees us before we see him. Feel me?"

The crowd soon dispersed, drug dealers piled out. Some hurried to get guns and others ran to make phone calls about what just transpired. Melquan, Mike Copeland and their goons withdrew from the horseshoe too. Expecting retaliation, they re-strategized and reinforced their ranks with additional troops.

Mike Copeland puffed on the Newport, staring at Melquan as they walked. He seemed to be deep in thoughts. He glance at Melquan's eyes and exhaled then he spoke.

"A wise man once said, 'You can lead a horse to water but you can't make him drink it.'"

"But he ain't say nothing about force feedin' 'em," Melquan replied.

A big sarcastic smile made its way across Mike Copeland's excited grill. He enjoyed beef. This was a way to enhance his already lengthy reputation as a shooter. It didn't take Mike Copeland long to come to terms with the violence associated with his chosen profession. His code of shoot or be shot, was what he lived by and the latter wasn't appealing.

Melquan and Mike Copeland knew that the process of taking over the projects could take anywhere from a few days to weeks,

possibly months.  Still they were undaunted in their quest.  They had assured themselves that there were greener pastures and brighter days ahead, for the both of them.

## What's Beef?
Chapter Eight

It wasn't too long before the attempted coup exploded into retaliatory violence. The following morning, all hell broke loose. Melquan was sleeping comfortably at his mom's house when his cellphone went off.

"Yo," he groggily said.

Melquan half expected to hear India's voice on the other end of the phone. He was surprised to hear Mike Copeland.

"We gotta problem," the voice quickly said. "Get the biscuit, my nigga. These niggas just shot one of our workers, lil' Jay."

"What da fuck? He dead…?"

"Nah, but he in da hospital… He caught one in the shoulder and one in the leg or sumthin."

The bad news quickly brought Melquan to his senses. There had to be repercussion. He was now in war mode.

"Grab the toasts and meet me at the spot," Melquan said, using pre-arranged codes.

"A'ight! One." Mike Copeland fired back.

This was a reality check for Melquan. For the first time he truly realized just what he had gotten not only himself, but his entire team into. There was no turning back now. It was either fight or take flight. Do or die.

Melquan quickly donned all black pair of jeans and hoodie. He laced up the most comfortable pair of black sneakers he could find. He grabbed his gun and slipped on his bulletproof vest, beneath his outfit. He pulled the pair of black leather gloves on his hands. Ready for war, he cautiously exited the building. He was on full alert for the police as well as his enemies.

Nearby Boston Secor projects was Melquan's honeycomb hideout. Not even Precious or India knew about the place, for good reason. The apartment belonged to Vanessa, a female friend who Melquan was using for sex. She worked the eight to four shift for the housing department in Edenwald projects and wasn't home this time of the day and neither was her kids. Vanessa was big on Melquan and kind enough to give him a spare key to the apartment that he could use whenever he liked. This was a safe haven when he was hiding.

Melquan and Mike Copeland had currently turned it into a war room. Every soldier that they had at their disposal was summoned there. Melquan and Mike Copeland exchanged ideas and received reports about the shooting incident that transpired. They also heard about what they had seen and heard in the projects after the shooting. The pieces of the puzzle were put together, separating fact from fiction.

"Anyone heard who did it?" Melquan asked no one in particular.

"I heard it was that nigga Wiz," someone said. "He hustler on the avenue but he run wit those niggas from the horse shoe… He said Lil' Jay couldn't pump out there no more. He didn't care who he was pumpin' fa either. Wiz told Lil' Jay, if he made one more sale that he was goin' ta pop 'em. Lil' Jay did and Wiz popped off."

"Did Nashawn have anything ta do wit this?" Melquan wondered aloud.

"I don't know," the kid said. "I heard that the nigga Nashawn got bagged for some ol' ass warrant a few days ago. He ain't on the bricks yet. But you know all 'em niggas from the shoe run together."

Mike Copeland couldn't fathom how any foe had the courage to shoot one of his workers. Although the situation had angered him, outwardly he remained calm. He wanted to be in this situation, not necessarily under these circumstances. He was a shooter, and shooters shoot. It was now time to put up or shut up. Drama made mice out of men. It could also turn boys into men. The big question was who would rise to the challenge? Everybody was a soldier until the war popped off.

"Look, I could give a fuck about who done what. I ain't got time to be lookin' fa certain niggas. We see them then we see them. We give 'em the bizness. It's that simple. As far as anything else goes, I say we run up in the shoe and just start blastin'. Niggas violated. So now they gotta git it! Let's go head shoot first and ask questions last. They drew first blood and playtime is over," Mike Copeland coldly explained.

"No doubt," Melquan added.

He wasn't in a talkative mood. His mind was focused on the task at hand. Quickly Melquan began to place a series of calls.

"Hey, Vanessa what's up? It's me Melquan."

"Long time no hear from…" Vanessa excitedly answered. "You know I'm startin' to believe you only call me when you want some. I know we got an understanding but I thought we was better than that."

"Vanessa, don't take it like that. You know a nigga, busy. Grindin…" His sweet talking perked her ear. "But look I just wanted ta let you know that I'm in ya crib. I was in the area and had to use the bathroom real bad so… Anyway, I'm gonna chill out fa a few handle some B.I. with my man, Mike then I'm gone… I'll leave a lil' sumthin' fa you in ya room under the TV."

"Okay," she replied. "Just make sure you leave my crib the same way you found it. I ain't got much, but it's mine."

"A'ight. But don't I always do?"

"Yeah… You gonna come back through later?"

"I'll see what I can do. Shit is a lil' hectic right now… I'll holla at you later!"

Melquan wished he could have every female wrapped around his finger the way he had Vanessa. Life sure would be easier. Thoughts of India flashed across his mind. It wasn't the right time to call her. He had business to tend to. Melquan made another call.

"Yo, this me… I know you heard what happened this morning," Melquan said.

"Yeah…"

"Do not talk about it over my line. Anyway, how it look out there? As far niggas and po-po…?"

"Where are you, Mel?" Precious immediately asked.

"Damn, don't worry bout that. Just answer my questions."

"It was a lil' hot a few hours ago. But things have quieted down now. There's only a few heads out."

"Okay listen, I want you stay inside ya crib. Don't come outside, understand?" Melquan ordered."

"Why?"

"I'll explain later," he said, assuring her. "For right now, I just need you to keep me posted on to what's happenin' in the shoe. Lemme know when niggas start getting' comfy and come outside. Once that happen, hit my jack ASAP! One…!"

Precious stared at her cellphone, rolled her eyes, and shook her head. She was pissed that she couldn't be where Melquan was, despite the danger. Although she had close association with Melquan, she knew he wouldn't put her in harm's way. Precious didn't care. She was his ride-or-die-chick. No matter what the weather, she wanted to be by his side.

For the rest of the morning and early into the afternoon, Melquan, Mike Copeland and company, chilled at Vanessa's apartment. They knew it wasn't in their best interest to retaliate right away. They waited a few hours, in the hopes time would be on their side. Everyone would be expecting them to come through. They had to move when they were least expected.

A few hours passed, finally Melquan got the call he had been waiting for.

"Mel, them niggas out here…!" Precious said. "It's like nothing ever happened."

Melquan said nothing, he hung up the phone. His light mood turned tense.

"Mike, call us four cabs. Request the windows be tinted too… We out…!"

The dispatcher for new Laconia cab service found the request for four-tinted window cabs odd, but complied anyway. The four cabs rolled to a stop outside Boston Secor projects, and lined up back to back. Melquan and company boarded the cab, two men per taxi. Melquan and Mike Copeland rode in separate cabs. Each person gave the cab driver a different direction in which to drive. They all had the same destination, Edenwald projects.

The cabs dropped them off at designated points, some at 229th Street drive, some at 226th Street and Laconia Avenue and others at 225th Street drive. When everyone was in position, they all received a chirp on their phones from Melquan. They descended on the horseshoe in pairs from different direction. School buses and kids provided the perfect camouflage they would need to move undetected.

The crew met up in the horseshoe, simultaneously liked they had planned. They spotted the suspicious parties and gunshots rang. Mike Copeland was the first to pop off. No words were exchanged only a barrage of bullets.

Horrified residents looked on in pure terror at the shootout that had erupted in broad daylight. Grabbing their children, they quickly darted for the safety of the buildings. Ducking for cover, they went inside the burgundy brick buildings, knowing that it would provide them with their only safe haven. Bullets were flying all over the place the horseshoe was transformed into a war zone.

Not wanting to hit innocent bystander, Melquan's crew was careful how they engaged the enemy. Mike Copeland didn't care, he was shooting at everybody.

"Fuck it! Let the police sort out the guilty from the innocent. Right now they all looked the same to me," Mike Copelamd said, firing his automatic weapon. "Damn!" he cursed when the hammer of his gun flew backwards. It was smoking, but he was out of ammunition.

Fortunately, for him he was near Precious' apartment window when it happened. With no one returning fire, Mike felt safe enough to attempt to get another gun.

"A yo," he shouted up to the window. "Throw me that thing."

Precious's nose had been jammed to the window, watching the entire gun battle. She was on point.

"Here," she called out.

Mike Copeland tucked the other pistol he had just emptied into his waistband then caught the silver .45 Precious had conveniently dropped out the window. He cocked it back and started firing without missing a beat.

Although shootout had only been going on for a few minutes, to the participants it felt longer. Especially once their fire started to be returned. Some of the dealers who had escaped went inside their apartments. They ran up to the roof to return fire. Melquan and company were forced to take cover behind a row of parked cars until they could locate the shooters.

"They on the roof…!" Melquan pointed, from his crouched position. "Niggas up there shootin' at us…!"

Melquan's crew focused all their attention on the rooftop and began firing. The great volume of shot successfully put an end to the sniping. Sensing that the police might be on their way, Melquan waved to Mike Copeland, signaling to him and everyone to fall back. It was time to go. They had riddled the horseshoe with bullets and vanished into the maze that was the project.

In their wake they left countless spent shell cases and few wounded victims. Miraculously no one was killed. If the projects didn't know they were serious, they knew now.

After that incident, Melquan, Mike Copeland, and their team moved deliberately through the projects everyday, from North Side to South Side, building to building, performing routine shooting and shakedowns. It would take them whole month and then some to implement the plan. They sent messages to their rivals, and residents through non stop violence that the local police department could do little about. The takeover would be a stark reminder for anyone who had forgotten about the good old bad days in Edenwald projects.

## Gettin' a Rep

Chapter Nine

It was month later and two weeks fresh off his latest punishment, Jose Torres Jr. sat inattentively during his final class of the day. He attended a strict parochial school. Jose was agitated and seemed more interested in his watch than the curriculum. It was geography, but Jose Jr. kept his eyes on his watch. Glancing at his wrist for the umpteenth time, he began quickly packing his textbook in his book bag.

Even though it wasn't time to go, Jose Jr. jumped out of his seat, disturbing the class in the process. The teacher, Sister Saunders looked up at him. She stopped the class, and addressed him.

"Mr. Torres, where do you think you are going? Class is not yet ended," she said, looking at her watch.

"Excuse me, Sister, no disrespect. But school is over," Jose said, holding up his wristwatch.

"Young man, please sit down. School isn't dismissed until the bell sounds. And according to my calculations you still have several more minutes left. Please be seated so I can continue on with my lessons plan for those students who are interested in learning—"

The bell rang, interrupting the teacher. She stared menacingly at Jose Jr. The rest of the class started to laugh. The teacher quickly addressed the class.

"Please make sure you read chapter twelve. That is your homework assignment. Tomorrow you will be quizzed on what you have read."

Jose was already out the door, he hadn't heard a word she said. He was running out the schoolyard and already waiting to pick up Maria. A few seconds later, she joined him and they started their journey, walking home.

In no time flat they were back home in the projects. Jose was busy getting out of his school uniform. He slipped on a pair of blue jeans complete with a black hoodie. Maria remained fully dressed in her parochial school attire. Taking off her shoes was as comfortable as she got. While sitting in the living room she saw her brother quickly trying to duck out the door.

"And where do you think you're going?" she asked.

"Shut up!" Jose snapped. "Who you think you are? My mother or sumthin...?"

They were just about to engage in a big argument when suddenly their father walked into the apartment. Maria jumped into his arms.

"Daddy..."

"Hey princess... Jose where'd you think you're going?"

"Oh, hey dad, I was gonna ask you if I can go to the library?"

"For what…?" Jose Sr. asked with a suspicious scowl on his tired face.

"I've gotta use their computer to check on some research for a social studies paper I have due next week."

"I bought a brand new computer, what do you's think it's for? Just to download songs, instant message your friends, go on Myspace and watch videos on Youtube huh? If you gotta go down to the library then why the hell did I buy it for then? It was for schoolwork, things like this research…"

"Daddy, I use it for that," Maria chimed. "Unlike some people…"

"Dad, the information I need is only found at the New York City's public library online data base. You have to physically be in the library and use one of their computers to access it."

"Oh alright, I guess you's can go. But why don't you's bring along your sister so she can keep you's company."

"Dad, I don't need no company. I see her enough… Plus, she's not even dressed. And you know Maria,s she's a girl and she be moving too slow. She's gonna hold me up. Then she walks real slow… Can't I just go by myself?"

"Forget you, Jose. I hope you can't find what you're looking for and you fail. Then I'd really laugh. Ha! Ha!" Maria chided.

"Maria, that's enough. That's not cute," Jose Sr. cautioned.

Jose Sr's expression hardened when he heard the animosity in his son's voice. He didn't like it one bit. All he ever wanted was for his kids to be close. Outside of him, they were all that each other had. If he only they could realize it. He wanted them to build a bond. God forbid something was to happen to him, he hoped that they would be there for one another. Whether his fears of disunity were real or confirmed, it didn't matter. His children's bickering was a major cause of concern.

"Alright my princess, stay home with papi. Go ahead," Jose Sr.

said, following his son to the door. "You shouldn't act like that toward your sister. It ain't like you two come from a big family. It's only you and her. There's no reason for you to be carrying on like that."

"Okay dad," Jose said, walking out the door.

Out on the street the evening air was becoming cooler. Jose slung his hoodie low on the left side of his face. He was headed towards the horseshoe driveway. Jose slowed and changed his bop when he saw a group of teens.

"What up Jose?" they greeted.

"We 'bout to go puff this L." one of them said. "You wanna be down."

"Yeah, why not?" Jose answered.

Jose walked over and gave a familiar dap to all the teens. Then they disappeared inside a building free from prying eyes and the police. One of the teens pulled out the blunt, and said, "Yo Jose, you wanna spark this shit up my nigga?"

Jose Jr. stared at the blunt long and hard before giving an answer. Before he could comment, another blunt was brandished.

"I ain't waitin' on y'all. I got my own trees," one of the other teens said, immediately lighting the blunt.

He had a strong pull on it, and exhaled a cloud smoke. He inhaled deeply again, and passed the blunt to another teen, who started puffing. Two blunts were in rotation, and full fledge smoke session was going down. The blazing blunt finally reached Jose. He nervously took it and fumbled the hand off, causing the blunt to hit the floor.

"Damn yo you comin' in here and fuckin' shit up already, huh?" one teen asked. "Everything was goin' good 'til we passed the damn blunt off to your clumsy ass."

"Don't let the blunt drop in no piss, nigga," another teen said.

"Hurry up and hit the blunt, Jose. Other niggas in the cipher. Is you scared or what?" another asked.

"Yo, if he don't want none of that, pass it here, my nigga," a teen yelled.

"Nah skip him, give it here, I'll show him what to with that," another laughed.

"Yo, this nigger too scared his pops gonna find out!" someone said. "Don't worry we won't tell on you. We'll keep that on the low-low," he laughed.

They all joined in laughter at the red-faced Jose's expense. He looked around them taunting him and flipped.

"Shut da fuck up! I ain't even thinking about my pops. And what he don't fuckin' know ain't gonna fuckin hurt him!"

"Alright, stop frontin' and smoke that shit," a smiling teen prompted Jose.

Jose stared at the blunt. Finally, putting it to his lips he inhaled too hard. Too much smoke, too fast, too soon, left him coughing and clutching his throat. Jose was coughing so hard, his face got redder and his eyes became inflamed. It appeared he was about to pop a few blood vessels. The teens burst into uncontrollable laughter. Caving in under peer pressure, Jose became the brunt of their jokes.

"Gimme that shit 'fore you bust a blood vessel and bleed to death," one of the teens said, laughing.

"Yeah take that form that novice before he kill himself," another teen laughed.

"Here, you can have this shit! I don't want anymore," Jose said, coughing and holding the blunt like it was a time-bomb.

His head exploded even after Jose gave up the blunt he continued gagging, choking, and was totally disorientated from the weed. Doubled over, saliva was drooling from Jose's mouth. Another teen walked over, and started patting him on the back. The others were puffing, and their laughter rang loud in the lobby.

"Damn, Jose sound like he gettin' ready ta die over there," one of the teen observed, laughing.

"This nigga's a new jack. I can tell by the way he coughing," a teen said, trying to sum it up.

They continued the cipher, smoking and getting high without Jose. He was chewing on a piece of candy offered by someone.

"Let's go check out some girls," one teen suggested.

"Yeah, let's go over to the center," another said.

"I'm about to go upstairs and play Madden, my niggas." another joined in.

They were surprised when the building door suddenly swung open. Melquan and Mike Copeland walked into the lobby. The teens held their collective breaths, when Mike Copeland instinctively reached for his nine millimeter under his NY Yankee warm–up jacket.

Fear swept through the crowded hallway. Both Melquan and Mike Copeland quietly surveyed each of their faces. Jose Jr. attempted to straighten up. The gun in Mike Copeland's grip held the teens in check. Melquan sniffed the air.

"I know y'all lil' niggas ain't up in my buildin' smokin' no weed, now?" Melquan shouted. "I better not catch any a y'all violatin' like this, ever. Don't none of y'all even live in this building." Melquan looked at all their faces before saying, "Get fuck up outta here!"

Jose tried to run off with the rest of the crew, but started in a coughing fit and was unable to flee the scene. Melquan approached Jose with a look of concern.

"Hold on Mike," Melquan said, walking to Jose. "You a'ight, shorty…?"

"Yeah, I'm good," Jose said.

"Fuck is all that coughing about then?"

"I guess some smoke went down the wrong way," Jose said, trying not cough.

"How about this…? Maybe your young ass shouldn't be

smoking."

"Yeah, I guess you right…"

Melquan stare caused Jose top straighten up. Embarrassment crossed his face when he saw the wrinkle of a smile on Melquan's face. He looked away, keeping his head straight ahead.

"Yo, what's ya name?"

"Um… Jose."

"Jose, you seem like a smart kid right? So what the fuck you doin' hangin' out here with these knuckleheads in this buildin'?"

"I live around here. They're my friends. I'm from da projects too. Just like you," Jose said, nodding his head.

"Hmm really…?"

"Yeah, those kids are my friends. I used to go to school with them, and grew up in the same building with some of them."

Melquan stared at the now relaxed youngster and was able to see his face. He recognized him immediately.

"Oh…yeah, now that you said that, you do look familiar. Don't you be with this lil' girl all the time…?"

"Yeah, that's my sister—"

"Yo Mel, we ain't got time to be playin' social worker gettin' familiar with everybody in homies family… My nig, I'm dirty. Let's get da fuck up outta da lobby," Mike Copeland said, moving closer to Melquan.

"You're right. Jose, do me a favor and leave 'em knuckleheads alone. They're goin' nowhere fast. Believe that! Now go on home."

Jose walked out the building and looked back just before the door slammed shut. He saw Melquan standing there steadfastly looking at him. It was as if he knew Jose would look back, Melquan was waiting to stare him down. Something about this kid told Melquan this wouldn't be the last time their paths would cross.

# Armed and Dangerous
Chapter Ten

Although things were simmering down in the projects, Melquan and Mike Copeland were actively stepping up their recruitment for their drug organization. Each guy that they knew of that returned home from prison they made a pitch to each individual to run with them. To sway their decisions they often took these guys shopping for clothing or whatever they might need. In certain cases, they also armed these dudes giving them handguns that they had either taken from rivals or bought on the streets.

Routinely they made it a point to check up on dudes and see how they were doing. They gave them weekly monetary allowances until they got on their feet. By doing little things like this their numbers began to swell.

Melquan and Mike Copeland's drug operation was expanding along with the duo's reputation for violence. Everyday they would deliberately move from building to building, from North side to South side, and all points in-between. Once they got wind of Nashawn returning home from a brief stint on Riker's Island, they immediately paid him a visit.

Rolling two deep, Melquan and Mike Copeland were able to move through the projects virtually unnoticed. They quietly slipped into Nashawn's building and quietly lay for him either entering or exiting, it really didn't matter.

When Nashawn suddenly walked downstairs into their trap, Melquan couldn't be happier. Upon hearing his voice and the sound of footsteps descending Melquan and Mike Copeland suddenly appeared from their hiding space beneath the stairs. Mike Copeland was ready with his weapon already drawn.

"Oh shit!" Nashawn exclaimed, raising his arms shoulder height.

"Long time no see," Melquan greeted. "What's crackin'? Put you guns down and lemme holla at you real quick, Nashawn."

"What da fuck y'all doin in my buildin'?" Nashawn summoned the courage to ask. He took a few steps backward.

"Don't even think about turnin' 'round, nigga. I'll put a bullet in ya fuckin' back!" Mike Copeland warned.

Nashawn, like everone else was well aware of Mike Copeland trigger happy reputation. Out of fear of being gunned down in his building, Nashawn dared not move a muscle. At this moment, Melquan and Mike Copeland had the upper hand, he conceded that much.

"Look fam, I know you been away for a second, but more than likely you got the word about what was happening around here. I'm a make a long story short. You either git down wit us, selling work for us, or buyin' weight from us, it don't matter. Those are the only two choices you have. If you got a problem wit what I just said let it be known right here, right now…" Melquan said, interrupting Mike Copeland harder approach.

Nashawn was never the one to fight when the odds were against him. He didn't stand a chance going up against a loaded gun. For a moment Nashawn remained silently scheming while staring a Melquan's smirk. He grimaced looking down the barrel of Mike's gun.

"So what its gon' be?"

"Mel, fuck this shit, man! Let's just smoke this nigga right now and git it over with," Mike Copeland fiercely suggested. "We don't need this nigga!"

The loud sound of a squeaky apartment door momentarily distracted all parties. Their eyes gazed upstairs at the source of the sound. An old woman suddenly appeared. Gingerly, she slowly took each stair, one at a time. Mike Copeland lowered his gun slightly, to the side of his leg.

A wicked smile suddenly spread across Nashawn face. He knew that the woman was his ticket out of this predicament.

"Nigga, who the fuck you think you are…? The mob…? You and Mike Copeland is a joke, man. Fuck you and your meetin'!"

"What?" Mike Copeland shouted, raising his gun slightly. "You faggot ass nigga!"

"What you gon' do? Shoot me?" Nashawn said, wanting to be overheard.

The old woman by now had come into sight. She could see the tension escalating between the parties, not to mention what she just heard.

"Nigga you pull that trigger, you better kill me!" Nashawn announced at full volume.

He was acting bold because he knew Mike Copeland's smirk was not enough to harm him. Mike watched him silently shaking his head.

"Fuck you, Melquan and the rest of your weak-ass team! I'd never join y'all bunch o' pussies! I'm my own man. I'm gonna sell my shit whenever and wherever I damn well please!"

"Then you're gonna have a problem with my team," Melquan said, wearing a cynical smile.

"Mel, please lemme kill this piece of shit! Let's settle this shit right here!"

"Melquan…?" The older woman asked, straining her eyes to see his facial features. "Is that you?

"Yes, Miss Butler," he said. "How you doing…? He quickly added.

"I thought that was you," she said.

"Damn!" Melquan uttered under his breath.

He silently cursed himself for the calamity he was in. This woman knew his entire family. There was no way now he could allow gunfire to erupt. He stepped in front of Mike Copeland while simultaneously grabbing his arm that he used to clutch the gun. Not only did he shield the weapon from the old woman's eyes, Melquan also signaled him to be easy. The situation was still a volatile one.

"How's Miss Tina doing? Tell her she could come see me sometimes. You know I'm still here… Right in apartment 2D…" She continued.

"Oh alright," Melquan said, his eyes riveted on Nashawn.

"What you doin' in my building, anyway…?" She smiled, wondering.

"I'm just visitin' my real good friend here, Miss Butler," he said.

When Melquan spoke, Nashawn glanced at him sideways. All of a sudden Nashawn turned and walked out the building unharmed.

"Peace out, friend. I'll see you suckas later," Nashawn said with his middle finger held high.

The sound of a car horn distracted Ms Butler's and grabbed her attention. Nashawn had already disappeared into the still night.

"Oh, excuse me, baby. That must be my ride. Be sure to tell your mother what I said," she said before hobbling off.

"You got it, I'll tell her, Miss Butler. Goodnight," Melquan said, holding the door.

"Goddamn!" Mike Copeland cursed. "I don't believe this shit. We had that nigga right where we wanted him. Ol' bitch showed up and fuck shit up!"

"Calm down. We'll settle this another day. I don't want no innocent bystanders caught up when bullets start flyin'. Besides that, I known her since I was mad young," Melquan said.

Mike Copeland swallowed hard and shook his head before he spoke. They were both looking outside on the project's night sky.

"That nigga real lucky, I was about to body that mufuckin-runnin'-mouth nigga," Mike Copeland said, tucking his gun back into his waistband.

Old friends and business associates, Melquan and Mike Copeland kept talking. They walked out the building.

"I'd a let him feel the heat. Mel, I'd just hit da nigga twice, one for you and one for me. Nah, make it three times. The third slug be for his direspectfulness."

"I know. I saw you were ready to give that moron the bizness. Don't worry, we gon' see da nigga again. Believe that," Melquan said, assuring him.

"I don't know what da fuck you were thinkin', Mel? Why did we even bother to come at dis nigga talkin'? You already know what type of nigga he is. According to the plan, we was supposed to smash this fool early."

"No question."

"To a nigga, like Nashawn, we look like we came here to cop a plea. Da nigga gon' be feelin' himself way too much now, ya heard me?"

Silently, they slipped inside the building where Precious resided. Her apartment was used for stashing their weapons. Melquan was contemplating the events that just transpired. He could hear Charlie Rock's voice in his head saying, 'Man didn't I teach you better than that. We only pull out guns for a reason, not for the season. A true hustla only uses gunplay as a last resort. Life or death…'

When they reached Precious' door Mike stared at Melquan. They knew the job was not complete until they were completely rid of Nashawn.

"When you come at a killa, you can't come talkin' they don't understand that language. Now we really got watch our backs, Melquan. I ain't scared of Nashawn, but I know he's gon' be a problem," Mike Copeland said, pounding his fist.

Precious opened the door and smiled when she saw Melquan and Mike Copeland standing in the hallway. They walked in and silently secured the weapons. Precious followed them around like a pesky child. She was dying to find out the 411.

"So what happened with Nashawn?" Precious asked. "I know y'all handled that lame, right?"

Her eyes were wide open, darting from Melquan's to Mike Copeland's face then back agan. She anxiously awaited a response, but never got one.

## Real Niggas Do Real Things

Chapter Eleven

He had a strong craving for Jamaican food. This hunger led Melquan to 225ᵗʰ Street and Laconia Ave. Melquan wasn't about to let his ongoing drug turf disputes keep him from satisfying his hunger. The .380 tucked in his waistband was strictly for defensive purposes. He donned a hoodie to help camouflage his identity. Melquan walked to the restaurant like normal people do.

On entering the Jamaican restaurant, Melquan removed his hoodie and immediately chilled in a far corner of the restaurant next to the Snapple machine. In this strategic position he retained the element of surprise. He was able to see whoever entered the restaurant after him. He patiently waited to place his order.

"So what ya wan…? Curry goat, peas, and rice? What size… small… medium or large?" the cook asked in thick Jamaican accent.

Prior to his beef, Melquan used to frequent the restaurant so much the cook knew his face, and his favorite order.

"Yes sir," Melquan nodded.

The cook grinned, grabbed a Styrofoam food tray, and hurried filling Melquan's order.

Unexpectedly, Nashawn suddenly entered the business establishment. He didn't even see Melquan laying in the cut. Nashawn walked to the counter, glancing around.

"Yo bombo-claat, Ras, where you at…?" Nashawn shouted. "Where you at my man…? I ain't got all fuckin' day. Come hit me off now, Jah!"

Nashawn could feel someone watching him and immediately scanned the surrounding. He jumped back when he spotted Melquan in the cut.

There were no words exchanged between the drug adversaries. Melquan stared menacingly at Nashawn. When the shock wore off, Nashawn did the same.

Melquan gripped the gun he kept in his waistband. Nashawn saw the outline of a gun and knew Melquan had the advantage. From his vantage point, Melquan could drop Nashawn if he wanted.

"Can I help you?" the cook's sudden request broke the impasse.

"Matter fact, I'm good." Nashawn said without taking his eye off Melquan.

Nashawn backpedaled out the store with his eyes peeled on the man in black hoodie, standing next to the Snapple machine. Once across the street, Nashawn was in the wind. He quickly disappeared into the projects.

"Me nah like dat blood claat yout'… Ya hear me. Your order is eight-fifty," the cook abruptly announced.

"Me either!" Melquan chuckled and nodded his head.

Nashawn's presence had made him uneasy. Even though he had the advantage, Melquan felt like a sitting duck. He paid for his food and quickly left, vowing not to take a chance like that again. The next time he wanted anything from the store, he would send someone to get it for him. On the way back to his building, Melquan called Mike Copeland's cellphone.

"Yo, guess what?" he immediately said. "I just seen faggot-ass," he continued without waiting for an answer.

"Nashawn... Where...?" Mike Copeland replied.

"At the Jamaican restaurant on the Ave..."

"Please tell me he still there...? I'm on my way right fuckin' now."

"Nah, that nigga bounced soon as he saw me. He ain't even order or nothin'."

"Damn, I wish you would a called me earlier. We coulda finished his punk-ass off."

"Yo, I was thinkin' from what I saw that nigga ain't no threat. Truth be told, that nigga ain't even worth it. If we hit 'em up and he don't die, da nigga's the type that might tell on us... Shit's startin' to go good right now. I don't wanna fuck shit up over that dumb ass nigga."

The brief silence on the phone was long enough to let Melquan know that Mike Copeland wasn't particularly feeling his idea for a ceasefire.

"Yo, I don't agree with you on that one. I say we smoke him. Save ourselves the trouble of having to do it later..."

"We good I'm tellin' you. He'll be no problem, he don't want beef."

"So da nigga just gon' back down like that...?"

"I'm tellin' you, he don't want it."

"A'ight, if you say so then..." Mike Copeland spat, like the end of a eulogy. "And so we lay it to rest…"

Early evening and Melquan jumped from the cab, heading to a neighborhood sneaker store in Bay Plaza. His on again, off again relationship with India was sinking into jeopardy. Melquan thought of buying India and Zach couple pairs of sneakers. He hoped gifts would smooth things over with her. India liked when he bought things for Zach and spend time with him. The boy's father was currently not giving his kid the time of day and file custody papers for the boy out of spite.

Stomping into the store, Melquan was spotted by Nashawn. He was at the Plaza catching a movie.

"Yo Butta, stop the car!" Nashawn ordered after spotting Melquan. "You gotta ratchet up in here, kid?"

"Nah, who be ridin''round wid fuckin' guns in they whips these days? It's too hot uptown. The gun squad is definitely pullin' cars over, big homie. And I ain't tryin a go back up north," Nashawn's friend, Butta said.

"Damn!" Nashawn cursed. "I'd lay that-fake-ass-gangsta down right now, if I had a ratchet."

"Who you talkin' 'bout…? That kid you was just talkin' 'bout that pulled out on you earlier? What's his name?"

"Melquan…"

"Yeah, you talked da muthafucka up. Where he at?"

"He jus went inside da sneaker store, kid. Damn, this a moment whe you need the gat."

"Nashawn, I got an idea, son. Let's just follow da nigga and see where he goes. If you know where da nigga resting his head, it'll be easier to do him."

"Yes son. You a fuckin' genius Butta… Yes let's follow da

muthafucka 'round for a minute. He don't know your whip, anyhow."

"And dese tints… Nigga ain't gon see you no way, Nashawn."

"Word up…"

After purchasing the sneakers, Melquan walked a short distance to the entrance of India's apartment building on Driesler Loop, Co-Op City. It was a cool evening and he pulled the hoodie over his head. Although the hoodie may have hidden his identity, it also obscured his vision. Melquan was completely unaware of the car, occupied by Nashawn that was slowly following him.

From a safe distance, Nashawn watched Melquan enter the building, taking note of the building address. A few minutes elapsed before the Nashawn made his move.

"Yo, what you about to do…?" Butta asked with concern. "Remember you ain't got no ratchet. What if Melquan sees you? You said da nigga had a ratchet on him earlier?"

"Son, son, be easy," Nashawn assured him. "I got this, a'ight?"

"A'ight, if you say so. Only you know best," Butta said. "So what you want me to do?"

"Just chill right here, nobody knows you, nigga," Nashawn said exiting the car.

He walked over to the building and entered. Pretended to be looking at the buildings intercom list, Nashawn struggled to select the right bell. Finally, he gave up and tapped lobby door and motioned for the security guard.

"Ah, excuse me, sir. I'm lookin' for my friend who just entered the building a few minutes ago. He was wearing a sweatshirt with black hoodie. I had to find parking and he didn't tell me what floor he lives on to buzz his intercom… Would you happen to know, sir?"

Before answering, the Hispanic security guard quickly

scrutinized Nashawn. He found his mannerism non-threatening and his speech to be very polite.

"Who are you talking about Melquan?"

"Yeah...Mel," Nashawn smiled.

"He live on the seventeenth floor, I think, ah, it's seventeen G. You can go up if you would like."

"That's just it I can't find parking and…"

"Yeah, parking is bad around here at this time of the evening. Go around the block—"

"Nah thanks, man. I'll just buzz him when I find parking. If not, I'll wait for him outside in the car a just lil' while longer. He should be comin' down soon anyway."

Nashawn walked out the building with a smile on his face. He got back in the car and Butta drove off. He knew Melquan's exact location and there was no need to stick around.

Heading back to the projects, the devilish grin smeared Nashawn's rugged face. Now, he wouldn't be the only one watching his back when he entered a building. His mind started scheming a way to send Melquan a mesaage. Put him on his p's and q's.

Upstairs, Melquan labored with the keys trying to open the door to India's apartment.

"Damn!" he hissed aloud. "So much for a fuckin' surprise, I can't even open the fuckin' door."

The more he struggled with the lock, the more Melquan thought he was tripping. He couldn't open it to save his life. He checked the apartment number, seventeen G, this was the right door. Melquan thought as he tried the key again and again. He removed the key, looked at it, and began blowing his breath on it. He tried to open the door again, to no avail. It suddenly hit him like a ton of bricks. India changed the damn locks. Why else wouldn't his key work? Melquan sighed loudly, and banged his fist against the door.

India peeped through the peephole before opening the door. Melquan had a blank look on his face. They pause for a moment. No one says a word. Long stares replaced what they had to say. Finally India spoke, breaking the icy silence.

"Well are you just going to stand there, staring and saying nothing? Or, are you coming in?"

"I'm waitin' on you. You the one changin' locks and blockin' the door," Melquan said, bravely controlling the anger raging through him.

India watched him with concern in her eyes. She wondered where he was coming from. And why he was acting as if he had an attitude with her. India wanted to hug Melquan just to be engulfed in his warm embrace. She missed him, but now wasn't the right time to display those feelings. Instead she stepped aside and Melquan entered the apartment. If there were going to be a scene, it wouldn't be in the hallway. Having her nosey neighbors in her business was the last thing she wanted.

Melquan walked into the apartment and headed straight for the bedroom. India followed closely behind him. She watched him threw his bag that been on the floor in the corner of her closet. Reach underneath the bed, Melquan pulled out his stash box. He removed all the money from it and stuffed it into his pockets. Then he removed every article of clothes from the closet and placed it on the bed.

"What are you doing? Are you leaving?" India asked, watching Melquan from behind.

"It's obvious you don't want me here anymore. You changed the locks. So I'm a just pack my shit, and bounce…" his voice trailed as he continued packing.

Melquan grabbed a duffel bag, and started putting his clothes inside. He was too vindictive to even realize how emotionally charged this process was. In his mind it was over and there were no two ways about it. India didn't have to tell him twice. By changing the locks the message was loud and clear.

"You're just going to let it all end like this, right Melquan?"

India moved to face Melquan. She wanted him to look her directly in the eye. There were more than questions on her mind. Melquan wasn't in the mood for any of her mind games. He tried to walk by her, but she blocked him.

"There's no way we can talk it out?" India asked in the softest of tones.

She got his attention by holding him in a bear hug. Melquan hugged her back. India smiled up at him.

"Please Melquan," India requested. "Don't be like that."

"Please don't be like what? Huh? You're the one who keep kicking me out. Every time we have an argument or a disagreement it be 'Melquan please go'. What's up with that?"

"I would rather you leave than have a heated argument with you. My son lives in the apartment. Was I wrong last time? Put yourself in my shoes. What would you do? You left me no other choice. You've cheated and you've lied, done me wrong over and over, Melquan. It's gotten to the point where I have to question everything you tell me."

"Oh really…? So whatever I say don't matter, you just gonna think it's a lie anyway, right? Those things are accusations, figments of your imagination. You know nothing have ever been proven."

"Melquan, you're acting like I'm doing something wrong. You've got to recognized that you're the one causing these situations. I'm not the one to be faulted here, I just reacted, I never acted."

"No baby, you overreacted. You blow things way out of proportion. All you had to say was take that out of my house. Or, don't come back with that shit on you… I could respect that if you say it in a nice tone of voice."

"Okay, I agree, I can be a little nasty at times. And I'm sorry but, Melquan I've told you that same thing before. It's not like we haven't had similar conversations, Melquan. On top of all that, I've been calling you for the past few days. You don't even return my calls, Melquan. I've called your mother's home and left messages. And still there were no phone calls from Melquan. Which leads me to believe something ain't right."

India threw her hands up and was about to walk away. Melquan grabbed her and kissed her hard. When they were both out of breath, he let her go.

"Baby, sometimes it ain't what you say, it's the way you say it. You got a way of makin' a nigga feel like he ain't shit," Melquan painfully explained. "It's like I ain't on your level, or sump'n."

"I'm so sorry, honey. It's not like that, really," India said, kissing Melquan's lips. "I'll try to be more understanding. But sometimes I panic because the custody thing, you know that."

"Look, I want everything to go right for you and Zach. I ain't tryin' a fuck shit up. But you know how I'm living right now. I'm eating off the streets. Sometimes shit just happens. I don't plan on bringing the bullshit to your door. I'd never knowingly jeopardize your custody situation."

India moved back away from Melquan and stared at him incredulously. Then she smiled awkwardly as tears welled up in her eyes. She spoke softly.

"For whatever its worth, I love you. And I really care for you, Melquan. I don't want you to leave me… I don't want you to go anywhere. I want you right here with Zach and me. I want us to be a family. We can work this out, Mel," India reassured him, clinging to Melquan.

The close proximity of their bodies was causing Melquan to calm down. He rather enjoyed touching India in such a sensual way.

"You know, married people go through this all the time. There will be arguments, fussing and fighting, but at the end of the day, the only thing that keeps them together is an open line of communication…

Let's talk it over, boo. Melquan, let's do what married people do…" her voice trailed.

Her tongue was down his throat and words would not suffice. They kissed passionately for another couple minutes, breathing each other's essence. Melquan embrace became firmer, his arms gripped her shoulder tightly, and India was lifted off her feet. She marveled at his strength.

"Let's take a shower together…" India whispered warmly against his ears.

He carried India into the bathroom and turned on the shower. They quickly pulled off each other's clothes. Their bodies were continually drawn to each other, with India sitting on top of the sink way before the shower got warm.

Melquan's nature hardened and soon he penetrated India. She willfully accepted every inch of his manhood as it went deep into her womb. Hot water produced steam and it formed a thick mist. Their naked bodies were joined together in passion.

"Oh baby yes! Give it to me!" she demanded.

"Yeah talk that shit." Melquan said. "Take this dick!"

He fucked her good and she screamed loudly with a care, the way he remembered her. It was just like in the beginning when the sex was new, and their passion was hot. Cries of pleasure constantly escaped India's body and only served to excite Melquan even more.

"I'm about to come…" he sighed heavily.

She kissed his lips and sucked hard on his tongue. Melquan continued to rhythmically pump India with rapid succession. India raised her hips to meet his every thrust. Their bodies moved easily against each other in an enticing sexual dance. Finally, India wrapped her legs around Melquan's waist, pulling him deeper inside her.

"Come in my pussy," she seductively whispered. "Come all inside me."

"Oh ah, ah… Ah ugh…!" Melquan screamed.

India worked her back and Melquan shot his load. His knees buckled as the semen raced from his body. Momentarily weakened, Melquan collapsed against India. They were both lost in the moment.

"You were kind a loud, where's Zach?" he asked, regaining his senses.

"Oh, he's with his father. We got the whole house to ourselves. I'm glad you asked. You really care Melquan. C'mon, let's do it again."

"Hummmm, sounds like a plan to me," Melquan excitedly exclaimed.

Melquan lifted himself off India. She climbed down from the sink.

"C'mon," she suddenly proclaimed. "Let's do it in the shower."

She grabbed his hardened dick and led him. Melquan didn't reply, he merely followed her lead.

# A Gangster's Gambit

Chapter Twelve

About a month later, Melquan's dreams of taking over the project's illicit drug trade turned into reality. To witness how a slim possibility had morphed into a certainty, even to him, was an amazing feat. His crew now controlled the crack trade throughout the entire projects and that meant more customers. Having beat back all challengers, Melquan and Mike Copeland, were now free to concentrate on profits rather than strategizing for beef.

Shop was set up in the horseshoe; it was the cartel's primary place of operation. The choice was logical one, there was already drug flow and Precious lived there. This meant they could access weapons and drugs all day, making profit and be protected at the same time. Melquan and Mike Copeland took full advantage of both.

Taking a break from overseeing their drug empire, Melquan and Mike Copeland spotted Charlie Rock. Mike Copeland sighed loudly.

"Yo Mel, here come ya man," Mike Copeland announced. "Unk Leech," he laughed.

"Mike you one disrespectful bastard. You know that, right?" Melquan replied.

"Yeah, tell me about it," Mike answered. "I just don't like seein' muthafuckas I know, git played outta position. Am I wrong for that?"

"Play me out how? Tell me how he playin' me out?" Melquan insisted.

"Niggas think I be talkin' just cuz I like hearin' myself. Runnin' 'round here hatin' on niggas for no apparent reason. I got my reasons Mel! Like they say, what's done in the dark will come to light. One day what I'm sayin' will all make sense."

"Yeah, one day...? Cause right now, you talkin' in riddles, my dude."

"Whatever Mel. I'm out like last year. I don't even wanna witness da bullshit he 'bout to lay on you. When he bounces, I'll be back."

Silently, Melquan watched Mike walked away in the opposite direction. He smirked, shaking his head in disbelief and turned his attention to Charlie Rock rapidly approaching. Melquan's expression went through a quick change. He was doing everything to hide his emotions. His megawatt smile greeted Charlie Rock.

Stylishly dressed in a dark blue Champion sweat suit, his three-sixty waves protected by a matching Yankee baseball cap, and pair of white and blue shell toe Adidas. Charlie Rock was looking fly. They exchanged daps and hugs then Melquan took a break from his drug activities to kicked it with him. It was gesture of respect, from the young guard to the old guard. He was never too busy for Charlie Rock.

"Hey you know what, nephew?"

"What's that Unk?"

"I'm really proud of you, nephew. You did what you said you were gonna do. I got to tip my fitted to that," Charlie Rock said, raising his baseball hat. Many are called but the chosen are few…"

"Unk, it just had to be done, man. I just thought to myself if not me then who? And if not now then when? Unk, just like you, I been out here all my life, doin' what you always talkin''bout, throwin' rocks at the penitentiary. Things change and I feel it's only right that I get this money."

"Yeah, there you go. That's the only way to think, get yours. But I'm a tell you sumthinI learned from experience. When you start gettin' money, the wolves come out. That money is the scent they follow to the source. So be careful. The same thing that feed you must feed them--the streets…"

From his seat in the wheelchair, Charlie Rock stared directly at Melquan. His tone was serious and Melquan immediately noticed the change.

"I know you got a lot on your mind. But hear me out, nephew. I'm tellin' you sumthin' for your own good."

Melquan remained tightlipped and didn't utter a word. He held his breath, bracing for the words the wise OG had for him.

"A'ight, hear me out. First and foremost you cannot sleep on these niggas. Shit might be good now, but it won't stay that way. Hope for the best but expect the worst. Keep your ears to the street. I'm tellin' you what I know. You've gotta have eyes in the back of your head. Stayin' alert is stayin' alive! Don't take any rumor pertaining to you lightly. Many times the streets will get the word before you do."

Melquan nodded and let the words resonate. Charlie Rock was speaking from experience. He had been around the rise and fall of many major criminals. Melquan felt he had to heed these jewels. Charlie Rock didn't drop them on everyone, and this made Melquan feel special.

"Watch 'em dudes around you. Besides Mike Copeland, they all suspect. Find out who built for the drug game, and who built for war. Don't let 'em good-time niggas fool you. Don't let 'em tell you they thorough. Make 'em prove it. Remember, everyone's a soldier until it's time for war. Then what you got? A bunch of spectators…"

Nightfall had descending upon the projects and Melquan's team hand over fist made that dough. It was now time to go home. Unlike most drug dealers Melquan preferred to run his crack operation similar to a dope operation. There was a specific time to open and shutdown the business every day. This time restriction lessened the chance of anyone on his team getting knocked.

However he knew, if Mike Copeland had it his way, shop would be open twenty-four-seven. Melquan saw no reason for this. It would only build more animosity for his crew if they took all the money. Rivals drug dealers may resort to calling the police on them. It was better for all to let rivals eat for a couple hours. In the projects, the only people out late at night were cops, stickup kids, and drug users.

Directly across the drive, Nashawn and one of his cronies hadn't faired too well. Having taken over a crackhouse in his building their sole objective was to cut Melquan's throat on drug sales in and around the building. Their customer trickled in light and intermediate, making their money slow. They loved when Melquan's team closed shop for the day. It was a real chance to make a few more dollars.

Nashawn was fighting a war he knew he couldn't possibly win when it came to quality and quantity of drugs. He didn't have the connection to compete with Melquan's crew. Nobody in the projects did for that matter. Melquan had it good and plenty. He didn't have to chase Nashawn out of the projects with guns blazing. He was going to force him out by taking away his ability to make a drug profit to support himself or his team. Soon his crew would start to defect. It was only a matter of time. Nashawn would die a slow death. Humiliation would weaken him faster than a bullet wound. He saw Melquan's crew making all that money, right where he lived, everyday was beginning to sting like a slap in the face.

Nashawn was angered by the vast amounts of customers venturing across the drive to purchase Melquan's product, all day long. Some were his loyal supporters and had deserted him. By the time Melquan had left, Nashawn's frustration was close to boiling point. He went outside and approached one such turncoat crack addict.

"Yo fam, come here lemme holler at you," Nashawn growled at the man.

"Okay," the man answered, sounding intimidated. "Wha- what's up…?"

Nashawn put an arm around the man's neck like they were long lost friends. Expecting a beatdown, the man was acting nervous. He tried to spring himself from Nashawn's grip. Nashawn was strong and leaned hard on his former customer.

"Why you always running over there to cop, huh? You live in my fuckin' buildin', and still you ain't showin' me no love? Why?"

"It ain't even like that Nashawn," the man answered in a pleading voice.

The steel in Nashawn's glare had him in check. This former customer could sense trouble heading his way.

"Why then…?" Nashawn quizzed, looking perplexed.

"It's just…" the former customer's voice trailed.

Nashawn watched him with a glint of anger shielding his face under the black NY Yankee fitted.

"Just what?" Nashawn repeated, releasing the man. "Huh? Please explain this bullshit to me."

They were standing face to face. Nashawn sized up the man. Feeling the fear building in the man's throat, he realized the man didn't want to say anything. If the man did speak, he might just be making up something to get away. Nashawn calmly waited.

"Nashawn, I ain't even gonna lie, man. They st-stuff is big-bigger and bet-better than you-yours," the crack addict stuttered, wincing.

He was expecting the kicks and punches to follow. Then he heard the anger in Nashawn's voice and started shaking.

"What da fuck you mean? Talkin' 'bout they shit's bigger an' better than mine, huh?"

"C'mon man, I ain't lookin' for no trouble, man. You asked me a question and... Look man, I don't cause trouble, I don't bother nobody, I don't burn nobody, man. All I wanna do is smoke my shit and get high," the addict explained. "I don't want no problems."

"Nigga, I really don't give a fuck 'bout what ya want. Homie ya got some trouble now," Nashawn said, landing a two-fisted combination to the crack addict's jaw.

He had no time recover from Nashawn's suckerpunch. Then Nashawn's boys jumped in, beating on the crack fiend. They made short work of him. In a brutal New York minute, the crack addict was laid out unconscious on the pavement. Nashawn and his boys walked away from the injured man like nothing ever happened.

"Yeah muthafucka, if I ever catch ya ass goin' cross 'em streets to cop again, I swear I'll kill you!" Nashawn spat. "And that goes for all of you muthafuckas," he said, pointing to the bevy of onlookers.

Mike Copeland reappeared when the time the altercation ended. He was going up to Precious' apartment to secure today's drug profit. Glaring across the drive at Mike Copeland, Nashawn was now feeling himself. Mike Copeland was always strapped and the smirk on his face said he was unimpressed. He was looking for any excuse to gun Nashawn down.

"Nigga, I wish you'd just attempt to do dat shit to me," Mike Copeland suddenly loudly announced. "I ain't that fiend, nigga!"

Silence like the nightfall descended over the horseshoe. Mike

Copeland's laughter exploded into the night's air when he had no takers on his offer. He swaggered away and moved on to handle his business.

After being absent for a couple weeks or so, Melquan joined Mike Copeland back in the horseshoe. It was a rare appearance because lately, he been playing India's house real close. Melquan had been reserved and was not running the street as much. He was doing this in an effort to make the relationship work.

To the casual observe it may have looked like Mike Copeland was calling the shots. It wasn't the case. Melquan was still holding the reigns. He was fine with Mike Copeland receiving all the attention. At the end of the day they both knew who was captain.

Precious got wind of Melquan's presence and she quickly joined them. In the past few weeks she hadn't seen Melquan. Precious was curious and wanted to find out why Melquan hadn't returned her calls. She had learned that his relationship with India had been blossoming at the detriment of his relationship with her. It was strained to say the least. Precious was still playing her part, holding down Mike Copeland, and supplying the team with re-up whenever the need arose.

"What's up stranger?" Precious smiled warmly.

"You…" Melquan replied with a wink.

"How you been, huh? Ain't seen you in a long while, Mel…"

"Good…"

"You're a sight for sore eyes. You can't call me, huh?"

Melquan glanced at the smile on Mike Copeland's face, shaking his head in disgust. The moment she came outside there would be high drama.

"Here you go," Mike Copeland announced.

"Shut-da-fuck-up, Mike!" Precious immediately lashed out.

"Mind ya fuckin' beeswax."

Turning her attention back to Melquan, Precious stood before him with her arms folded over rapidly rising chest, waiting an answer.

"Precious, let's not go there right now. We'll talk about that later. A'ight…?" Melquan insisted.

Precious saw the scowl on Melquan's grill. She knew just how serious he was, and decided not to make a scene. Precious would roll with the punches for now. She had made a promise that once they got in private then she would give him the business. There was no way Melquan was going to get off that easy.

"Okay, okay, whatever you say, Mel," Precious replied smugly.

Melquan had been chilling and had to get used to the routine of standing again. He perched himself high on the park bench in front of the building. Precious seized the opportunity to immediately sit between his legs. To the left of them, Mike Copeland was standing guard. They watch the drug operation make transaction after transaction. Soon Sheron approached them.

"Sheron, what up, shorty…? Where you been? I ain't see you in a while," Melquan greeted the boy.

"I been around. Where you been at? I ain't seen you in a long, long time, Melquan. I went by your mother's apartment a couple times, but you never there," Sheron emphasized.

Precious interrupted, "Don't worry, shorty. I can't find him either."

"Word, my moms ain't even tell me, shorty. I gave you my number… Why you ain't hit me up?" Melquan said, ignoring Precious.

"I lost it, Melquan," Sheron answered.

"Wow…! Anyway how you doin'…? You a'ight…?"

"No, I'm hungry. And I need a haircut, Melquan."

Much to the chagrin of Mike Copeland and Precious, Melquan immediately handed Sheron couple bills. It looked like short money, but vexed the onlookers.

"Here you go, shorty… Do what you gotta do with that money. Keep the change. Hide it in your sock. Don't even let your mother know you got it," Melquan instructed Sheron.

"Good lookin', Melquan," Sheron said, accepting the money.

When Sheron ran off, Melquan could hear the snickering of Mike Copeland and Precious. He was annoyed at them and let them have his wrath.

"I don't know why y'all fuckin' laughin'? What's so fuckin' funny? I pray to God it ain't at shorty!"

"Nah, we ain't laughin' 'at shorty. We laughin' at your ass, nigga," Mike Copeland answered, still laughing.

"That lil' nigga playin' your ass and you don't even see it. That's what's so fuckin funny," Precious said without a hint of humor.

"Mel, you ain't doin' nothin' 'cept feedin' his mom's crack habit," Mike Copeland said.

"What the fuck you talkin' 'bout?"

"You really think she ain't shaking shorty down for some bread? C'mon Mel. She know you lookin' out for shorty too. She probably sent him over here to see you just now. You feel me?" Mike Copeland spat in disgust.

"Mike, ya buggin', my dude. I don't fuckin' believe that. I ain't even gonna let you put that shit in my head. Shorty ain't like that. That lil' nigga would never do sumthin like that," Melquan said.

"Mel, how you know Tess ain't puttin' pressure on him? I mean she sees her son everyday on a regular, and you see him every now and then. You just can't tell for sure," Precious reasoned.

"A'ight, next time I see shorty, I'm gonna ask him myself, what da deal is," Melquan said.

"And you think he gonna tell you? That's his mother you talkin' 'bout. To you and me she a fiend, but to shorty, that's his mother, first and last. And he gonna do everything in his power to protect her."

"You got that right, Mike. If she was my mother, I'd surely be doin' just that," Precious said.

"Melquan, look what you got yourself into? This what you get for bein' kindhearted and all. That B.S. will only get your ass played. You gotta start bein' more ruthless like me. If you don't got it, you can't get it from me, you feel me? Nothing personal but muthafuckas ain't gave me shit. I'm just returning the favor, man."

Melquan paused for a second, analyzing what had gone down. Thing were beginning to make sense. The thought of Tess roughing her son up or conning him out of money disturbed him. He didn't want to believe the obvious, he gave Sheron the benefit of the doubt.

The day wore on and the trio kept their eyes on the flourishing drug organization they had established. Melquan was content to observe it all. Mike Copeland and Precious meanwhile took a more hands on approach. Giving out packages to workers, they were collecting major paper.

Precious would reposition herself back between Melquan's legs after each run. A blue Honda Civic suddenly pulled up into the drive. Slowly the driver steered the car toward the trio and stopped. Before Precious knew what was going on, Melquan abruptly pushed her from his legs, jumped up, and was making his way to the car.

India stared at him from inside the parked vehicle, smiling. Melquan was clearly not prepared for this surprise visit. He did not immediately return her greeting.

"Houston, we have a problem," Mike Copeland laughed out loud.

Melquan turned and glared at Mike Copeland. Precious watched in earnest as Melquan walked over to the car and leaned into the window.

"Where the fuck is that nigga think he goin'? Who da fuck is in da fuckin' car, huh?" Precious spat venomously.

"You know what they say, right? Never ask a question, when you really don't wanna know the answer..." Mike Copeland's voice trailed.

They watched Melquan getting into the car. India quickly greeted Melquan with a passionate kiss. Melquan didn't know what it was all about, but had a good idea. He broke the lip-lock and motioned for India to drive off.

"What's going on, boo?" India smiled.

"You tell me. What you doing here? Ain't you supposed to be at work?" Melquan asked, looking at India with disbelief splattered all over his mug. "Thought I told you to call me first before you come... What if I wasn't out here and shit? A lotta shit be goin' down that I can't really get into right now. For future reference, baby, please, please, call before you come through."

"Whew... I never knew it was that serious. All I wanted to do was to see you. I missed you. I had a dental appointment and decided to take the rest of the day off."

India looked at Melquan as she emerged into traffic at the end of the drive.

"Is there someone here you don't want me seeing or...?"

"Look, India you're gonna think what you wanna think. That's just how you do. But seriously, ain't nothin' like that goin' on," Melquan lied.

"Oh really...? This is just a place where you conduct your biz right...?" India said with a sharp tone. "Other than that ain't nothing happening, huh Melquan?

Melquan looked over at her and smiled, shaking his head. He waited for her sarcasm to die before he spoke.

"Look India, I can't change how you feel. I ain't even gonna try. I ain't tryin' to beef with you no more 'bout this ol' bullshit anymore. You can say and think what you wanna. That shit's on you... But I'm not feedin' into it… So, anyway… You hungry…?"

"Yes…"

"Let's go get sumthin to eat then."

"Whatever you say Melquan… Whatever you say..."

The car drove off and a surprised Precious was furious. Holding her gaping mouth, she couldn't believe Melquan had just suddenly driven off with his main chick.

She stared evilly at the car until it disappeared from sight. Precious now knew exactly who it was that Melquan had left with. The heartache hit her like a ton of bricks when she realized the woman was India. The mixture of emotions stirring through Precious' veins soon became rage.

"I hate him! I so hate dat dirty, no-good muthafucka!"

"Ah, you just sayin' that cause your feelings hurt. But you already knew what time it was."

"Shut up, Mike! Please mind your fuckin' business, already!"

Oh really…? You should shut up! My mind is my business. I can't help it if you open off my man. But the funny shit is you know what it was when you started fucking with him. You knew he had a main girl… Precious, it is what it is, not what you want it to be! Ah, just deal."

"You know what? I will. I'm tellin' you, niggas ain't gonna like the way I play my hand."

"You better make sure you know what you doin'. And further more who you doin' it to? Don't take this shit out on everybody… Make sure you get the right person back…"

"I will," Precious assured.

"Better yet, you need to wake and smell the coffee, 'fore you find yourself by yourself! You feel me?" Mike Copeland said, grinning and walking away.

Precious was left sitting on the park bench by alone and herself. Evil thoughts did laps on the tracks of her mind. She was emotionally devastated, and glanced around the horseshoe feeling sorrow. It seemed like everyone in the horseshoe was watching her getting played. A lone tear escaped and Presious bowed her head in shame.

# Love's Blind
Chapter Thirteen

Applebee's in nearby Co-op city became their destination because of its close proximity. Melquan and India had met there for lunch before. It was restaurant where they were familiar with the menu and the cozy atmosphere. Although it was going to be the first time in a long spell the couple had gone out. With her job and her son Zach, India had her hands full. Besides she was a hell of a cook who preferred to showcase her talents for Melquan.

They were seated quickly in restaurant. The lunch crowd was thick, but people were moving in and out due to the prompt service.

Music videos, weather and sports highlights were on the television screens. Melquan and India settled into seats at a table that was out of the way lunchtime rush.

"I haven't been here in a long time, but I know exactly what I want… Some Jack Daniels barbecue chicken…"

"Yeah, that's so crazy, baby. I had a taste for some of dat Barbecue chicken my-damn-self."

"No, you get what you always get. That way I can eat off your plate. I'm having the barbecue chicken… It's to die for. Mel, I gotta go to the bathroom. Order some drinks for us."

India walked away, leaving Melquan alone with his thoughts. His mind flashed back to India's sudden arrival at the horseshoe. Melquan crossed his heart, thanking his lucky stars that India didn't see Precious sitting between his legs. Chuckling to himself, Melquan looked at the menu to see if Apple Bee's had added any new delicacies. He had dodged a bullet.

"Sir, may I take your order," the waiter said, interrupting his musing.

"Lemme get a shot of Hennessey, and an Apple Martini. Bring me an order of the Jack Daniels barbecue chicken for my lady, and I'll have a steak. Well done…"

The waiter took the order and left. India returned to the table, smiling brightly. Soon after, the waiter returned with their drinks. He placed them in front of India and Melquan, respectively then walked away.

"Hmm, this is really good. Wanna try it?" she asked, sipping her drink.

"Nah, you know I can't fool 'round with 'em girlie drinks. India, you dealin' wit a man, not with a mouse…"

"What does your manhood have to do wit it? C'mon Melquan, please try it…" she whispered throatily.

That tone made India sound like she was requesting him to

fuck her, sending chills down his spine. Melquan quickly took a look around before taking a sip of India's drink. India stared curiously at his facial expression awaiting Melquan's verdict. His blank expression never let on.

"Mel it tastes good, right?"

"It's a'ight," Melquan admitted. "But it's too damn sexy for me. Look at that sexy glass and that cherry. I need sumthin hard. Now this glass of Henny will put some hair on your chest," he laughed.

"Oh really, Mel? Hair on your chest, huh…?" India laughed. "You can keep it. I'll stick to sexy drinks."

The food arrived and both of them got busy eating. India was really pleased with her choice. She cut the chicken into small morsels, devouring it. Melquan went to town on his steak and potatoes, sitting directly across from her.

"Hmm… Melquan, this barbecue chicken is to die for," India said, licking her lips and smiling.

"It must be, I heard ya the other six times ya said it."

"I have to give credit where credit is due. It's really good."

"Well, maybe I ordered the wrong damn thing then. My steak taste just like steak, nothin' to write home 'bout. And you won't hear me hootin' and hollerin' over it."

"Don't be mad, Mel. Here, try some of my chicken. I guarantee you'll like it."

India picked up a piece of chicken on her fork, dipped it in to the sauce and affectionately attempted to feed Melquan. Eyeing her, he opened his mouth, and accepted the offering of food. Melquan slowly chewed the food, still looking into India's eyes. Their eyes seemed to search each other's soul. Smile overcame their queries.

"Wasn't it really good?" India asked, smiling.

"What? That chicken was bangin'. I'm orderin' that, the next time, for sure. What's the name of that shit again?"

"Melquan, would you please watch your mouth. This is a public place there's families with children here, hon. Its grilled chicken with Jack Daniel's sauce, okay?"

"My bad," Melquan said, looking embarrassed.

"Here's another piece," India offered.

Melquan gladly accepted and chewed with a smile. Everything was going great with their nice impromptu date. They shared laughter and small talk. Melquan and India were caught up in the moment and they seemed to be enjoying their quality time together. This was a side of Melquan that made India fall in love with him in the first place. It was the street persona of Melquan that she could do with less of. They were from two different worlds. India came from a two parent, middle class, household in New Rochelle, New York. Melquan was the product of a broken home. He grew up in the Edenwald projects.

There was a bond between Melquan and project life that India felt she couldn't comprehend. It was like a magnetic force field that kept pulling him back in. She was trying to help him become a better man, but his occupation and familiarity seemed to play a huge factor in Melquan's decisions. The mood remained light until India's insecurity reared its ugly head.

"So, Melquan who was that girl I saw sitting in between your legs?" India asked.

Melquan was caught off-guard by India's line of questioning. He thought he had gotten away with that act. Melquan fumbled with his thoughts, he knew his answer had better be justifiable good.

"What? Oh her…? That was nobody."

"Oh really…?" India asked, raising her eyebrows in suspicion.

"Yeah, she's nobody…?"

"I wonder… Hmm is that what you say about me when I'm not around, Mel? Who is she to you? And please, don't tell me she's nobody, Melquan."

Sipping her third Apple Martini, India watched Melquan squirming under her direct line of questioning. Melquan didn't want to go there, but India was giving him no choice.

"Is that all you got to say? She's nobody…? Melquan, I know you. If that was me, there had better be a good explanation. That man had better be my father. Or there would've been hell to pay."

"Look India, if you must really know, that's Mike Copeland's cousin. True story, we stash guns and drugs in her crib. She works with us. And that's all! We had drugs stashed in da area, so she just sat there to make it look good. Just in case five-oh roll on us. Whatever's goin' down, we'd just look like we together. Matter fact, she came right before you rolled up."

Searching for the truth in his expression, India stared deep in Melquan's eyes. Feelings of compassion were returned. She reached over and gently kissed his lips.

"Thanks for explaining that to me. I don't know the ins and outs of all your business, but seeing another woman up on you like that, makes my skin crawl. That's why I'm so happy you took the time out of your day to spend it with me. I really feel so special, Melquan."

"That's cause you are special, India."

India reached out and grabbed his hands and stared lovingly at Melquan.

"I'm glad you believe me…" Melquan started to say, but India put her finger on his lips.

"Oh, I believe you, Melquan. I just don't want history repeating itself. I told you, the next time, I'm gonna hav'to take a stand. And you might not like the stand I take."

"A'ight, you got that. I can respect that," Melquan smiled.

"You understand me now, Melquan? Cause I don't wanna have to get ghetto all on a bitch. Ya know…? Throw on my sneaks, hoodie and jeans, grease my face up and go whip a bitch ass for my man…" India said, putting on her best ghetto girl act.

"I couldn't picture that with a Sony camcorder," Melquan laughed.

"Don't get it twisted, kid. It could ugly when I spaz out. Lucky for you, I'm way past that. I'm too much of a lady, a mature one with a son. I learned a long time ago that you can't keep a man anywhere he doesn't want to be."

"I hear that. Check please," Melquan said, waving at the waiter.

"It's my treat, Melquan. You're always doing something for me. Let me do something for you once, please…?"

India pulled out her credit and checked it. She put it back and pulled out another out of her purse.

"You good, hon? You know I got this, right?"

Melquan pulled a fat bankroll and paid the waiter. He placed a big tip on the table. India eyed him and kept her eyes peeled on the amount of money in the hustler's hand.

"Gosh Melquan, business must be really, really good," she said, eyeing the money.

"Yeah, it's doin' a lil' sumthin, sumthin," Melquan quietly smiled.

"You've got to be walking around with about six months of my salary in your pockets."

"I don't know 'bout all that now," Melquan smiled.

"I do," India laughed. "If you pull out any more money, I'll be very tempted to rob you," India laughed.

"Oh, I see you got jokes, huh? You don't have to rob me. I'll easily get butt naked and empty my pockets for you, baby."

"Okay, okay stop tempting me. You know I gotta go get Zach from his after school program."

They laughed effortlessly, leaving the restaurant. Maybe this will work Melquan was thinking getting into the car. India walked to the passenger side with him then she opened the door, and shut it after he got inside. She ran around to the driver's side and jumped in.

"India, what's wrong with you, girl?" he asked. "You just grinnin' from ear to ear.

"I'm happy," she smiled. "For the first time in along time, I got somebody that I truly want to be with and who wants to be with me. Life is soo good."

# Geting a Rep...

Chapter Fourteen

It was an evening after school. Fall was bum rushing the projects. The air was crispy and new. Jose Jr. locked the door to his apartment with a smile because he had put one over on his dad. Again his father fell for the library routine, this time it was even easier. Maria did not attempt to block, like she had done in the past. They had a conversation and he made her realized, she had been causing him to be on punishment too often. She agreed, relaxed, and now he could breathe.

One of the building's elevators was temporarily out of service. Jose decided to take the stairs. He heard loud voices and smelled the strong scent of weed when he entered the staircase. Jose loosened his waistband, and his jeans hung low. He twisted the red NY Yankee fitted, pulled it down to his nose and let his backpack sagged.

Quickly Jose began his descent toward the buildings lobby. In no time he was with a group of teenagers, all of whom he knew.

"What's good, Jose?" one of the kids said.

"G mackin'..." Jose replied.

Showing him love, the others gave him dap and hugs. There were changes in his demeanor. That squeaky clean catholic school image was quickly fading. Jose's street persona was now in full affect.

"Whatcha gettin' into now, Jose…?"

"I'm getting' ready ta go do my thing in da shoe, son…"

"Oh word?" one kid shouted.

"Do me…" Jose bragged.

"Be careful out there," another teen said. "We goin' over to the center to see what's poppin' in there."

"A'ight, I'll holla at y'all later," Jose said.

Jose walked down the rest of the steps, bopping. His swagger was at an all time high. His new Nike ACG boots squeaked whenever he took a step. He was ready, jeans sagging and his black hoodie low on his face. Jose was walking the walk.

Mike Copeland was the first to see him and smiled. Jose walked over to him like a soldier reporting for duty. He gave Mike Copeland a firm handshake and awaited further orders.

"What up, Jose? You ready for work or what…?"

"You know it…"

"That's da fuck I wanna hear," Mike Copeland answered with authority.

He nodded to one of his workers, who quickly walked over to Jose and handed him a package of crack. Jose's heart began pumping faster. Blood rushed to his head and made him dizzy. Mike Copeland looked at the transformed Jose, and a smile pasted his lips.

"A'ight Jose, let's see da fuck you made of, right now. Cuz, here comes your first custie," Mike Copeland said, turning away.

A strong craving for crack cocaine brought Tess through the horseshoe. She was looking for the best crack available, and knew exactly who had it. Mentally she had already bypassed other drug dealers, preferring to look for those with more familiar faces. She hoped, they would give her the best deal.

Tess stopped in front of the building Melquan's operation was run out of. Mike Copeland disappeared into a nearby building, anticipating her begging.

"What's good?" Jose called out. "I got what you need, right here. Come check me out!"

His new face so automatically drew a suspicious stare from Tess.

"Who you…?" Tess wondered aloud.

"Why?"

"Cause I asked," Tess replied. "I ain't never seen you out here before."

"Just cause you ain't never seen me, don't mean I ain't been out here."

"Oh, you gotta smart mouth too, huh?" Tess commented. "You seen Mike?"

"Mike? Who dat…?"

"Mike Copeland! Don't play stupid, I'm a grown ass woman."

"Oh him…? Nah he ain't out here right now. But I'm holding down his thing."

"You are, huh? Why didn't you say that? Lemme see it."

Jose was shook at first, but impressing Mike spurred him to action. He reached into the bag and pulled out a handful of dimes of crack. Tess carefully inspected the drug, looking for the biggest rocks. When she found them she placed them inside the palm of her hand.

Tess announced, "All I got is ten dollars. Can I get these two dimes for ten? Mike's my peeps and he always hooks me up."

"Well, I ain't Mike," Jose snapped.

"Please, please," Tess begged in her softest voice. "Maybe we can work sumthin out. I do a lil' sumthin, sumthin for you, and you take care of me."

"Look Miss. You can't do nothing for me. I'm good. All I want from you is that paper."

"Well, fuck it then. Take this lil funky-ass ten dollars. I ain't got time for your bullshit. I'll see Mike another time… You know what you ain't never gon' get no money being so petty," Tess erupted, handed him the ten bucks turned to walk away.

"Yo Miss, wait a minute, you forgettin' sumthin. Where's my other dime at?"

"What?"

"Yo, don't play stupid with me, Miss," Jose warned. "I know what I gave you. Open your hand."

Tess started to make a run for it, but was sure the kid would catch her. Once he did there was no telling what he might do. Tess didn't know this kid and there was no telling what kind of beating he was capable of inflicting. Tess thought better of the situation and decided to return the drug.

"Huh…?" she said, pressing the crack back into Jose's palm.

Jose quickly inspected it. Satisfied the package was the same that he had given her, Jose didn't utter another word. He watched her walk away.

"Heads up, here comes another one…"

Jose snapped back to reality when he heard Mike Copeland's voice. Alerted back to his grind, he reached into the bag to for more of the product to pitch another potential customer. Under the watchful eyes of Mike Copeland, Jose set about his grind. He never noticed the other eyes who were watching him. A pair belonged to someone who was very friendly with his father.

Charlie Rock rolled into the horseshoe unannounced. The man in the wheelchair was completely disappointed watching his friend's son get his grind on. His stomach turned when he saw Jose Jr. hustling. His father didn't get out the game and make other great sacrifices for his family's sake, just so his son could hustle drugs.

The game wasn't for lil Jose, plain and simple. Charlie Rock knew he had to do something about the new drug dealer in the horseshoe. He tugged at his silver and black goatee, racking his brain for an answer. Charlie Rock wanted to do something would curtail Jose's chosen career path.

According to his street indoctrination, snitching was done by snitches. He found fault in himself for what he wanted to do. Telling his friend would be going against everything he ever stood for in the game. Talking to the boy's father weighed heavily on his mind. Charlie Rock would have to contemplate this thought long and hard before he could make a decision.

Jose Jr. was making drug transaction after drug transaction, when he noticed a wheelchair bound man coming his way. He reached into his stash and removed a handful of crack. Jose was well aware that addicts come in all shapes and sizes, normal and paralyzed. Seeking to get a closer look, Charlie Rock guided his wheelchair over to the new drug dealer in the horseshoe.

"What up, my man," he greeted. "This the first time I seen you out here."

"Well get a good look, daddy, cuz it won't be the last. You a'ight? Need sumthin. Holla atcha boy…" Jose's reply was smooth.

Hustling was in his blood. His father was a damn good one before he was born. Charlie Rock's mind was distracted sizing up the young man.

"Ya want sumthin' good, or what?"

He heard the young hustler's chant and Charlie Rock looked at him and smiled, shaking his head.

"Nah nephew, I'm good!" Charlie Rock assured him.

With the prospect of making a sale gone, Jose turned his attention to other would-be customers. Charlie Rock maneuvered his battery-powered wheelchair a few feet away and continued to watch in disbelief. He was unable to shake that sickening feeling gnawing at his stomach.

# To The Victor, The Spoils

Chapter Fifteen

It was still early, seven in the morning, and Melquan was resting comfortably in the bed. His manhood was suddenly aroused once more as soon as he spotted India walking out of the bathroom, just a towel clinging to her wet, shapely body. Melquan fondled her ass when she passed by him. Whether it was pure physical attraction or animal magnetism, Melquan had a thing for India. He couldn't deny that.

India knew Melquan wanted morning sex from the first touch. It was the normal routine for him. Even though India couldn't always accommodate Melquan's yearnings, she tried to satisfy him. She was well aware of the fact that Melquan was the type to stray. Whenever she could help it, India didn't want to give him any excuses.

"I got to go to work and you're gonna make me late, Melquan," she protested in vain.

Melquan's fingers were already rubbing her clit. It was no use resisting, India opened her legs and gave him more.

"Damn Melquan, you're making it difficult for me to say no...!" she screamed when he raised her.

She hoisted and wrapped her legs around his waist. India threw her wet hair back and kissed Melquan when she felt the deep penetration. Her ass rose up and down in rhythm with his thrust. Her kiss dragged on long and sweet. Their passion was real and she sucked on his neck. It was the first time. Melquan's body bucked faster and she did it again and again. Melquan's mind was reeling from tasting ecstasy. He sucked on her breasts harder, while she bit his neck and earlobe. Her mouth drove him over the edge and he exploded.

"Ooh yeah, Melquan. Give it all to me!" she begged, moving her ass faster.

Melquan crammed his dick to the hilt inside her hot pussy. The friction of their lovemaking set her on fire and she erupted into an orgasm, holding her breath.

"Oh God, oh my no… This feels soo good!" India screamed.

She ran back into the bathroom and Melquan fell against the bed panting. He was ready to go again. By the time he got to the bathroom, India had already taken a quick shower and was getting in her bra and panties. She threw a towel at Melquan.

"Boy, I've got to go to work. Will you be here when I get home?" India asked, slipping into her nurse's duds.

"I'll probably step out for a few, but I'll be back. More than likely, I'll be here by time you get home."

"Okay Melquan, make sure you lock up when you leave. And be careful out there. I'll see you later," India said, kissing him flush on the lips.

"A'ight, see you later. Have a good day at work."

Melquan could afford to relax. Mike Copeland had the business under control. He was doing a good job of running the show. Still whatever he needed Melquan would always be there to assist, be it physical, maybe just giving advice. Melquan would continue to hold Mike Copeland down anyway he could. When it came to making money, Melquan didn't have an ego. He knew that Mike's success was his success and vice-versa.

Melquan was feeling good. His day was off to a good start. It was eleven a.m., and time to get down to business. He smiled at the prospect of counting money with Mike Copeland. He was on his way and Melquan chuckled not knowing which one made him feel better. Was it pussy or money?

He pondered this question in the cab, riding from Co-op City to Edenwald projects. The ride went by quickly and Melquan was still pondering. He paid his fare, hopped out the cab, and entered his building with money on his mind.

Inside his room at his mother's apartment, Melquan and Mike Copeland counted out money. They sat on Melquan's small bed, dividing the loot. His mother knocked periodically on the door, pretending to be checking on them. All she wanted to do was be nosey.

Melquan ordered that the bulk of the money was to be kept out of sight. He knew that his mother was a money hawk. She would continuously spy on them and if she saw too much money she wouldn't hesitate to ask for some. On cue, Ms Tina walked into the room unannounced. Melquan shot Mike Copeland a smirk.

"You know this room has not changed one bit since you were a boy, Melquan," Miss Tina noted.

"Ma, what's good?" Melquan asked. "Don't you see we takin' care of bizness up in here."

"Boy, lemme tell you a thing or two. First of all, ain't nobody think about y'all. And secondly, I've seen lots of money getting counted before?" Miss Tina asked.

Miss Tina had tried to unsuccessfully quell her son's suspiciousness, her eye betrayed her. They were continually drawn to the bed, where stacks of money were being counted and stacked.

"Okay ma, it's not that serious. We just tryin' to handle our bizness and be out."

"Well, ain't a damn soul stopping you," Miss Tina said.

"You are!" Melquan insisted. "Talkin' to us while we doin' this can throw off the count."

"Anyway, now that you getting big money don't you think it's time you buy some new furniture," Miss Tina said, walking out the door.

"Ma, I gave you more than enough money for yourself. If you really wanted to you could have redecorated this room a few times."

"That money was for me! Not no furniture, boy."

The room went silence for a moment. Melquan and Mike Copeland continued to take their individual money count as Miss Tina looked on.

"Ma, do me a favor, please?" Melquan suddenly asked.

"What?" she answered.

"Could you get me and Mike sumthin to drink? We a lil thirsty, back here…"

"Oh okay. I got some Pepsi or some Orange juice. Which one y'all want?"

"Pepsi sound good," Melquan said.

He winked at Mike Copeland when Miss Tina exited the room. The two shared a private joke. They knew that Melquan had purposely made the request to get rid of his mother's domineering presence. Continuing with the divison of money, they quickly packed most of it away. Melquan stashed it in a Nike shoebox and closed the closet door.

"Yo Mel, you know ya mom's is right, right? You do need some damn new furniture up in dis piece."

"Oh yeah…? Then why don't you buy me some, huh?"

"I may damn well have to…"

"Right now, none of this shit matter to me. I don't even be up in here that much no more. You musta forgot that I lay my head at India's crib. Besides, I ain't doin' my mom no more favors than I have to. Shit, all that money I done gave her, she should buy it. It's about ten years overdue!"

"No question. That's your mom's my dude, break bread!" Mike added.

Miss Tina suddenly reentered the bedroom with two tall glasses of soda in her hand.

"That's right Mike tell him a thing or two. Melquan is too tight with his money. I don't know where he get that stingy habit from? Must be his father's side of the family… Cause it sure ain't mine."

Mike Copeland stared at the gorgeous older woman and nodded. He looked over at Melquan and said, "You gotta learn how to enjoy this money while we gettin' it like this. And start takin' care of Ma Dukes a lil better."

Melquan listened, but wasn't about to change his mindset. Not to accommodate his mother's strong craving for money.

"What about them rainy days? What about puttin' away lawyer and bail money? Funny I ain't hear nobody mention that."

"My dude, we seein' way more than enough cake to cover all that…"

"You think…?"

"I know my dude, c'mon. Look how much dough we just finish countin'?"

"And if the man run down on us right now, it could be all gone. Bottom line is, we don't know when this run gon' come end," Melquan fired back.

"I hear you, my dude and I'm a sum it up like this, let's live until we die."

"Amen, Mike. That's sure saying a thing or two," Miss Tina cheered. "Well put, Mike."

Mike continued, "I don't know about you, but I'm a take a few stacks and make a trip to the car lot. Why don't you grab a few and hang with your boy. I'm tired of havin' a closet full of money and no riches. I think it's time to let niggas know. We gettin' crazy dough..."

The trio jumped in a cab and headed to National Auto Sales on Boston road. This car lot wasn't big, but had lots of fly whips on the lot. Melquan, Mike Copeland, and Miss Tina fanned out in different sections of the lot. They were searching for the vehicle that appealed to them the most.

"Yeah, my man, this me all day, right here," Mike Copeland said to a salesman.

"Sir, this is a two thousand and eight Porsche Cayenne. It goes zero to sixty in six point four seconds and can go up to a hundred and fifty-five miles per hour. It's got dual airbags and rear entertainment system and the girls love it..."

"Yeah, say no more. I want to test drive this bitch right now," Mike Copeland said excitedly. "I'll look good in this shit. Huh, I'm a lil' nigga too..."

"This vehicle will definitely make you popular if you're not already... The fellas on the block will hate on you for sure," the salesman laughed.

"They already do... Fuck 'em though! I'm a really give 'em a reason to hate. This one for my bitches..." Mike Copeland said. "Yo Melquan, peep this!"

Melquan was busy checking out a black Range Rover Sport. He smiled when he saw Mike Copeland hop in the Cayenne sport and take it for a test drive.

"Yeah Mike, get that. It's a good look for you," Melquan said, barely able to take his eyes off the Range Rover Sport.

Melquan now officially had succumbed to the pressure of his peer. Watching Mike actively car shopping made him want get himself a nice whip too. Totally disregarding what he had said earlier about saving money for a rainy day, Melquan joined the fray. He was about to wear out some major dollars.

"Yeah, this really me right here, you feelin' me Mr. Salesman...? Let's go test drive this bitch. If it drives as good as it looks, you just might have a sale."

The sales man smiled and ran off to retrieve the keys to the Range. Miss Tina, not to be outdone, also found a convertible Nissan 300ZX, a ride she liked. She sat inside and slammed the car shut. Taking a deep breath, she soaked up the new car scent. A car salesman came by, and began to seriously stroke Miss Tina's ego.

"This is a sophisticated car for a classy woman like yourself. Damn Miss, you're a really fine woman but you driving this car, now that would really stop traffic."

"Thanks," Miss Tina said with a toothy smile. Turning her head, she shouted. "Melquan, come here I found something I like. Come over here for minute, boy."

Melquan walked the short distance over to where Miss Tina sat in the red convertible.

"I thought you wanted to get the X5 over there?" Melquan asked.

"Can't a girl change her mind? Don't I look better in this though?"

"Yes, ma," Melquan deadpanned.

"This the one I want. Melquan, so you gonna get it for me, huh?"

"Yes ma. But lemme do me first. Before I get your car, I need to get mine."

"Okay, I'm ready. And I promise not to change my mind

again."

Melquan nodded and walked away with the salesman. Miss Tina followed closely behind them. They all walked into the business office and began to negotiate.

About twenty minutes later, Mike Copeland returned. He walked into the business office, singing the Cayenne's praises.

"That shit is no joke, Mel. I took that shit for a test run and I was out, my dude," he exclaimed. "Zero to sixty in six seconds, purring like a cat. Man, I'm coppin' that bitch."

The others looked at him smiling. All were pleased and looking happy. Melquan was visibly pissed. He didn't like the fact that Mike Copeland was showing the car dealers just how much he liked the car. He on the other hand was the complete opposite. If the numbers weren't right, Melquan was prepared to walk off the car lot without the car he liked. To him this was nothing more than business, an investment.

"Mike, lemme holla at you for a minute," Melquan abruptly announced.

They both walked a few feet away, just out of the earshot of Miss Tina and the car sales people.

"Look, Mike you gotta be easy. Be hyped about coppin' a whip later. Right now I'm tryin' to bring the sticker price down on all three of 'em whips. They keep hearin' you holla about how great da car is, then I ain't gonna have no kind a leverage. So fallback and start hittin' these cats with your best ice grill."

"No doubt..." Mike Copeland said, nodding in agreement. "Say no more..."

Melquan went back inside and began to negotiate vigorously with the big boss, Joe. He drove a hard bargain and the dealers pushed back. Then he produced cold hard cash, and the dealership relented. They agreed to accept the numbers Melquan proposed.

When the agreements were signed and money was paid, it was

time to enjoy the lifestyle that came from hustling drugs. Melquan, Mike Copeland and Miss Tina entered their vehicles that had been issued temporary tags.

"Good lookin' Joe," Melquan announced. "We gon' do bizness again. Just as long as ya continue to show me love like that…"

"Love is love, fam." Joe said. "Money talks and bullshit walks."

"Meet y'all back in the 'jects," Mike Copeland shouted.

"Y'all…? Just keep ya cellphones on I'll hit on ya da jack," Melquan suggested.

"A'ight," Mike Copeland said. "Cuz, I'm about to blow it."

"Drive safely," Miss Tina said, pulling off. "I tell you one thing. Get back to the projects in one piece now."

One by one the luxury cars exited the car lot. Mike Copeland was a blur in his new Cayenne. Once he merged into oncoming traffic, he put every ounce of his car's horsepower to the test. Melquan tailed him closely for a few seconds testing the power of his Range. It had power but he decided to fall back. Miss Tina took her time deciding to slowly style, and profile in her new 300ZX convertible.

By early dusk all three vehicles were parked in Edenwald projects. Shiny and new, the cars were attracting a lot of attention. Miss Tina went upstairs and called all her girlfriends to brag about her new car. Melquan and Mike stayed outside in the public eye, soaking up all the admiration.

"Let's go to Smitty's tonite, my dude," Mike Copeland suggested. "That a nice spot from all I hear."

"Bet, I heard the same thing…" Melquan added. "I heard they got plenty ho's up in dat piece too."

"You already know my dude…" Mike Copeland laughed.

"A'ight, that's what's up? I'll meet you out front in a couple hours."

"Get fly my dude, you know I gotta look good in da new ride."

# Dealing with haters...

Chapter Sixteen

Melquan and Mike Copeland entered the building looking like millions. Fresh to death, Melquan was outfitted in white Versace button down shirt with turquoise cufflinks, blue True Religion jeans, and Louis Vuitton loafers. Mike Copeland was Ed Hardy down, jeans, hat, shirt and black Prada shoes. The only thing lacking was jewelry. Melquan and Mike Copeland both felt like they didn't need any. Their luxurious whips would provide any X-factor.

An unmarked DT car drove through the drive as the duo were about to get into their rides. There were three officers riding in the undercover car, slowly rolling by. All eyes were focused on Melquan and Mike Copeland getting into their expensive rides. Mike Copeland coldly stared back at the detectives. Melquan avoided all eye contact with their icy grills. The cops nodded and kept on driving.

Mike Copeland and Melquan from the projects getting in posh European cars burned them up. On their present salary, none of the cops could afford any of those vehicles. One detective couldn't help but speak on it.

"Tommy, can you tell me where the hell these bastards are getting all that money from?" the detective asked.

"What do you know something that I don't know," another said. "I'm interested in finding out."

"Crack baby. This is the crack cocaine city! These sons of bitches are making a fortune pushing that poison," Tommy answered.

"You know what Tommy?" the first detective asked. "Maybe we're in the wrong business. What you think?"

"Hey, maybe... It looks like now is a good time to be a bad guy, huh?"

Occupants of the undercover car exploded in laughter. They drove though the horseshoe, observing for awhile then they drove off.

By the time Melquan and Mike Copeland arrived Smitty's on Tremont Avenue in the Bronx, there was a line in front the club. Mike Copeland gave the bouncer a hundred dollar bill and the duo breezed through the door and security checkpoint. They were inside once admission was paid. The hot spot was crowded and swarming with fine women.

The club's sound system pumped the latest R&B and rap records. Swigging bottle after bottle, Melquan and Mike Copeland were thrust into an intense party. Bouncing to the club's atmosphere, the stress from the streets quickly dissolved. The duo relaxed and were blending in.

Young Jeezy featuring Jay Z and Fat Joe, Go Crazy blasted through the speakers. Melquan and Mike Copeland smiled at revelers dancing and mingling.

> When they play a new Jeezy all the dope boys go crazy
> and watch the dope boys go crazy!
> I pop my collar then I swing my chain
> You can catch me in the club, pimpin doin my thang
> Aye...

"Da spot's jumpin', you smellin' me, my dude?"

"Yeah, it's a good night to be out gettin' that groove on," Melquan observed, surveying the room. "Stay on point Mike. I seen a few heads from the hood up in here."

"I got you, my dude."

"Let's go sit up in VIP," Melquan suggested. "Just feel like sittin', chillin' watchin' these broads."

"That's what's up," Mike Copeland said, looking at the girls dancing in the club.

They were seated and drinks were ordered in the VIP section by the time Fat Joe's verse rang through.

> What up Jeez
> Cracks...life, what's the matta wit yo head?
> Cracks...life, all you niggaz gon end up dead
> Cracks...life, everybody servin rat till he ride
> Everybody think they somebody, till somebody end up shot
> Listen, I'm in that GT, Choppa on the passenger side
> No skeets skeets, choppa on the passenger side

The sound of popping champagne bottles attracted the girls' eyes and in a hot New York, Melquan and Mike Copeland became the center of attraction.

"Yo, Mike, cheers," Melquan announced. "Here's to us. May our run be long."

"Yeah, yeah you already know my dude. Edenwald projects in da buildin'…!"

Toasting and laughing, the duo danced around with a group of party hearty girls while Kanye West and Lupe Fiasco remix of Touch The Sky, thumped through the club's speakers.

> I gotta testify, come up in the spot looking extra fly
> For the day I die, I'm a touch the sky
> Gotta testify, come up in the spot looking extra fly
> For the day I die, I'm a touch the sky

The night wore on and pretty young ladies for the picking, flocked around the duo's table. Mike Copeland already helped himself, grabbing up on every pretty face that passed. Meanwhile Melquan eyed a voluptuous dark skin cutie. He corned her and began rapping to her, feeding her drink after drink. Melquan and Mike Copeland felt like they had the keys to the city. They were having fun when suddenly out of nowhere Precious appeared. Looking stunning in her simple black dress and jewelry, she was seething in her six-inch heels. Mike Copeland's jaw dropped when he saw her.

"Damn! Precious is that you…? Ooh-whee…!" Mike Copeland whistled and laughed. "You stepped your game up! I take back every bad think I ever thought about you."

"Mike, shut up!" Precious snapped, brushing him aside.

She couldn't resist smiling at the backhand of a compliment, but she was not in the mood for Mike Copeland's sarcasm, no matter how true it was. She wanted Melquan to shower her with compliments. Precious was here to make Melquan see her. She waited for a few minute. Nothing came. It was as if she was not even there. Precious turned away and moved closer to Mike Copeland.

"Mike, what's the matter with your friend?" she asked.

"Fuck I'm 'pose to know? I can't even speak for the next man.

He right there, why don't you ask him?"

"Hi Mel," Precious leaned over and said. "What's wrong with you? Can't speak?"

"I'm chillin'. What the fuck you doin' up in here anyway?"

"Nigga, I'm grown! I didn't know I needed ya damn permission to go out!"

"I ain't sayin' that, but I wish I would've known you was gonna be up in here."

"Nigga, pul-leeze, this a few muthafuckin' country last time I checked… Anyway, I heard you, Mike and ya moms copped some whips today. What's up with that? I thought I was gonna be the first bitch to ride up in your new joint?"

"You thought wrong."

Melquan was tight, he wasn't feeling Precious' drama queen act. It turned him off, and turning away, he totally ignored her. Melquan continued eyeing the good looking, butter Rican. He raised his champagne glass to the cutie he was admiring before Precious' rude interruption. Precious saw him smiling, and was about to explode.

"Yo ma, don't leave here without givin' me 'em digits," he said, knowing the comment would bother Precious.

Jealousy raised its ugly head and Precious was pissed. She purposely bumped the table spilling drinks. The mess she created forced Melquan, Mike Copeland, and their groupies to temporarily vacate the vicinity. Precious was planning on bringing the drama, and walked away while a Mexican porter cleaned up.

"You wildin' right now," Mike Copeland said. "If you gon' act like dat you shoulda stayed yo ass home! Can't take you niggas nowhere, I swear!"

Precious could hear Mike Copeland's comment and fired back. "Fuck you Mike! I ain't in the mood fa ya shit."

Melquan continued to flirt with all the pretty ladies drifting by him. Mike Copeland stayed as far away from Precious as possible. It was clear from her stink attitude that at any given moment, she was ready to black out on Melquan.

Once the area was all cleaned up, Melquan and Mike Copeland settled back into their spot. Precious eventually followed.

Couple more bottles of champagne and Melquan was really getting loose. Dancing around with several flirty women, he was laughing, enjoying himself. The women walked away and with champagne glass in hand, Melquan was left two-stepping to the beat of Game featuring Fifty Cent, Hate It Or Love It.

> *Hate it or love it the under dog's on top*
> *And I'm gon shine homie until my heart stop*
> *Go 'head and envy me…*

Precious walked up on Melquan. He was in full grove, holding his drink and two-stepping.

"Melquan, dance with me…?"

"Nah, I don't dance," he replied easily.

Precious glanced at Mike Copeland, trying not to show that was pleading. He shook his head, sipped and spoke.

"Don't bother even lookin' dis way. You know gangstas don't dance."

"Whatever, Mike. Melquan will you please dance with me…?"

"I thought I answered that one already."

"Melquan…?"

"What I say?"

Precious moved nearer to Mike Copeland. She was feeling dejected. Mike Copeland glanced quickly at her, and turned his attention to a brown skinned beauty walking by close. The gorgeous butter Rican pecan returned and grabbed Melquan. Dragging him to the dance floor, she moved closer to him. Much to the dismay of Precious, Melquan willingly danced with her all over him.

"Did you see that shit, Mike? What your man did is soo foul. Fuck him!"

"Why you gettin' mad at me for…?"

"Y'all are the same! I could be out fuckin' with mad niggas. But nah, I'm thinking that the nigga wants me a little bit. But he playin' me, Mike," Precious screamed, breaking down emotionally.

"I ain't the one doin nothin' so why you screamin' at me fam?"

"This nigga don't appreciate the sacrifices I'll be making for his ass. How he gonna just straight up dis me like this…? But you watch... Watch, I got sumthin for his muthafuckin' ass!" she said, sashaying away.

"Precious do me a favor and make sure you get ya revenge on the right person." Mike Copeland warned. "Miss me wit da bullshit. Whateva y'all got goin' is between y'all so keep it that way, a'ight?"

Precious said nothing else, but rolled her eyes at Mike and walked away. She gave no indication that she would comply with his request. Mike Copeland watched the sway of Precious' hips. Damn! She sure came dressed to win her man. Mike's thoughts were abruptly disturbed by another fatty swaying his way.

Meanwhile, on the dance floor, Melquan was enjoying himself. It had been a minute that he had really rocked out, and was doing it up to the max. He never saw the two guys grilling him from the bar. Mike Copeland came to his rescue, alerting him. Melquan instantly saw the haters scheming.

"Okay, Melquan that's enough of this dancing shit. Fuck you think you is? Usher?" Mike Copeland said, brusquely interrupting the dance. "It's about that time to bounce, my dude."

Melquan was having so much fun and didn't realize that Precious had disappeared. How fast the time had flown. Mike Copeland downed another drink while Melquan wiped beads of sweat from his forehead with a napkin. Always security conscious Mike Copeland began to survey the crowd. Once again he spotted the same two dudes at the bar.

"Yo, don't look now" he said between clenched teeth. "But

there's two muthafuckas at the bar. They been gettin' they hatin' on all fuckin' night, my dude."

Melquan coolly scanned the bar with his eye until he found the two men in question.

"Yeah, Mike, I see 'em."

"They been eyeballin' me for the longest, Mike. They ain't been drinkin', talkin' to no bitches, lookin like they havin' no kinda fun. Them niggas just straight sizin' nigga's up. Starin' at us like they want beef," Melquan said.

"They don't want no trouble, Mel."

"Mike, they sure actin' like it. We gotta be careful goin' back to da whips this ain't exactly our neck of the woods. If they gone try sumthin' they gonna try it then."

"You a'ight, Melquan? You not drunk or nothing like that, right?"

"I'm good, Mike. I can drive. Now, I'm ready for whateva, and that's my word!"

"A'ight my nigga, let's get da fuck up outta here then," Mike Copeland said.

They immediately got up and walked out of the lounge area and made it to the bar. Suddenly Mike Copeland stopped and smiled.

"Hey man, don't I know y'all from somewhere? Y'all look real familiar like I seen y'all before?" Mike Copeland said, wearing a fake smile. "Riker's…? Up north…?

"Nah nigga, you don't know us. We ain't from 'roun here," one of the mean-mugging thugs said.

"You might be mistaken, you know?" the other said.

"Yeah, my bad, I feel you," Mike Copeland said, quickly pulling the burner out.

It lit up the place in a hurry, and happened real fast. No one but the parties involved saw the flash from the muzzle. Then three shots rang out. Some patrons couldn't hear the explosion over the music.

They danced on like it was a sound effect from the deejay. Others who were close enough to see the spark, ran for the exits. The hysteria quickly spread like wildfire, and mayhem broke loose.

Patrons reacted to what they saw others doing, and raced to the exits. Mike Copeland shot the pair of haters. One man was hit in the stomach, and the other in the back. They were both left leaking and squirming on the floor.

"You right, you don't know me either! If you did you would've known not to front on me," Mike Copeland said, and casually walked out of the chaotic nightclub.

## Risking It All… Blowin' The Spot
Chapter Seventeen

It was around noon when Melquan and Mike Copeland met with members of their cartel in the horseshoe. Smoking blunts, they spoke of the day's business. The conversation soon turned to the previous night's escapade in the club. The partying, the beautiful broads, and the shooting that ensued were discussed. Mike Copeland took center stage, recounting last night's events. He loved the fact that rumors of the shooting had already reached back to the hood.

"So I don't know where these niggas from. I think Webster Ave or some ol' place like that..." Mike Copeland started. "I really ain't give a fuck. These niggas were up to no good, lookin' fa trouble and recklessly eye-ballin' niggas all nite."

Mike Copeland was animated, acting out the episode. With the crowd huddled around him, he was in rare form.

"So sumthin tell me, go look fa Melquan. The dance floor was crowded so it took me a minute ta spot him. Mel two steppin' wit da bitches. The goons in the cut eyein' my dude like he food. While niggas pointin' and whisperin', I snatch Mel off da dance floor, give him da four-one-one. When we get ready ta bounce, I walks over to da niggas on some humble shit and play their asses out. Once I got they minds off what I really came to do, then its blam, blam. Niggas runnin' up out da piece like Godzilla comin'. You should a been there to see what happens when shit hit da fan."

Just then Melquan walked up to the group, and caught the end of Mike's tale. He couldn't believe his ears. Mike Copeland was not only talking about last night's events, he was bragging about them. Melquan was furious.

"Mike," he shouted. "Lemme holla at ya for a minute…"

"Yeah, niggas got what they hand called for. Phony-ass-muthafuckas!" Mike Copeland spat. "That shit was straight gangsta, my nigga. I just walked up to 'em muthafuckas and gave 'em da bizness."

"A yo, Mike…! What's good?" Melquan repeated, gesturing directly at Mike.

"Calm down my nigger. I'm comin'," Mike replied.

By the time Mike Copeland strolled over. Melquan was visibly upset. Mike Copeland pretended not to notice Melquan's mood.

"What's good, my dude?"

"I don't know you tell me?" Melquan spat. "What's the deal wit da shit? Why ya tellin' these lil' niggas our bizness? We don't know what happened to them niggas. They coulda died for all we know. And if they did da charge just went from an attempt to homicide. Bet you didn't think about that, huh?"

Mike Copeland hissed, shook his head, and stared coldly at

Melquan before he spoke.

"Yo, stop bein' so muthafuckin' paranoid, my dude. These niggas already knew 'bout da shit before I even said a muthafuckin' word. Let's not forget there was a few heads from da hood up in there all night long. Niggas talk, I didn't even have'ta tell 'em a muthafuckin' thing!" Mike Copeland growled.

"What niggas know, and what they can prove, is two different things. You just added fuel to the fire by speakin' on it. Now you got about half a dozen witnesses that heard you say sumthin," Melquan replied.

"I wish a nigger would go to the grand jury on me. I'll body anyone of them fuckin' lil' niggas… That's my word."

"Yeah, but why even put yaself in da position, broadcasting ya BI?" Melquan said, turning away in disgust.

Mike Copeland stood dumbfounded, watching his boy hurt and walking away. His tough guy stance was the only defense Mike had. It proved to be a weak one.

Charlie Rock wheeled through the projects. He stopped to speak with a few residents, and saw two figures approaching him. Charlie Rock squinted to get a better view of them.

He saw a tall, stocky thirtyish man, walking with a limp and another shorter one with dreads. Charlie Rock recognized the taller man immediately.

"Oh shit is that you Justice…?" Charlie Rock asked, greeting the men.

Justice reached down and gave Charlie Rock a handshake that lacked any emotion. His friend looked on without saying a word.

"What up, ol' timer?" Justice greeted.

"Old timer…?" Charlie Rock repeated. "Where you goin' with

that? You know my name just like I know Justice. Ain't that yours?"

"Like I says, what up Ol' timer?" Justice reiterated.

Charlie Rock shook his head. "I ain't doin' nada, man… Just takin' things easy… What about you…? When did you get out?"

Justice glanced down at Charlie Rock. His expression was saying something other than what he was asking Charlie Rock.

"I came home da other day. I beat da case at trial," Justice smiled.

"That's a good look for you. I love it when my people beat 'em peoples in court. That's what's up. Anyway, how's your mother doing?"

"Fuck ya askin' 'bout her fa?"

"Man, I been knowin' that woman a long time now. What…? I can't ask about her?"

"I could give a fuck about how long ya know her fa. Just make this da last fuckin' time you speak 'bout her…"

"A'ight, yeah, I hear that. You got it, big man. Anyway, who that you with right here?"

"Nobody…"

"Don't he got a name he go by?"

"If he wanted to tell you his name, he'd have done so already. My man ain't too, too friendly. He don't like when certain peeps try to get too familiar either."

The man with Justice threw a menacing stare at Charlie Rock, and held it for what seemed to be an eternity. Charlie Rock fumbled for a cigarette.

"Lemme git one of those," Justice demanded.

Charlie Rock quickly complied. His sixth sense was tingling regarding these two. He could smell trouble.

"When you started smokin'? Musta picked up that bad habit in the joint, huh?"

"Look I ain't out here to rap to you about no cigarettes, and jail?

What's poppin' out here?" Justice snapped.

"Ya guess is as good as mine."

"You know everything. Fuck you think you talkin' to?

"A'ight Justice, you gettin' a lil too disrespectful fa me. I ain't got no time fa da BS. I got places to go and people to see. This convo is now over. Later!"

Charlie Rock attempted to maneuver his powered wheelchair away. Justice reached out and grabbed a hold of the wheelchair, preventing him from moving. Charlie Rock turned around to see the mean mugging of Justice.

"Now where da fuck ya think you goin'? I ain't through talkin' with ya crippled ass yet muthafucka!"

"Yo…?" Charlie Rock said, wearing a puzzled expression.

"Maybe I was away too long. I'm not in the know, but I been hearin' that there's a lot of money out here. Who holdin' all da dough ol' timer? I know ya nosey-ass knows. So start talkin' muthafucka!"

"Look man, don't start me to lyin'. I don't know a muthafuckin' thing!"

"Ya ass better stop lyin' to me, you ol' ass muthafucka! I already know ya know who holdin da dough."

"Look man, I be mindin' my own business. I don't care 'bout other people's shit. I don't be knowin' a damn thing—"

"You keep lyin' and I'm a turn this muthafuckin' wheelchair over with ya ass right in it."

Charlie Rock began to squirm in the wheelchair, struggling to break free from Justice's iron grip. Justice choked, laughing at the weak attempt.

"Justice, you got me fucked up with all these other lames out here. I'm paralyzed, nigga! I ain't no fuckin' bitch! Now I told you, I don't know nada! And that's what's up, muthafucka!"

"I know you know sumthin, ol' timer. You can bank on that. I hear you out here all the time, and you don't know shit…? I ain't buyin' da bullshit."

"I don't know shit! I done told you. I don't know nada, muthafucka! Those who know don't tell and those that tell don't know..."

"While I was on the Island, I heard that dis nigga, Melquan makin' all kinds of move in da projects. They say right now, he da nigga..."

"I don't know a damn thing 'bout that. I don't be makin' other people bizness my bizness. Who does what, that ain't none of my concerns. What another nigga eat don't make me shit."

"So, you don't know Melquan?"

"Who that...? You expect me to know every Tom, Dick, and Harry who peddle crack''round this muthafuckin' projects? I don't fuck wit these dudes...!"

"Really? That's not da word on da street."

"If the street told you that, then that means da street can tell you better than I can."

"Listen ol' timer, you better start talkin'. I'm two minutes off ya cripple ass. So stop playin' games wid me!"

At the same time an unmarked DT car cruised by. Justice stopped harassing Charlie Rock and watched the unmarked police car rolling by. The car stopped, and the three plainclothes cops paused looking at the gathering outside the project building.

The plainclothes cops got out, and all the workers around Melquan scattered, running off in different directions. Melquan was the only one left standing. Justice and Charlie Rock saw the commotion. Justice was smiling when he saw everyone running away.

"Melquan, what's poppin my man? How's business today?" the first cop asked.

"Melquan, why did your boys run off when we were just dropping by? They dirty? You dirty Melquan?"

"Nah, officer you got the wrong man."

"You think so?"

"I know so."

"I got a message for your buddy, Mike Copeland. Tell him we got a Billy club with his name all over it. Let him know its six more stitches every time he runs!"

"Why don't he man up, Melquan? He got no heart, now? His name is starting to ring bells. Better tell him if he doesn't chill, we'll have a case with his name on it too."

Melquan remained silent. He had nothing to say to that. Justice realized that he couldn't touch Charlie Rock. Not with the police around. The thought of bullying Charlie Rock suddenly left his mind. Justice would rather avoid police contact at all cost. Suddenly he released his grip on the wheelchair.

"Whateva, whateva… This ya lucky day ol' timer, get da fuck outta here! And you better not let me catch your ol' ass out here again," Justice warned.

"Yeah, you got it this time," Charlie Rock said, sounding frustrated.

Nashawn was watching a safe distance away. He saw Justice and Charlie Rock. The police were questioning Melquan. He turned to his worker when the police left.

"Yo, wait till po-po leave then go upstairs and get 'em gats. I see some heads that shouldn't be out here today," Nashawn smiled wickedly.

Later that day, Melquan was passing through the horseshoe in his Range Rover. He was about to drive out the projects when he spotted Charlie Rock. It surprised him to see Charlie Rock standing with George, a well-known crack head. He pulled to a stop and George limped way. Melquan let down the window and spoke to Charlie Rock.

"Charlie Rock what you doin' hangin' with fiends?" Melquan shouted through the opened window.

"I known him for a long time, he wasn't once who he is now."

"I know him a long time too. And he always been a fiend," Melquan said, spitting in disgust.

"True story, but at the end of the day we all human. And we ain't perfect, we all got our vices. Ask me, I know that shit. Whether sellin' or usin', or reapin' the rewards from it. We all addicted to this drug game. At some point or 'nother we all get caught up."

"Without question," Melquan responded, nodding.

"Anyway, this whip the real deal, nephew. Fit you well too," Charlie Rock said, complimenting.

Looking cautiously around, he directed the wheelchair and moved closer to the shiny, black SUV. Melquan turned down the volume on the Jay-Z's 534 CD when Charlie Rock lowered his voice.

"Yo, I gotta tell you sumthin real important, nephew."

"A'ight Unk, what's really good?"

"Your man Mike Copeland is really foul. He ain't playin this game fair!"

"What he do?"

"He got that young Puerto Rican kid out here sellin' crack! And that's not a good look," Charlie Rock complained.

His voice was so low his words came out in a hiss. He glanced furtively around then shaking his head, he continued.

"Don't you know that if da lil' boy's father find out, it ain't gonna be a good look. Da boy's father ain't no slouch. Y'all don't need them kinds of problems. Mike has to respect the game! A man's family is off limits."

Melquan nodded his head, intently listening to what Charlie Rock had to say. He thought carefully before responding.

"Charlie Rock, I already warned Mike about certain shit. But he's who he is. Shit just goes in one ear, and out the next fuckin' one."

"But that's your right hand man. It's not a good look for your organization, man! Ask me, I know that shit."

"Yeah, you right Mike Copeland is my man. Sometimes I even have to question some of his moves. I'm gonna have a talk with him about that," Melquan said in an even tone.

"There's one more thing I wanted to tell you, nephew. But I was so upset 'bout that other shit, I done forget what it was…"

"You slippin' Unk," Melquan chimed in.

They both chuckled. Charlie Rock thought for a second then waved Melquan on.

"Ah, forget about it. Soon as you drive off, I'll remember," Charlie Rock said.

"We'll talk later, Unk."

"Yeah, go 'head. It'll come to me later," Charlie Rock announced.

Melquan drove off leaving Charlie Rock scratching his head, perplexed in his thoughts. He glanced out on the avenue and suddenly his memory returned. Charlie Rock immediately turned his wheelchair, and headed the other way.

# Can't Stop It
Chapter Eighteen

Melquan rode down East Gunhill Road. The sound of Jay Z blasted through his speakers. He nodded his head while listening to the lyrics of Dear Summer.

> *Dear summer, I*
> *know you gon' miss me*
> *For we been together*
> *like Nike Airs and crisp tees*
> *S dots with polo fleeces*
> *Purple label shit with the logo secret*
> *Gimme couple years,*
> *shit I might just sneak in…*

The conversation with Charlie Rock weighed heavy on his mind. He finally turned down the volume on the track and dialed Mike Copeland.

"State your business…" Mike's tone was authoritative.

"Meet me in Bay Plaza by Red Lobster," Melquan said.

"What's good? Everythin's a'ight? Wha', we got beef…?" Mike replied.

"I'll talk to you about it when you get there," Melquan said, hanging up.

He waited patiently for Mike Copeland while listening to the 534 CD by Jay-Z.

> *Niggas can't fuck with me*
> *I'm in a good mood, you lucky,*
> *I got a good groove*
> *And I ain't trying to fuck my thing up*
> *But I will lay down a couple green bucks,*
> *get you cleaned up*
> *Now I'm Pulp Fiction, Colt four-fifth and*
> *Young niggas that blast for me…*
> *blasphemy, no religion…*

He could hear a loud thump getting closer. Melquan turned his music off when he heard the sound blasting and getting closer. It felt like there was an earthquake in the mall. The Cayenne Sport pulled to a stop and Melquan could hear the spitting of Fifty Cent and G-Unit.

> *Well tell 'em niggas they could pop this*
> *and stop frontin'.*
> *You heard a nigga*
> *do you know how I get down*
> *Stay with my vest on and*
> *roll with a couple of trey pounds*
> *In case you motherfuckers want to jump bad now*
> *Start some bullshit*

Mike Copeland jumped out the whip in a hurry. Melquan's improv meeting was cause for concern to him. Although they hadn't seen eye to eye lately, Melquan was still his man and partner. He entered Melquan's car and showed gave Melquan a pound.

"What's good, my dude?" Mike Copeland said. "What was so important that you needed to see me right away?"

"Look Mike I'm a get right to the point," Melquan said. "What's this I hear ya got some lil' Spanish kid, named Jose sellin' fa us?"

Mike Copeland looked at Melquan with a puzzled expression on his grill before speaking.

"Nigga, who da fuck told you that, huh? Who da fuck be spyin' on me like that…?"

There was no answer coming from Melquan and the questions hung in the air like foul odor. Mike Copeland thought about it for a while and sardonically smiled, shaking his head.

"Never mind you ain't even gotta tell me I already know. It's da ol' muthafucka in da wheelchair. Fuckin' snitch-ass, Charlie Rock…!" Mike Copeland angrily said. "Tell me sumthin, since when you start takin' da word from a crack-head?"

"Wha…?"

"You heard me! Fuck dat nigga! Da kid stepped to me. He talkin' bout he wanna rock. It ain't like I went out and purposely recruited his ass. If he didn't get it from me, he was gonna get it from da next man. He coulda been puttin' in work for da competition, Melquan. So I put him on before somebody else did. What da fuck is da deal?"

"Regardless of how it happened, it can't go down like that. It's a problem. And let's nip shit in da bud before it goes any further."

"Yo, lemme ask you sumthin man. What's your problem? Why everything I do startin' to bug you?" Mike Copeland asked, getting emotional.

Melquan stared at him blankly, unaffected by Mike's mood swing. He couldn't believe that Mike couldn't see the moves that he was making, if left unchecked would lead to their downfall.

"In ya eyes, ya never do nothin' wrong. I told ya before, I ain't into corruptin' no kids, Mike—"

"Da fuck you hollerin' 'bout? These kids already corrupted! They certainly don't need no help from me."

"Mike, this shit's not open for discussion! When shorty comes around again, send him on his way. Do not give da kid another package."

"You buggin' da fuck out my dude. But you know what I'm eat this one. Next time approach me when you got a real issue. Not on some he say-she say, ol' bullshit, a'ight? And furthermore, I ain't really been feelin' da way you be talkin' to me lately. Who da fuck I am, and how I do, nigga! Respect me like I respect you, my dude."

An angry Mike Copeland got out the car and slammed the door. He swaggered to his ride and peeled out of the parking lot. Mike Copeland did not once look back at his friend.

Jose Jr. walked out of his project building. He was now an official part-time crack dealer, putting in limited hours, everyday on his new job. Everyday he made up a different lie to tell his father about his whereabouts. Jose Sr. seemed to actually believe it. Jose took the long way to the horseshoe, just in case his father was watching out the window. This was an added precaution.

Mike Copeland spotted Jose coming, and a cynical smile appeared, lighting up his face. He greeted the young boy with a solid handshake.

"What's good, my nigga?" Copeland asked.

"You and da package you got fa me," Jose said.

"Look, shorty, I got some bad news fa you," Mike Copeland said. "Today's gonna be your last day on da team."

"What?"

"Yo, believe you me. You're a natural at dis and I don't really wanna let you go. But from what I know, this got sumthin' to do with your pops. Certain people gotta lotta respect for him. They don't want no problems. You feel me, shorty?"

Mike Copeland went on to explain the politics behind the decision, without naming any names. Jose was depressed, but understood for the most part. When his last package was handed to him, Jose hustled harder than he ever did.

Unbeknownst to Jose, Maria followed him to the horseshoe. She stopped a distance away, watching him and Mike Copeland. She had discovered her brother's secret life, and bit her lips, holding back the tears she felt. There was confusion about what she was supposed to do. She felt like her brother had been taken away. This caused tears to sting her eyes. She walked back home feeling alone.

Precious walked past the weeping young girl, without giving her a second glance. Sashaying across the street, she jumped into a waiting cab. Her timing couldn't have been better. The car sat at the curb for couple seconds. Nashawn exited his building, entering the cab from the opposite side door. The cab pulled off and Mike Copeland, wearing a grimace, quickly dialed on his cellphone. He was anxious and couldn't wait to tell Melquan what he had just witnessed.

# Living Lavish
## Chapter Nineteen

Melquan was chilling in the apartment, watching television with Zach and India. Suddenly his cellphone vibrated. He unraveled his body from the comfort of India's warm embrace to get at the ringing cellphone.

"Yeah, what's up?"

"You got to get here, my dude. You gon' bug da fuck out," Mike Copeland said.

"Mike, what da deal?"

"Wait a minute… Is you with India right now?"

"Yeah… Why?"

"I suggest ya come take a look for ya-damn-self."

"A'ight, Mike, I'll be right there…" Melquan said, ending the call.

He pulled on his jeans, and threw a hoodie over his T-shirt. Melquan was reluctant, but knew Mike Copeland wouldn't call on him if it wasn't an emergency. There was no getting around it, he had to go. He was already dressed and getting ready to walk out the door.

"I'll be right back, baby," he said to India.

"Where are you going now, Melquan?" she asked with an unsympathetic ring to her tone.

"I have to go handle some important BI. Mike needs me right now."

"Melquan, I need you!" she said, sucking her teeth. "I need you here with me."

"India, this ain't gonna take too long. I'll be right back."

"What's the sense of having people working for you if you have to leave home every time something goes wrong? Can't Mike handle these emergencies? Can't it wait until tomorrow?" India asked, sounding very irritated.

"Look, I don't know what this 'bout. Mike Copeland refused to talk over the phone. So my guess is that it's pretty serious."

"Can I go with you?"

"And who's gonna take care of Zach, India?"

"Shoot, you right. I totally forgot about Zach. I swear from now on, Melquan when you come inside please turn your damn cellphone off, once you close that door. When you're inside with me, you're here with me. No exceptions. You just can't be running in and out, like this some damn store."

Melquan left India's apartment, and quickly linked up with Mike Copeland. After the two discussed the situation, they decided to wait outside for Precious to return. Their patience paid off. A couple hours later, a cab pulled to a stop in the driveway.

"There they go right there," Mike Copeland said, pointing across the Avenue.

Everything looked peachy when Precious and Nashawn got out of the cab together, and walked inside the building. Nashawn was walking alongside her like they were more than just friends.

"See, what I was talkin' 'bout, my dude? Bet you thought I was makin' shit up, huh? A picture is worth a thousand words… This bitch's in violation!"

Mike Copeland was laughing and making light of the situation. Melquan was quiet and thinking. He looked at Mike, rocking with laughter.

"Mike, why's everythin' so fuckin' funny to you?"

"Cuz it is. It's 'specially funny how a dude that supposed to not give a fuck about a bitch is lookin' kind a pussy-whip right now."

"I don't give a fuck about her! I don't give a damn who she be fuckin' creepin' wit. We got 'em muthafuckin' guns and drugs stashed inside her crib. And that's my concern. Mike, I got a bitch ten times badder than Precious. And she's home alone waitin' on me!"

Mike Copeland looked at Melquan in disbelief. They had known each other for a long time. He could tell that Melquan was pissed.

"Word, that's what's up, my dude."

"Get ready, Mike, we gettin' ready to go over there, right now."

Mike Copeland removed the 9mm from his waistband. He checked the clip and cocked the weapon. Then he replaced the weapon in his waistband. They walked across the street and quickly entered the building.

"Mike, lemme do all the talkin'. You just hold your tongue, and don't say nothing," Melquan warned.

Melquan and Mike Copeland swiftly made their way up the stairs to the third floor. They walked cautiously down the hallway, passed the elevator and Melquan leaned against the wall as if he listening in from the outside. He stayed out of site while Mike Copeland knocked on Precious' apartment door.

"Who is it…?" Precious hollered, checking the peephole.

She saw Mike Copeland, and opened the door. Dressed in a red halter top dress, revealing heavy cleavage, Precious was looking beautiful. She was still wearing her high heels and her hair was tightly drawn back. It showed her entire face, and she was stunning. Mike Copeland's eyes were wide, staring blankly.

"Mike, what the hell you doing here…?"

Precious was very surprised, and stared wide-eyed at Mike Copeland who had a gun in his hand. He put his finger to his lips and crept inside the apartment. Precious stared at him seemingly confused. Suddenly Melquan revealed his position, and greeted her grimacing, carrying his nine millimeter.

She was scared watching them moving silently about her apartment. They checked each room, making sure no one was home. When the duo was satisfied, they returned to see Precious' surprise gaze following them through the two-bedroom furnished apartment.

"He ain't up in here," Mike Copeland said.

"He ain't up in here…?" Precious repeated incredulously. "Who ain't up in here?"

"Nashawn. Where da fuck is he?" Melquan asked.

"Nigga, please. Is this what all this is about?" Precious asked.

"What da fuck you doin' with Nashawn, huh? You switchin' up sides?"

"Melquan, you don't want me, at least not like I want you. So why you now gonna front like you even care about me, huh? You go home to your girl every night… How could you even be mad at what I do, huh Mel? Not after all the love I've shown you… And you still take me for granted."

Caught between anger and hurt, Precious' face had an appearance of picture of beauty. Her voice rose with the emotions she felt, causing her breast to rise and fall. They seemed as if they were on the verge of busting out of her sexy top. Silently tears rolled down her cheeks. Melquan and Mike Copeland put their weapons away. All three stared at each other, saying nothing. Melquan and Mike Copeland glanced at each other then they both stared at Precious.

Her curves were on display and the dress displayed her figure very well. Even without makeup, Precious still had a very pretty face. Melquan bit his lips tightly, and spoke between clenched teeth.

"I don't care who you fuckin'! Just let it not be da muthafuckin' Nashawn!"

Melquan's words thundered through the room. Precious stared at him, standing there, confident and cocky, telling her what to do.

"You gonna keep being my damn father? I really need you to be my man," Precious said, playing with his emotions.

"C'mon, don't act like you don't know. Shit could pop off at anytime on any given day. Nashawn is da fuckin' enemy! I'm sure you know that much!"

Melquan was front and center in her face. They were cheek to cheek, and staring each other down. His warm breath blowing on her made hot and bothered. The heat of their bodies was melting the anger they both felt. Melquan reached out and grabbed her by the throat.

"You need some attention, huh Precious? Come here. I'm gonna show you all the attention you need!"

Melquan picked up Precious and took her down the short hallway to the bathroom. Mike Copeland immediately rushed inside Precious' bedroom. He packed all the weapons and drugs in a duffel bag. Mike Copeland was quick about his business, and was ready to leave the apartment.

He gave Melquan a three fingers and a circle signal with his free hand, walking past the opened bathroom door. Melquan was in the process of ripping off Precious' thongs and winked at his partner. Mike Copeland was smiling when he quickly fled the apartment.

Melquan was quickly deep in Precious' gusy pussy. He fucked her hard while standing. She was bent over against the closed toilet seat, throwing hips back his way, meeting his every thrust. Precious was going buck wild and Melquan was smiling. Bouncing on her toes, she threw her hips right back at him.

"Ooh yes, Melquan," Precious screamed.

They were fucking so hard, she didn't even hear when Mike Copeland slammed the door, laughing, going down the stairs. "My dude's in there blowin' da bitch out," Mike said to no one in particular.

Meanwhile, India was tossing and turning while lying awake in bed. She rubbed her stomach, and India's hand wandered to her Venus mound. She was feeling really horny and missed Melquan. It was after two in the morning. Where was he? Her mind raced.

India turned on the television and channel surfed for a moment. She turned off the television and walked to her bedroom window. She saw the lights of the city, and could see clear to the Bronx from her window. India couldn't picture what Melquan was doing. What kind of business would he be handling at this hour? She wondered.

Impatiently India glanced at the time and her cellphone. India wanted to call him, but she kept telling herself over and over again, she didn't care. She had a difficult time convicing herself of that.

## Messin' With The Devil

Chapter Twenty

Monday went by too slowly for Jose Jr. in school. He was able to get through the day with no problem and couldn't wait to get home. Jose Jr. rushed to get his sister Maria and together they hurried home. About an hour later Jose Sr. arrived home from another stressful day at his job. He smiled when he embraced his daughter.

"Oh my little princess," he greeted.

"Hey daddy," she screamed excitedly.

"How're you feeling, dad? I'm going to the library, okay?"

"Okay, but you've been spending an awful lot of time there.

What you got a job there?"

"Dad I've got more than one project. I got a science project and then the geography teacher said she wanted us to be there and…"

"Oh, alright then. You better let me see some A's at the end of the semester, that's all."

Jose left to get his jacket from his room and Maria followed behind him. He looked at her, hoping she doesn't want to go with him.

"Jose, so you're going to the library, huh?" she asked sarcastically. "Jose, I know where you're really going."

"What? You better shut up. You don't even know nothing."

"Really I do, Jose. I know you're not going anywhere near the library, Jose," Maria said with a knowing smile.

"Shut your mouth! You don't even know what you're talking about. Alright, since you know so much, where am I going then?"

"You, Jose, are going to," Maria said, pausing to recall in her mind every exact detail of what happened.

She nodded her head before continuing. She may have been younger in years, but Maria was way ahead of her older brother.

"Go ahead and say what you don't know," Jose said, daring his sister.

"Alright, you're going to the horseshoe! I saw you be—" Maria almost shouted.

But Jose wouldn't let her. He immediately grabbed her and pulled her inside his room. Jose looked outside his room door to see if his father was about. Satisfied, he turned his attention back to Maria.

"Shut your mouth, girl!" he said, putting his index finger to his lips.

He stared at her for a couple beats as if studying her. Now he had to find out how much she knew.

"Maria, you better be quiet before daddy hears you. Maria, tell me what exactly did you see?"

"I saw you standing around with these other boys. Then they handed something to you. Then you handed to another man and he gave you money for it."

His whole secret life was unmasked by a nosey little sister. He couldn't take it out of her mind but maybe he could distort the picture.

"Oh, ha, I was just doing a favor for one of my friends. Ahem… ah and he was waiting for his dad. So his dad's friend came and got it from me," Jose lied, confusing even himself.

He could feel sweat formed around his cheeks as he spun his yarn. Jose tied himself into knots. His stomach tightened and his legs weakened.

"You are lying. Daddy don't want us to go there because they sell crack—"

Fifteen year old Jose was sweating bricks. He had been busted by his thirteen year old sister. She glanced at him like a judge about to execute sentence on the guilty.

"Maria, Maria tell me… Did you tell dad?"

"Nope, but I've been thinking about it," she said firmly.

"Good, please, Maria, please don't tell dad, please. Maria you know dad, he will kill me if he found out I was even closely there," Jose pleaded.

"Then why are you doing it, huh? If you know that he will kill you? That's really stupid, Jose. Are you crazy?"

Jose offered no answer. He stared dumbfounded by his sister, thinking of the death penalty he was now facing. There was no explanation, but maybe there was another way out of this. The idea clicked in his mind. Jose smiled then hugged his sister.

"Maria, I can give anything you want. You name it. Money…?"

Jose reached into his pocket and pulled out a small knot. He peeled off couple twenty dollar bills. He offered it to his sister.

"No…" she muttered. "I'm okay."

"Maria take it. I'll give you a hundred dollars right now. Just please don't tell daddy nothing."

He tried to shove a couple bills at Maria she stared at his hand as if he was giving her trash. There was a look of disgust on her face. The contours of her expression quickly transformed, and soon Maria was in tears.

"That's dirty money. Just like daddy says, Jose. The bible says money is the root of all evil!"

Maria was crying and Jose hugged her. She pushed him away, staring at the money he was still holding in his hand. He lined his pocket with the dirty money. Jose saw the tears in his sister's eyes, and his heart cried.

"Jose, please stop going there to the horseshoe with those boys. I don't want the money. I just want you to stop."

"Alright, Maria if you stop crying, I promise I will not go out there today. I will not go out there ever again."

"Okay, if you promise then I'll stop."

A few minutes later, there was a knock on the door. It was their father wandering through the apartment. He pushed on the door.

"Jose, you seen your sister…?"

"Yes dad, she's in here," the boy calmly said.

"What's going on in here?" Jose Sr. asked, pushing on the door. "Open the door, now."

Jose Jr. stared at Maria then he quickly opened the door. His father presence in the room made it even tinier. He walked in sniffing the air.

"Hi dad," Maria said.

"There you are. I was looking for you. What you doing in here?"

"Hey daddy," Maria said, laughing. "I came in to see this video on BET."

"Princess, why are your eyes so red? You's crying or—"

A great hush fell on the tiny room. It landed awkwardly, and Maria stared through her dad's perception. Jose looked on, guilty as charged. He sprang into action.

"Oh yeah, she was. This real sad documentary about the life of Aliyah came on. Then they showed the video, Missing You. And it made Maria cry. You know her, she cries for everything."

"It made me think about her. She died so young," Maria said sadly.

She seemed to be on the verge of tearing up again. Jose moved closer to her and gave her a hug.

"Oh, don't worry about dying, princess. You've got a lot of living to do," Jose Sr. said embracing his daughter. He glanced at his son and said, "I thought you's going to the library?"

"Dad out of nowhere I caught a migraine headache. I ain't going nowhere. I'm gonna try to find what I need online. I'm leaving that library thing alone for now."

Maria and her dad walked out the door. He had his arm around her. Just before exiting, she turned around and winked at her brother. He nodded seemingly deep in his thoughts.

# Living It

Chapter Twenty One

Last night, Precious had gotten all the attention she craved from Melquan. Things were back to reality when she awoke the next morning. She was alone and Melquan was with his main chick, doing only God knows what.

Precious checked the time on her cable box. It was 11:30 a.m. Her next move was to check her cellphone to see if she had missed any calls from Melquan, Mike Copeland, or any of the workers. There were none. Slowly she began suspecting something was wrong.

She began wondering what Mike Copeland was really doing

in her house last night. Precious looked where the stash used to be and that was gone, so were the guns. It finally dawned on Precious. Melquan had clearly left and shitted on her. she quickly dialed his digits and he picked up.

"Melquan that shit ain't funny. What you did last night was really fucked up! Hold up, I can't hear you," Precious screamed into her cellphone.

"What ya talkin' 'bout…?" he asked still chuckling.

"How could you pull some bullshit stunt like what you fucking did..?"

"I don't know—"

"Melquan don't play stupid with me. You know exactly what I'm talking about! You had Mike Copeland take all da guns and drugs out of the apartment while me and you were in the bathroom. Then I'm sitting there wondering why nobody ain't call me all day…? Why you do that?"

"A'ight Precious, ya want da truth? Ya violated. Like I told ya before, anybody but him..."

"Oh, so I'm not down no more, Melquan?"

"Ya ass his-story now!"

"Mel, Nashawn and I didn't even do nothing. He took me to the movies and then we went and got sumthin to eat. Ain't nothin' happen, Melquan… Please believe me. I only did it to make you jealous."

"Yeah, you really expect me to believe that shit, huh? A bitch like ya could easily set a nigga up."

"Melquan, after all this time we been dealin' with each other, you just gonna cut me out of your life like that, huh?"

"Bitch, ya shouldn't have put yaself in this position. So ya only got ya ass to thank."

"After all I did? This how you reward me, huh? I held you down. Kept your stash, I sucked your dick when you need me to, fucked you whenever, wherever you wanted. And you straight shitted on me,

Melquan!"

There was a moment of silence, but Precious heard what she thought was laughter coming from the other end. It made her furious.

"You dirty muthafucka!"

"Chill with all da name callin', just go see Mike Copeland. Tell him to give you a couple a dollars for ya pockets. It's your severance pay, bitch! After that we even."

There was a long pause between them. It was as if the line had gone dead. Precious swallowed back the tears.

"You there?" he asked.

"You know Melquan, you can't be possibly serious. You can't just fuck me over like that! I don't deserve it. All I was doin' was tryin' to get your attention."

"That you did… Precious, ya can take it how ya wanna take it. Our business is over for now, and that's all I got to say."

"What!"

"At the end of day, I still got mad love for ya, but I certainly ain't in love with ya ass!"

"Melquan, fuck you alright! Fuck you! You can take that shit and shove it up your fuckin' ass! You're gonna get yours, Melquan! You hear me, muthafucka!" Precious screamed loudly.

Standing and gazing out of the window of his project building, Melquan and Mike Copeland gave each other daps on the execution of their plan.

"I told you, Melquan, I knew she knew sumthin when I seen da bitch earlier today. She just rolled her eyes at me."

"Yeah, she was tight. When I told her she wasn't down anymore, she fuckin' screamed her fuckin' head off. She sound like she might do sumthin stupid…" Melquan's voice trailed.

Mike Copeland eyes were trained on him, anxiously awaiting his doubts to be revealed. Melquan was thinking too long.

"Whatcha talkin' 'bout, my dude? She gon' do sump'n? Like what?"

"Call po-po… I mean she still knows a lot—"

"I wish da bitch would. I'll murder her ass so fast!"

"Mike, did put that stash where I told you to?"

"You know I did. Don't worry about that, we good."

"Now you see why I told you to put everything up, right? You were careful so that nobody followed you, right? I mean you made sure, right?"

"Yeah, what you think my dude? I'm a security risk? I got this."

A sudden knock on the door alerted Melquan. Mike Copeland grabbed his gun. He had it cocked and ready before Melquan peeped out. Smiling, Melquan opened the door.

"What's good, shorty?"

"Melquan," Sheron greeted, walking into the apartment.

He gave Mike Copeland dap and walked over to Melquan, embracing him and showing him much love.

"Yeah shorty, that's da fuck I'm talkin' 'bout right there! How you?"

"I'm okay…"

"Yeah, that's good. So where you comin' from?"

"School…"

"How was school?"

"It's good. But today, my friend almost got me in trouble."

"Word…? What happened?"

"Well, he threw a paper at me. I threw it back. The teacher saw me and not him."

"So, did you tell on your friend?"

"No," Sheron immediately said. "That's my friend. Why would

I do that for?"

"That's good. Never tell, especially on your friends. You hear me, shorty?"

"Yeah, but I already knew that. I ain't no snitch, Melquan. I wasn't gonna tell."

"Yeah, and you better keep it like that, feel me, shorty!" Mike said, intervening.

"Be easy, Mike…" Melquan's voice trailed.

Mike walked to the kitchen, leaving Melquan beaming from what the kid told him. He was that proud of what Sheron did, and admired the quality he deemed good in Sheron. Melquan pulled out a knot, and peeled off a couple of bills.

"Get some new sneaks and jeans with that. Keep the rest on the low. You hear me, right?"

"Thanks, Melquan.

"Lemme ask you sumthin shorty, you don't give your mom any of that money I give you, right?"

"No, you gave it to me. So that means only I'm the one who's supposed to have it."

"That's right. Do not give your mother nothing, you hear me? Not even one dime…" Melquan's voice trailed and he sunk deep into his thoughts. After a few beats he spoke. "I don't know if it's my place to tell you this, but I will. Your mother's on drugs."

"I know," Sheron said, nodding his head.

"What…? How do you know?"

"Whenever she comes in from outside… She goes straight in her room. And when she comes out, she be actin' all funny. Like somebody is chasin' her. She makes me stay in my room and cut off the TV."

"Word…?"

"Word up…"

"How does that make you feel, shorty?"

"I feel bad sometimes, especially when there's no food. And she keep tellin' me she's goin' to the store to get something to eat... I feel bad when she starts walkin' around the apartment naked like she going crazy..."

"Sheron, when you get hungry and she ain't around, just come knock on my door, like you did today," Melquan said in a saddened tone.

"Okay..."

"I'm a leave word with my mother to take care of you. Whatever you want, you let her know."

"Yep..."

"I mean if you need a place to sleep, you got that too, right?"

"Okay..."

Melquan gave Sheron dap. By the time Mike Copeland returned to the room, Sheron was already out the door. Mike Copeland glanced around the living room before speaking.

"I know you think it real cool. But really, I don't think it's a good idea to have shorty up here. You be too trustin' my dude. See what we had to do with Precious, huh? We runnin' out a places."

"Nah, shorty's good. You heard what he said, right?"

"Yeah, but you never know who his so-called good ass be talkin' innocently with."

Melquan and Mike Copeland walked down the stairs and stood outside the building. Across the avenue, Justice and his dreadlocks friend were sitting in a late model tinted window Cadillac, observing them.

"There goes that nigga, Melquan right there. He wearing the blue Yankee fitted and the other dude in the black Yankee is Mike Copeland, the shooter," Justice said, pointing out the window of the

Caddy.

"That's him, huh?" the dread asked. "You sure 'bout dat…?"

"Positive…"

"How we gonna bag that nigga? Him and his man always together and shit."

"Yeah they are, except when they're home. I'm sure they don't sleep together. Divide and conquer," Justice smiled.

## Gotcha Open
### Chapter Twenty Two

India and her son, Zach, were finishing dinner at home. They had been having a great time, but it was almost time for Zach to go to bed. She expected Zach to resist, instead he was cooperative. She was so pleased and allowed him an extra half hour to play videogames.

"Mom, dinner sure was good," he smiled, putting his empty plate in the sink. Zach hurried off to his room.

"I'll come in and see you, when it's time for bed," India called after him.

Melquan would be home soon. She started cleaning up, a chore she wasn't fond of, but it gave India her time to think. She was in the kitchen packing dishes away when her cellphone rang.

India picked it up expecting Melquan's number, saw the caller ID blocked. She thought about not answering and was about to put the phone away. The phone rang until she couldn't ignore it anymore. It was the same blocked number. This time she answered.

"Hello, who is this?" India asked.

"I don't know you, but I seen you. Precious is my name... I'm da bitch who was sitting between Melquan's legs in the drive over in Edenwald. Member that day when you rolled up on him...? Yeah, that was me. I don't know what he's been sayin to you about me, but we sleepin together too. Whenever he's not with you then we together. Melquan my part time boo."

The revelation dropped like a building on top of India. Wanting to nullify the caller's claim, she steadied herself from the blow.

"Melquan is doing what? Who is this calling me with this nonsense? I mean you could just be calling me to get me mad. You might just be playing with my mind. He's always home with me. That incident was at least a couple months ago. Anyway, how did you get my number?"

"One of the many nights your so-call man spent at my house. It was one night when I put his ass to bed, you kept calling, annoying us, and I copied your number from his cellphone."

India's anger was boiling so hot, her skin itched. She felt her stomach rapidly twisting into a knot. Frozen to ground, she suddenly felt like urinating, but her feet felt heavy, and perspiration broke out all over body.

"You alright...?"

"How long have you known Melquan, and how long have this been going on?" India asked, wanting badly to hear the full story.

"Since way back in high school me and Melquan been on and off. You see, he always have a lot of chicks and I just couldn't be bothered chasing his fine ass around. Then we got back together on some business tip, and all our feelings started coming back. On and off,

I'd say we've been in each other's lives about four to five years now. So I'd say that's a very, very long time…"

"Alright thanks. I don't want to hear no more, please!" India quickly said.

"Well I figure that I would just call you and let you know, he dogged me. And he's gonna dog ya ass too!"

"Really now…? Listen up little girl, whatever Melquan did to you, you allowed it to happen. You never called my number when everything was all good. So please don't call with the bullshit now!"

India was about to end the call, but even with the phone some distance from her ear, she could hear Precious' ranting. India put the cellphone back to her ear and listened.

"Bitch, you don't have to be all nasty about it. Ain't nothin' personal. I was just callin' to let you know, the man you claimin' is a damn, two-timin' ho!"

"Bitch, it takes one to know one. So you should know! Goodbye!"

India was way past any further conversation with the caller. Precious was still screaming when India pressed end call. She wanted to see Melquan in the worse way, and hear his version.

India was an emotional wreck and threw down the phone so hard, the battery case fell apart. She paced around the kitchen, wandering into the living room. India walked back and bent down, picking up the pieces of her cellphone.

She attempted to put the battery back into the instrument, but a task she had performed before, seemed almost impossible for the first time. She stared at the cellphone, struggling to put it back together. The heavy tears clouding her eyes wouldn't let her.

It was late when Melquan entered the darkened apartment. He shuffled through the place without pausing to turn on any of the lights. There was enough illumination provided by the city lights shining through the large living room window. Melquan walked directly to bedroom expecting to find India asleep. He was surprised when he got there, and didn't see her.

Melquan checked in on Zach. He was still up playing videogames. The boy turned around and devilishly smiled, knowing he wasn't supposed to be up at this time.

"What you doin' up? It's way past your bedtime… You better get some sleep. Where's your mother?"

"She's asleep on the couch."

"Why's she sleeping out there?"

"I dunno…"

"A'ight, thanks."

Melquan walked back to the living room and stood over India, studying her beautiful face for a couple beats. A smile creased his lips. Their lovelife was finally coming together. He stared out at the city's skyline, now he had attained a kingdom, Melquan wanted to build a palace for India, Zach, and himself. Melquan was thinking how much he was going to miss this view when he heard India stirring.

"Hey baby, get up. C'mon, let's take a shower together and go to bed," Melquan suggested with a smile.

"No, I'm very good just right where I am, Melquan. I don't want to sleep in the same bed with you anymore."

Melquan was taken aback by India's curt response. He looked at her seeking the humor of it all. Something had to be there to laugh about.

"Where's all this attitude comin' from, India?"

"Hmm, maybe we should ask your lil' project ho, name Precious," India deadpanned.

"Precious…? Who da fuck is a Precious. This some kinda joke

or sumthin…? I don't know no Precious!"

"Really now…? Playing dumb ain't getting you out of this one, Melquan. So for once come clean, and please don't start lying again."

"India, you trippin' right now! Lemme find out somebody been feedin' you some bullshit 'bout me!"

"Really now…? Melquan, please don't try my patience. You're such a liar! Precious is the bitch who was sitting between your legs on the bench that day. You lied about then and you still lying now. Who was she to you then? Please don't try that shit again."

"India, I don't know where you be gettin' your insane ideas from. But you, you're buggin' for real!"

"So are you denying even knowing a girl named Precious, let alone sleeping with her, huh?"

"What? you ain't heard da first time? I told you, I don't know no Precious, a'ight?"

"When I kicked your ass out, didn't you go running over to her place?"

Melquan couldn't get a word in, and he let India get whatever she had off her chest. He stared at her and waited for what was coming.

"Don't even try that my-poor-little-ghetto-story bullshit, on me. No, Melquan amnesia will not get you off this time."

"So come straight and say what it is…"

"Precious called my cellphone this evening. She told me she got the number that night when I kicked you out and you were at her place. She said and I quote, she had put you to bed," India said, raising both index fingers. "I remember very well, calling and calling and you asleep. So my calls disturbed your project princess, and she said she wrote my number down…"

Melquan stared at her in disbelief. She returned his stare, studying his reaction. Melquan was ice cold and never gave anything away.

"Oh, you're really buggin' now. First of all, I don't know no Precious, and now I'm beginnin' to think that you're makin' this whole thing up to start a fight. You just want a fight cuz you fuckin' insecure, India."

She stared at him with a smirk like she was looking for sympathy. Her eyes were clouded with dark sorrow of knowing when he was lying. This was leading her in a state of total confusion. She still loved Melquan that was the reason this incident hurt so much. India started crying, wallowing in her self pity.

India had feared the street life would come knocking on her door. She didn't know what would be next. First, someone called her cellphone and told her a story that was threatening to ruin her love relationship. The thing that bothered India was that she was now ready to believe the caller's story. She realized that there was some truth to it.

"Melquan, you've lied to me so many times. I don't really know whether I'm capable of believing you anymore. You've cheated before on me…"

"C'mon India, now whenever sumthin happens you gonna have to bring up the past, right? Let what happened stay in the past. We fuckin' arguin' 'bout some unknown broad… Some broad I don't even fuckin' know…"

She listened carefully hoping Melquan would slip, but he never changed his story. His denial unequivocal, he claimed not to know this person. India kept wondering why she couldn't believe what he was saying.

"I've been putting up with your shit for a long time now, Melquan. If it ain't one thing then it's another. If I knew you were going to shit on me the way you have, I would never let you in my life."

"Honey, c'mon…" Melquan said, reaching out to hold India.

She wiggled free and they were apart again. He could tell by her stance that she was fed up. He tried to hug her again.

"Get off, please, Melquan…" she cried. "Please, please, Melquan do not touch me, right now."

"I guess you gonna kick me out, now. Do you want me out, India?"

"Did I say anything about that…?"

"I'm just sayin' that's usually what comes next, right?"

"Melquan, if you want to leave then fine. I didn't say anything about that."

"Yeah, but you were actin' all crazy and shit. And when you ain't sayin' too much that means you gettin' ready to blow your top off on a muthafucka…"

"It isn't always about you, Melquan. I'm having a moment right now. I just need my space… So please, you're welcome to stay if want to. Nobody is forcing you…"

India turned her back and walk away leaving Melquan with his thoughts. Precious, Precious, Precious, she kept running through his mind.

Justice hugged and kissed his mother before leaving her apartment. She walked him to the door. Placing her hand on his unshaven cheek, she smiled.

"Boy your face is rough. You need to shave before you go to look for work," she said.

"That's tomorrow, ma. I'll shave then," Justice said.

"Boy don't be no stranger. Stop by and see me more often. You know I'm getting older and tomorrow ain't promised."

"Ma, don't talk like that. You know I don't like it when you do that… That's crazy talk. You ain't goin' nowhere."

"Yeah boy, I wish. But when the Lord calls me I gots to go… Just like everybody else. What makes me so special?"

"There you go, ma… Do me one favor. If the Lord calls when I leave, promise me that you won't pick up the phone, okay?" Justice said, kissing his mother goodbye.

He waved and left the building. Outside, he jumped into a waiting car and they peeled off.

"Yo, what took you so long, Just?" the driver asked.

"It's the old-earth, man. I had to show respect. I couldn't just eat and run. Just drive, and let's go pick up them guns," Justice said.

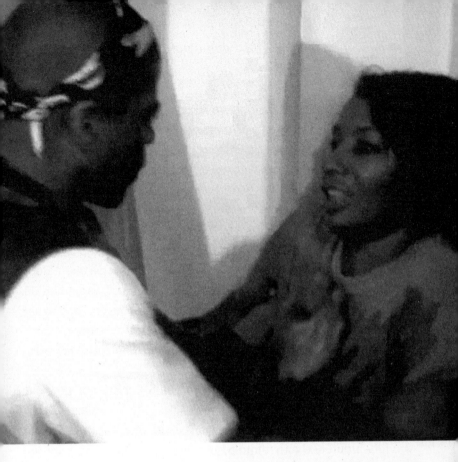

## Been About Money

Chapter Twenty-Three

Miss Tina was out late on the town and was just getting in. She got out of her ride and dressed in low form fitting skirt and a black butter soft leatherjacket that showed off her ample breasts.

"Girl, you ain't aged one bit. You still fine as ever," Charlie Rock declared.

"Stop it Charlie," she gushed, smiling she acknowledged the compliment. "I tell you a thing or two Charlie Rock, you're too much. You're too damn much."

Charlie Rock bit his lower lip and openly gawked at Miss Tina. With extra sashay in her hips, she seductively strolled by. He couldn't help but reminisce over their brief relationship a long time ago.

Miss Tina entered her building and quickly walked up the stairs. Her high heels were beginning to hurt, so she took them off. She rushed down the hallway to her apartment door.

Two men with their backs pressed up against the wall, silently stalked her. When she passed them, they eased out of the stairwell, preparing to strike.

Miss Tina placed her key in the lock cylinder, and unlocked the door. Two men pounced on her, bumrushing her apartment door. She was tackled from behind and two gun toting thugs, barged inside. Miss Tina fell on the floor face first. She recovered just in time to see one thug bearing down on her, and the other closing the door.

Miss Tina was a little woozy from the fall. She was so scared to death, she didn't even wince.

"Ah… What y'all want with me, huh?" Miss Tina shrieked. "What's going on? Why are y'all doing this?"

"Bitch you already know what it is! Just shut da fuck up before you fuck aroun' and turn it into a homicide," the gunman said, waving his gun.

Miss Tina watched both gunmen quickly walking through the apartment. One gunman checked inside the bathroom, both bedrooms and the kitchen. The other kept an eye on Miss Tina. Once the coast was clear Justice reached down and snatched Miss Tina off the floor by her hair.

"I don't know what y'all doing…?"

"Bitch, I don't told ya, shut your fuckin' mouth! One more word outta you and I'll personally shoot you," the gunman growled, holding the gun to her head.

"My son ain't—"

Miss Tina was moving slowly, and the gunman smacked her upside her head with his weapon.

"Bitch, I already know ya son ain't here," he said, pushing her down in a chair. "I need to know where he is."

Miss Tina was not able to think clearly and wanted the whole thing to end quickly as possible.

"Bitch, you taking too wid da fuckin answers… That means you lyin'. Where's ya bitch-ass son, lady?"

"I don't know?" Miss Tina answered in a cooperative tone. "Take anything you want. Please, leave me alone."

"Where your son keep da dough and da drugs…?" Justice demanded.

"In his room… There's a Nike box filled with money. Look in the closet. Take it and go, please."

"Stay right there with her if she so much as breathe too hard, clap her!"

"Please don't shoot me! I'll behave."

The gunman snatched Miss Tina up off the floor and threw her roughly into the chair. Miss Tina sat paralyzed by her fear, trying her best not to make eye contact. She feared that the gunmen might try to kill her to protect their identity. The other gunman returned with the shoebox filled with cash.

"Ol' head, you don't look too bad," the gunman smiled, lecherously admiring Miss Tina's body. "You lucky I ain't into takin' pussy like that. That ain't my M.O. But if I was doin' that, you could certainly get it. Ha, ha."

The gunman let out a sinister laugh that sent chills down Miss Tina's spine. She didn't know if he would act on his animalistic impulses. This kind of talk seriously disturbed her.

"Stop lookin' scared, bitch. I don't wanna fuck you," Justice roared. "But you tell that bitch-ass son of yours, he next!"

On the way out the apartment, he bashed her in the head with the butt of his weapon, and stepped over Miss Tina's unconscious body. They used the urine soaked stairway as an escape out the building, disappearing into the dead of a dark project's night.

A woozy Miss Tina awoke an hour later. She was lying on the floor with an intense migraine headache. Struggling to get to her feet, Miss Tina's legs were rubbery, and she collapsed on the sofa. Miss Tina reached for the house phone that sat on a nearby coffee table. Her first instinct was to dial Melquan. She dialed her son's cellphone, but it went straight to his voicemail. Melquan had turned his phone off for the night. Miss Tina tried repeatedly called, but only got his outgoing message.

She was so angry that she hung up without leaving a message. Unable to reach her son, Miss Tina dialed for Mike Copeland.

"Mike…" Miss Tina blurted into the phone. "I need you to get in touch with Melquan. I been robbed!"

"What?" Mike barked. "Where are you…? I'll be right there."

Mike Copeland was the first to arrive at Miss Tina's apartment. He had already alerted Melquan to the situation by calling India's home phone. Melquan was on his way. The door was still slightly ajar when Mike Copeland entered the ransacked place.

"Hey yo, Miss Tina?" Mike called out. His weapon was drawn. "Miss Tina…?"

"Mike, I'm in the living room."

Mike walked into the apartment gun in hand as if he were expecting to be ambushed. Once he saw the faint Miss Tina slumped down in the chair, he put his weapon away and rushed to her aide.

"Miss Tina, you okay? Who did this to you? How it happened?" Mike Copeland bombarded Miss Tina with questions.

"Mike, I don't know," she said. "Where's Melquan? How come he ain't here, yet?"

Mike did all he could to calm Miss Tina. He tried to aid her with the knot she had on the back of her skull. It wasn't enough. Miss Tina demanded to know why her son wasn't there. Why he wasn't the first person to come rushing through the door, and to her aide? Why he wasn't there to protect her from harm?

There were many questions swimming in her still aching head, Miss Tina was in a foul mood by the time Melquan arrived. He entered the apartment and everyone went silent.

"Oh, there you are!" Miss Tina erupted. "It took you long enough. I coulda been dead and you wouldn't have known it if it wasn't for Mike. Thank God for him."

"Ma, wha' happen?" Melquan asked, his voice straining with emotion.

Miss Tina cut him off. "Don't ma me. Do you know anyone who could've done this…?"

"I was about to ask you the same question," he said, getting closer to her. "Did you get a good look at their faces? Whoever did this is fuckin' dead! You hear me?"

"Melquan, see what you caused. This is all your damn fault. Take all your shit, the cars, the money, the clothes, and get out of my house, please!"

"But ma—"

"I wish I never had you! Them niggas came up in my apartment with guns looking for you. And you wasn't even here to protect me. They could've killed me and then what…?"

The question rang and Mike Copeland walked out leaving Melquan alone with his mother. He was surprised by her outburst, but she was still his mother. Miss Tina looked away from him after holding his stare.

"How many of them was it, mom?"

"There must've been like two of them. They came up behind me, outta nowhere. They took all that money… They acted like they wanted to take my life. It's all because of you, Melquan."

"But ma, it's not my fault."

"It's your fault. You the drug dealer not me…!"

"C'mon ma…"

"Take all that shit back, Melquan. I'm through with you. The cars, the money, the clothes… Ain't none of that shit worth dying for. I can't do it, Melquan. I can't live like this no more!"

Miss Tina turned her head away from Melquan. He stared at the back of her head. Melquan saw her wound, and it angered him even more.

"Ma, I'm sorry you feel that way. I wish this happened to me instead o' you. But I can't undo what's been done. I promise you this though, whoever did this is dead!" he said, walking out the apartment.

After a few tense minutes of trying to defuse the situation, Mike Copeland walked downstairs and caught up with Melquan.

"Mike, I don't know who did this shit. But when I find out I'm a body 'em."

"No doubt, my dude," Mike said, reassuring him. "You already know I'm wit you. We gone find out who did this. Don't worry about it, just keep ya composure, my dude."

They went out into the project and conducted their daily drug operation, hoping that would serve as the bait to lure the robbers to them. If that didn't work then at least they could question some talkative drug addict or drug dealer about last night's event.

Melquan was in a murderous mood, but he had no target to unleash his fury on. He kept hoping that it would all change before the day ended. Charlie Rock rolled through the horseshoe, Melquan didn't acknowledge him. He just wasn't interested in a long conversation with anyone. For the moment, all the friendliness they shared was dead.

"Lemme holla at you for a minute, nephew," Charlie Rock requested.

"Not right now, Unk!" Melquan answered. "I ain't in da mood. I got sumthin on my mind and I ain't really myself today."

"Nephew, what I gotta say is more than just idle chitchat. I gotta put a bug in ya ear. But everything ain't for everybody. Walk over here with me," Charlie Rock said, directing his wheelchair down the drive. "I'm sorry to hear about that situation with ya mom. How's Tina doin'?"

"She buggin' out and I don't know if the pain is physical or mental right now. Physically, she'll be alright, but mentally...? I don't know. She blames me for everythin'. She called me everythin', but her son."

"That's not a good look, but at the same time you can't take that too personal. That wasn't your mother speakin' to you and callin' you out your name. That was pain mixed with fear," Charlie Rock said.

"Unk, I'm ready to hurt somebody. I'm fuckin' ready to show these niggas that I ain't playin'. These niggas violated my mother. They gotta leave this earth for that!"

"Yeah, and they deserve everything and anything you dish out. Just make sure you get who's responsible for this. You gotta make the right man bleed. On that note, I think I got sumthin for you. I don't know if you know this nigga from the north side called Justice...?"

"Nah, I ain't never heard of him. Why...?"

"He a little older than you... Anyway one day he come around here talkin' about he heard this spot jumpin' and who gettin' all the money out here. Askin' me fifty questions... And he was with another dude a grimy lookin' muthfucka. You know me, I ain't telling shit. Ask me, I know that shit. Justice is a well-known stickup kid. He might be worth checkin'."

Melquan walked alongside him, staring straight ahead. He listened silently to Charlie Rock. His mind seemed to be in accelerated mode. He stared at Charlie Rock and knew his mind was made up. Justice was his prime suspect.

"You know where they stayin'?"

"No, but like I said the one named Justice is from the North

Side. I don't know where he lay his head. But I know his mother still live over there on Grenada Avenue. You know momma's crib is like magnet. Eventually everyone winds up there."

"You right, Unk. So lemme get her address," Melquan hurriedly said.

Charlie Rock gave him the necessary information and Melquan hit him with a C-note. Melquan signaled to Mike Copeland, and they hurriedly set off together.

"Charlie Rock just turned me on to a strong possibility. Justice, heard o' him?"

"Nah…" Mike Copeland answered, shaking his head.

"He's some ol' school stickup kid. I'm a put a bullet in that muthafucka's head. Let's go squat on his mom's crib!"

"Yeah, that's what da fuck I'm talkin' 'bout! Let's go light this shit up!"

# The One I Trusted
Chapter Twenty-Four

They were about to recon the project's ground and someone shouted at Melquan. He whirled ready to blast, but when he saw that it was Precious, Melquan put his gun away.

"What da fuck you want, bitch?" he asked, giving the dirtiest of looks.

"I heard about what happened to your mother last night. I wanted to know if she's alright, and say I'm sorry…"

"Whatever, bitch, you not on my team no more, right? So why you comin' 'round me for…?"

"I just wanted to let you know, I'm sorry to hear… I mean,

damn. I still got feelin' fa you. I still care what happens."

"Bitch, I don't have time to hear all da bullshit. If I find out you remotely connected to da situation, I'm a kill you too."

"Damn Melquan, why would I be even trying to get your mother hurt like that, huh? Tell me why, Melquan," Precious said, on the verge of tears.

Precious' pleas fell on deaf ears. Melquan ignored her. He walked away like he had not hear anything she had said.

It took around a week before Justice finally resurfaced. Unfortunately for him his visit did not go undetected. Melquan and Mike Copeland held an around the clock vigil on Justice's mother apartment building. When they weren't around they paid drug addicts and kids to be their eyes and ears.

It was popular knowledge by now about what had happened. The underworld of the project was more than happy to help Melquan. Something about hurting someone's mother spawned an outpouring of sympathy on Melquan's behalf. Melquan got the call that Justice was in the vicinity. He and Mike raced over to the building to watch and wait.

Inside his mother's apartment, Justice was enjoying some leftovers before he hit the streets. He had come to his mother's place to make sure she was taking her medication. She begged him to stay and offered him some food.

"Ma, ya food was good as usual. I hate to eat and run, but I gotta go do sumthin," Justice said, rubbing his filled stomach. "Ma, make sure you watch what you eat. You know you got high blood pressure. Stay away from all that pork."

"Oh boy, that pork ain't never hurt nobody," his mother countered. "Our people have survived for hundreds of years on pork.

So if I want to have me some chitlins, or some pig feet, every now and then, I'm havin' it. Shoot, ain't nobody gone tell me what to eat now. It's too late already."

"Here you go wid this again," Justice said. "All I said was watch what you eat. Ma, you real stubborn, you always hollerin' about goin' ta meet ya maker. I guess you wanna meet him wid a pork chop sandwich in ya hand. I guess the doctor don't know what he talkin''bout when he told you to lay off that pork, huh?"

"I'm havin' me some pork whenever the mood hit me," the old woman said.

"Okay ma, I done said all I had to say."

He got up from the table and headed to the door. Outside Justice's ride was getting impatient. The man began incessantly honking the car's horn.

Melquan and Mike Copeland didn't see the car before. The loud sound of the horn, clued them. They were able to put two and to the together. Discreetly, Melquan slipped out the car and took up a strategic position under the stairs in the building's lobby. He left the driver for Mike Copeland to handle.

"A'ight ma, goodnight... I gotta go. I'll call ya later," Justice said.

"Take care boy, and stay off da streets and outta trouble," she said, kissing Justice on the cheek.

"I will ma. I love you, bye."

The sound of footsteps descending down the stairs echoed throughout the hallway. The heavy thuds snapped Melquan out of his murderous trance. He removed the gun from his waistline, hid beneath the steps and readied himself for his date with destiny.

Going down the stairs was an afterthought for Justice. His mind was thinking about finding Melquan and finishing what he had started. He couldn't wait to run down on him, and hit him for his whole stash. He was about to do a sweep of the projects to see if they could spot Melquan. The home invasion on Melquan's mother's apartment was a nice come-up, but Justice wanted more. He hit the last step and suddenly he heard his name.

"Justice…"

Instantly he realized that there was no friendliness in the voice. Justice thought about reaching for his gun, but remembered he left it in the car. He spun around slowly, hoping it was all just a figment of his imagination. He soon realized it wasn't. Melquan stood face to face with the man who violated his mother's home. He clenched his teeth and tightened his grip on his gun.

"Yo, I heard you was lookin' me?" Melquan snarled. "Well you just found me, muthafucka!"

Justice made a weak attempt to turn and run. Melquan's quick reflexes wouldn't have it. His muscle fiber twitched so fast, that three shots rang out before Justice could successfully take a step toward the door.

Boom, boom, boom, three loud gun blasts shattered the tranquility of the neighborhood. The shots caught Justice's accomplice completely off guard. He opened his car door and attempted to rush toward the sound of the gunfire. Before he could aid Justice, Mike Copeland cut him down in a hail of bullets.

Melquan stood over Justice's crumpled body and pumped three more slugs into his head and chest. He spit on Justice's corpse on the way out the building. They fled the crime scene, vanishing into the project's maze.

The killings brought no cries of justice from anyone except Justice's mother. Good riddance was the only sentiment of the community. Since he was an adolescent, Justice had been a menace in the projects. By all accounts he had reaped what he sowned.

The murders had clearly taken toll on Melquan.  He wasn't accustomed to taking a man's life so easily.  Violence was one thing, murder was something totally different.  The act weighed heavily on his mind.  Melquan needed a break from the game, and he took one.

# Mo Money Mo...

Chapter Twenty-Five

"What's the matter with you, Melquan?" India inquired. "For the last few weeks you haven't been yourself."

Melquan took a deep breath and sighed. "Nothing is the matter with me. I just wish you'd stop askin' me that question. It's really gettin' to be annoyin.'"

"Well, how else I'm going to find out what's wrong with you, if I don't ask" India said. "I don't care what you say either something's the matter with you. You've been in a funk lately and you're quiet, and moody. Are you having problems sleeping? If I didn't know better, I'd swear you were getting high."

"Wow…" Melquan managed to say.

There was no way in the world that he was going to come clean and admit to India that he had killed a man. Even if it was desperate, India would never understand the code of the streets. Melquan felt that all the explaining in the world wouldn't help her comprehend the strange codes of ethics that belonged on the streets. Melquan chose to hide behind the estranged relationship with his mother.

"Is the way you're acting got something to do with the fallout you had with your mother?"

"Yeah…" Melquan lied.

"Maybe you should call her. Do you want me to—"

"Nah, she won't even take my calls. She'll just…" his voice trailed.

"Why don't you just go over there and see her?"

"You don't really know my mother. She doesn't wanna be bothered. Best thing I can do is leave her alone and give her some space."

"I can't imagine my mother not speaking to me," India injected.

"This isn't ya Cosby-like family household. Everybody deals with problems differently," he proclaimed.

Melquan walked away and went to the bedroom, leaving India in the living room with more questions than answers. India shook her head and mentally replayed the exchange. Her instincts told her there was more to the story than Melquan was telling. She just didn't know.

Melquan took a break from the streets, hiding out in Co-op City with his girlfriend. Mike Copeland conducted business as usual. He ran every aspect of the drug game. Mike Copeland liked the idea of being the man and was really enjoying it for the first time.

There were great responsibilities that came with being the man. Mike was now in charge of all aspects of the drug operation, paying the workers, counting the profit, purchasing the product, and bagging it up. He took it upon himself to perform all these tasks with no help. It was a lot of work for one man, but Mike Copeland loved it. This was his chance to prove that he had the business savvy to run the entire show.

Mike Copeland entered Tess' apartment, thinking to himself that he had seen functioning crack houses that were cleaner than hers. Although he had manufactured crack in this apartment plenty of times it never ceased to amaze him how nasty the place always was. He walked to the kitchen cabinet, and removed his crack cooking utensils, Pyrex pot, baking soda, plate and razors.

Tess mut have smelled him and magically appeared from her bedroom. She stood quietly at the enterance to the kitchen.

"Hey yo, don't start beastin' and shit," Mike warned her. "I don't need you on my muthafuckin' back, sweatin' me fa no blast, especially when da shit ain't nowhere near ready yet. Bye!"

"Whatever," Tess replied, rolling her eyes and walking back to her bedroom.

Mike started the tedious process of transforming the powder cocaine to the hardwhite the street was buzzing about.

The water was boiling and he opened several packs of glassine bags in preparation for the finished product. Mike had a lot of weight to cook up. There was no way in the world he was going to be stuck up in a crack house all day. He planned on preparing a half of the food now, satisfy the demand on the street and prepare the rest of the product later.

Mike busied himself with all aspects of the manufacturing of the crack and time was rapidly flying by. About an hour in, Tess reappeared at the kitchen door. Mike slowly picked up his head from his work, and stared evilly at her.

"You… You…" Tess stuttered. "You think I could get that blast now, Mike?"

"Bitch you get on my last muthafuckin' nerves. You always beastin'… Da shit ain't goin' nowhere," Mike spat, turning away from her.

He kept walking disregarding Tess's presence. Suddenly Mike reached down on the plate and tossed a fat piece chunk of the hardwhite on the floor. Tess' eyes lit up immediately, and she jumped on the floor, scrambling to locate it.

Mike laughed out loud when Tess began crawling on her hands and knees to get the piece of rock. Her ashy fist clutched the hardwhite, admiring like it was diamond for a second. Climbing to her feet, Tess scurried off to her room. All she needed now was a torch and she'd be zooming to space. Raucous laughter from Mike Copeland's belly filled the apartment.

"Crazy Bitch…! Bitch you done lost ya goddamn mind."

Tess was too heavily addicted to care that she had been humiliated by Mike. She got what she wanted and Mike Copeland enjoyed a hearty laugh at her expense.

The slamming of the bathroom door signaled Tess' whereabouts. This small enclosure somehow eased her extreme bouts of paranoia. Tess opened up her medicine cabinet and removed her glass stem. The dark soot of the pipe was a telltale sign of high volume of usage. Tess broke a large chunk of the hardwhite off the beige boulder, placed it in the end of her crack pipe, and laid the rest of it on the sink.

She jammed the stem between her trembling, overanxious, charcoal black lips. Tess simultaneously flicked the lighter with her shaking fingers. Tess inhaled the drug deeply, filling her lungs with a monster blast. The quick euphoric high, raced to her brain, quickly spreading through her bloodstream. Tess exhaled a large cloud of white smoke.

Her heart thumped so fast, it threatened to jump out of her heaving chest. Tess repeated the process again and again, but still couldn't satisfy her unquenchable craving.

In the kitchen, an assembly line of three packaging crack at Tess' kitchen table was now reduced to a one-man team. Mike Copeland hurriedly found out there was no glory in bagging up this much crack by himself. Going through the motions, Mike's mind quickly turned to other things.

Meanwhile in a span of less than an hour, Tess high had come and gone in the blink of an eye. She touched down and all she was left with was an ever present need for more. It haunted way deep in her brain, Tess was now faced with a major dilemma. She knew Mike wasn't going to be sympathetic to her crack addiction.

"Damn," Mike cursed under his breath. "I gotta piss bad like a muthafucka."

Shaking his head, Mike jumped up from the table, and went to the bathroom to relieve himself. He sucked his teeth when he saw that the door was locked. He knocked hard. The sudden pounding on the door frightened Tess. She was on all fours, searching for pieces of crack that she thought fell.

"Bitch, come up outta there!" Mike shouted. "I gotta use da fuckin' bathroom."

"Wait a minute." She hastily replied. "Just gimme a second..."

"Bitch, if you don't come up outta there right now, I'm gonna kick this fuckin' door down for real. C'mon, I gotta piss, man!"

Tess opened the bathroom door and the stench of burnt plastic assaulted his nose immediately. The tiny place was filled with crack residue.

"Goddamn bitch!" Mike shouted. "What you tryin' ta kill me up in here?"

Tess hurriedly brushed pass Mike with her head held low. Too paranoid and high, she was not looking him in the eye. This fact not lost on Mike Copeland.

"What da fuck wrong wit you?" he chuckled. "What's wrong? Can't say nothin', bitch? That hardwhite got you twisted, huh?"

Mike stepped inside the bathroom, and whipped out his penis. He was about to drain his bladder, but felt a sharp pain in his anus. He not only needed to piss, it was also necessary for him to take a shit. Mike instinctively grabbed his gun out his waistband and placed it on the sink. Turning around, he pulled down his pants and squatted on the toilet. He shut the door.

Tess was watching Mike from her bedroom door. Once she heard the bathroom door slam, Tess sprang into action. Creeping down the hall with cat-like quietness, she headed straight for the kitchen. When she came to the enterance Tess took one look at the table and her eyes became bright as headlights. Mounds of crack, more than she had ever seen in her life, just sitting there on her kitchen table, Tess took a helping.

In her mind, the amount she took was too small to be missed from this huge mound. It was her kitchen table. People shouldn't leave things on her table. It will eventually belong to her. Cautiously she made her way back down the hallway to her room seemingly undetected. .

Mike Copeland had finished taking his dump. Relieved, he cleaned up, washing his hands in the dirty sink. Placeing the gun back in his waistband, Mike exited the tiny bathroom.

The moment he walked back into the kitchen, he could tell that something was wrong. Although Tess had tried her best to straighten up after the theft, Mike knew the order he had situated the product.

"Fuckin' Tess!" Mike swore.

He did an about face, and ran straight to Tess' room. Running at full speed, Mike rammed the door with his shoulder, and it flew open.

"Bitch, where is it?"

"Wha-what…" Tess stuttered. "What you talkin' bout?"

"Bitch…!" Mike roared. "Do not play stupid. Ya know what da fuck I'm talkin''bout. Da muthafuckin' crack you stole. It was about an ounce of my drug, bitch. Don't dis bizness!"

Mike slowly strode over to where Tess stood across the room. Inching closer and closer toward her, his voice dripped venom. Anticipating violence, Tess began backpedaling.

"Bitch, I know how I left my shit. I can tell that ya took sumthin ya fuckin' crackhead. Now I'm givin' you one mufuckin' chance to give it back, I'm not askin' you no more," Mike barked.

"Mike, I really don't know what you talkin' bout," Tess said, backing into a corner of the room. "I been right here in this room the whole time you were in the bathroom. I swear, Mike. God knows… for real, for real."

Those were the last words that escaped her mouth. Mike Copeland struck quickly, slapping Tess repeatedly across her face, whipping her head from side to side like she was in an automobile accident.

"You better gimme my shit, bitch! I'm gonna kill you up in dis piece," he angrily shouted.

Returning the piece of hardwhite never crossed Tess' crack ravaged mind. She figured Mike would soon get tired of asking, and this entire ordeal would be over. All she had to do was convince him not to beat her to death. Then she could smoke the rock.

Soon the sting from the slaps turned into pain from punches. From every possible angle Mike rained down punches on Tess face and frail body. Tess tried to defend herself. Her wild swings caught Mike by surprise. He backed up off her and Tess charged him. Mike wasn't a big guy, and she was able to knock him off balance.

This infuriated Mike. After staggering, he went down on his ass. Mike quickly jumped back on his feet. He swiftly drew his gun. It was already too late by the time Tess saw the weapon. Mike fired quickly. The gunshot hit Tess in the chest. She collapsed flat on her back to the floor and died instantly.

In a mad rush, his rage subsided. Mike froze, surveying the damage. He grabbed his head, in disbelief. Blood oozed from her lifeless body. Mike continued to stare dumbfounded by the fact that he had just killed Tess.

"Damn! Look what you done made me do, bitch."

The sound of the door opening brought him back to not only reality, but severity of his situation. It got worse when he heard the voice.

"Mom…!" Sheron called out, feeling pain.

Mike Copeland was spooked and ran out the room. Guilt filled his eyes when he bumped into Sheron in the hallway. He made brief eye contact with the kid, before his street sense kicked in. Gathering up all the crack, Mike fled out the door.

Puzzled, Sheron watched Mike running out the apartment before he continued the search for his mother. Although her bedroom door was wide open, Sheron's attention was immediately drawn to the bathroom.

"Mom…" he said, pushing the door open.

He was surprised to find the bathroom empty. She was always in here when at this time when I'm home, Sheron was befuddled. Considering how much time his mother spent in there getting high it was strange that she wasn't in there. Sheron turned his attention to her bedroom. Half expecting to find his mother not in there, maybe she was high and fell asleep. Sheron's young eyes weren't prepared for what he saw.

"Mom..?" Sheron cried in agony over his dead mother. "Mom…"

# Dead Right

Chapter Twenty Six

A frantic 911 call came into the police dispatcher. Squad cars from the 47th precinct and the housing police responded with the quickness to the call. Mike Copeland was the prime suspect and he was considered armed and dangerous.

Cops swarmed the projects on foot. There was a police helicopter hovering overhead. The building Mike Copeland resided was where the police concentrated their main effort. They stood outside in assembly then they rushed upstairs with weapons drawn.

A battering ram smashed through the apartment door of Mike's grandmother. Seconds later, dozens of New York City's finest entered the apartment with their guns at the ready. The sight of the officers nearly caused the elderly woman a heart attack. Knowing his grandmother had a pre existing heart condition, Mike surrendered. The police threw theshackles on Mike in a hot second. He was taken downstairs to where a fleet of squad cars were parked. Scared and watchful eyes recorded the moment when the cops took Mike Copeland out of the projects.

"You have the right to remain silent… Anything you say or do can be used against you in a court of law…" the arresting officer said, serving notice on Mike Copeland.

"Save that bullshit! I ain't tryin' a hear that! I'm innocent!"

"Hey Tommy, I think we caught a real tough guy…" one of the cops said.

"Funny, but he don't look that tough to me," Tommy said, smiling.

They led Mike Copeland to a parked car. Before they shoved him inside, one of the arresting officers leaned over to Mike.

"Hey Mike, take one last look at these projects. By the time you get out… Provided that you do get out, the projects will be all condos…"

Laughter erupted and they shoved Mike Copeland into the backseat of a squad car. They packed up equipment and although a few remained, most of the officers instantly exited the projects.

All the commotion from the heavy police presence had many residents watching closely. They gathered by the dozens. Nashawn was amongst them. Puffing on a cigarette, he was grinning from ear to ear.

"Ha! Ha! Mike Copeland got arrested. Good for that nigga! Y'all know what that means… This whole fuckin' projects belongs to me!" Nashawn loudly proclaimed.

It was fifteen minutes later when Melquan entered the projects. He had purposely taken his time after being notified of Mike's arrest by one of the workers. There was nothing he could do for Mike at the moment. People were still up talking about the raid by the cop's on Mike's grandmother's apartment. The police showing up in great numbers would be the talk of the projects for some time.

"It was like they brought da whole four-seven. Yo Melquan, cops were up in here like roaches. I don't know how or why Mike ended up in his grandma's crib. Why that nigga just ain't bounce up outta Dodge is beyond me," a worker reported.

"Did he say anything when they bought him out…?" Melquan asked.

"You know Mike? He was spazin' on da cops. He went out like a soldier," another said.

Melquan heard the taunting behind him when he turned to walk away. There was no need to panic he had the strap on him. Melquan listened to Nashawn shouting over his shoulder without looking back.

"It's over, nigga! Ya finished muthafucka! It's my turn to rock now!" Nashawn shouted above the buzzing crowd. "I'm gon' make my run, hope ya lil' niggas had ya fun!"

Very nonchalantly Melquan pulled one of his workers to the side and whispered in his ear.

"Go git that," he ordered.

## My Love Is Strong
Chapter Twenty-Seven

Catholic school had just let out. Jose Jr. and Maria were walking home. Jose Jr. was ready to cut across the horseshoe driveway, but Maria stopped. She remembered the admonishment her father had given her brother and refused to go any further.

"Jose, what are you about to do?" she asked with concern.

Her brother turned around and stared at her. Shaking his head, Jose walked back to where his sister stood.

"Maria—"

"Jose, you made a promise that you wasn't going to hang out in the horseshoe anymore. You said if I didn't tell daddy, and I held up my side of the bargain. If you—"

"You don't have to remind me, Maria. I didn't come here to hang out. I came to see somebody, okay?"

"Who Jose? You ain't got no business with none of these boys. We're not even supposed to be here, Jose."

"I know, I know, but I just got to ask him something real fast then we can go. I promise you. Now c'mon already…"

"Okay Jose, you remember your promise though. And I'm watching you. Hurry up!"

Jose Jr. and Maria entered the horseshoe drive. He ran off and left his sister standing on the curb. He was searching for his connect, and asked Rodney, AKA Young Feddi, the rapper.

"A yo, Young Feddi, where Mike Copeland at…?"

"What up, Jose…? Oh, ya ain't heard?"

"Nah, I didn't. What happened?"

"Mike Copeland killed some crack head bitch. Mad Po-Po came and arrested him. That shit happened earlier today."

"Damn! I don't believe that shit. That nigga owed me money for working," Jose said.

"I don't know how ya gonna get paid, Jose. I already told you what happened. So you might as well take that as a loss…"

"Who out here you know can pay me, son?"

"I seen da nigga, Melquan. He was out here a few minutes ago. I think he went into one a da building. See him maybe he might hit you off, son."

"That nigga don't even know me," Jose said, sounding frustrated.

"True that. But it don't hurt to ask."

Not far away in the horseshoe, a crack addict was out chasing a high. He was walking toward the other side when a street dealer stooped him.

"What you doin' servin' my customer?" Sylk Smooth shouted.

"Nigga, I don't give a fuck. I was here first. And I'm gonna serve him," Rodney said.

The crack addict made the transaction, and quickly left the area. The verbal confrontation between the two dealers continued. Nashawn saw the commotion, and walked over to check it out.

"What da fuck is y'all arguin' 'bout?" he asked.

"This nigga just cut my throat on a sale. He knows that was our custie he just served," Sylk Smooth argued.

"Didn't I tell y'all niggas to stay on y'all side of the fuckin' drive, huh?" Nashawn angrily asked. "Fa real fa real, y'all niggas shouldn't even be out here."

Nashawn and Sylk Smooth jumped Rodney, and a fight ensued. Together, Nashawn and Sylk Smooth, were too much, and easily beat down Rodney.

"Them niggas over there wildin'," Jose said excited by the action. "Da nigga, Nashawn is gonna kill that boy, son!"

Someone ran in the building and informed Melquan of the skirmish that had developed. He quickly rushed out the door with gun in his hand. Maria saw the dustup and immediately wanted to leave the area.

"Jose, Jose, c'mon let's get out of here. Let's go, Jose," Maria shouted.

"Yeah okay, Maria, I'm coming. I'm coming!" Jose shouted back.

In a flash shots rang out, Melquan came running across the drive. The guns started blazing when Nashawn pulled out his gun, returning the fire. A reckless shootout ensued and Jose was smack dab in the middle of it. He hit the ground to avoid being shot.

"Jose, Jose c'mon…" Maria shouted.

She was screaming for him to get out when she saw her brother risking his life. Unfortunately for Maria she had no street instincts to rely on. She stood erect as bullets wizzed by her.

"Maria get down, get down," Jose shouted from his position on the ground.

It all happened so fast. Everything seemed to be a blur in slow motion. Bullets from an automatic weapon ripped into her body. With a thud, Maria fell immediately. Jose ran over to where she hit the ground.

"Maria… No-oh-oh-oh…" Jose screamed.

Bullets continued to fly in every direction and Jose got up off the ground. He ran to his sister, despite the imminent danger he had just placed himself in. Once Jose reached Maria, he dropped to his knees and tried to console her.

Jose looked around him and saw bullets flying everywhere. People were running in pandemonium. His sister was bleeding and not moving. Her face was contorted and her eyes were shut tight. Jose could tell his sister was in a lot of pain. Blood leaked profusely from her body.

"Jose, it burns. I can't keep my eyes open," Maria said, struggling to speak. Then her body went limp.

"Maria…" Jose cried. "Don't close your eyes!"

The gun battle continued despite the casualty. Both combatants were still shooting, and manuerving deadly closer to each other. Miraculously neither man was hit. Finally ceasefire, they both ran out of bullets.

They both fled the scene in opposite directions. Melquan ran by Jose and saw him cradling his bleeding sister. He wasn't sure what the boy was doing but he didn't stick around to find out. Racing to his vehicle, Melquan jumped in, and peeled off.

"Somebody help me! Please call an ambulance…! Oh my God! My sister been shot! " Jose screamed.

Melquan swerved recklessly through the city streets. Later he pulled into a dark corner of the valley. He turned off the lights and exited the vehicle. All of sudden, the urge to urinate swept through him and he did it right there. He felt like crying and bit his lips hard until he tasted blood. Pangs of nervous thoughts caused his stomach to tighten. He tried to make sense of what had gone down.

Jumping back in the Range, he drove and his mind wouldn't stop spinning. He envisioned the discharge of ammunition, bullet after bullets leaving his gun. He never saw the shot that hit the little girl. He only hoped he wasn't responsible. It could have been Nashawn's weapon that did the damage. Melquan remained unsure. Replaying the deadly exchange in his head, Melquan continued to drive aimlessly.

He sat outside on the bumper of his vehicle and dialed India's number. Melquan listened as the phone rang. India calmly answered the phone with tranquility that Melquan now wished he possessed.

"I need to see you and…"

"I'm home so you may come by, Melquan."

"Nah, I can't."

"What?" India exclaimed. "Melquan you ain't makin' no sense."

"Meet somewhere…"

"Why…?"

"Not now, India," he found himself whispering. "Just do as I say and I'll explain everything when you get here."

"Okay Melquan, I'll meet with you, but this better be real good."

"Meet me on…"

Melquan ended the call immediately. He went to stake out the rendezvous before India made it there. Driving slowly, Melquan began thinking about all the wrong moves he had made in the game. The realization dawned on him that some of his decisions were unavoidable. In the streets the rule was simple, kill or be killed.

When India arrived at the designated spot in New Roc City's

parking garage, Melquan was waiting in paranoia. He watched every car that passed with great interest including hers. India climbed out of her car and entered his.

"Melquan, what the hell is going on? Why we had to meet all the way up here? What's wrong why you look like that?"

Melquan heard the questions coming like bullets at him. He couldn't get out the answers fast enough to satisfy India's curiosity.

"India, I think I just accidently killed somebody," he suddenly blurted.

"What? Melquan what do you mean, you accidently killed somebody?" she asked with deep curiosity.

"I got into a shootout. It was with this other kid name Nashawn. A lil' girl got in the way and was shot. I'm not sure, but I think she's dead," he said, his voice starining with emotion.

He could feel her eyes staring at him. Melquan looked away. Everything he believed in was summed up in India's eyes. They used to be beautiful now they seemed afraid. He felt like he had let her down and turned into some kind of a monster. Nothing made sense anymore.

"Melquan, you're scaring me. Do you realize what you just said? You killed somebody? Melquan, I got my son to think about. What if some of your enemies come to my door looking for retaliation? And now you're here playing some type of cloak and dagger game with not only my life, but my son's as well."

"But India it wasn't my fault. I don't even know for sure if it was me who killed her."

"Melquan I don't know how you're going to take this but you've got to go. I can't have you endangering me or my son's life. Melquan it's over. Melquan you've got to turn yourself in and get yourself a good lawyer."

"So it's like that? It's over just that easy, huh? You ain't even gonna support me on this one. Stand by my side while I fight da case…?"

"I'm sorry, Melquan. I can't do that."

Melquan stared at the woman he loved in disbelief. Their eyes locked for what seemed like an eternity. When they broke off stares, he knew what he had to do.

"Git da fuck outta my car, bitch!" Melquan spat. "I knew I shouldn't a told you shit. I thought you'd understand, India. But I knew better."

India glanced at him in disgust. Her lips was twisted and trembled with the emotion coursing through her frame.

"Melquan, I knew you were going to take this like that. But put yourself in my shoes… I've got responsibilities. I can't have the police coming to my place. First you were a drug dealer, now you're a murderer, who doesn't know if he killed an innocent girl or not. I love you but, I didn't sign up for any of this, Melquan."

India got out of Melquan's car and slammed the door. She didn't bother to look back, out of fear that she might change her mind. It was definitely over. Their relationship had run its course.

# Get Up... Stand up
Chapter Twenty-Eight

In the aftermath of the shooting, Melquan played everyone like they were the enemy. New York City was a big place, and it seemed like he used every inch of it to stay a step ahead of the police. Living out of different fleabag motels, every night Melquan was hiding out in a different borough.

His first order of business was to trade in the Ranger Rover for a black Honda Accord. Melquan completely stopped visiting Edenwald projects. Even though he had severed several ties, the thought of an innocent little girl dying didn't sit well with him.

It ate at his conscious and kept him up nights. One day after another sleepless night, Melquan decided to give a call to the only person he knew for sure was still in his corner, Charlie Rock. Secretly they set up a meeting place in a desolate area near Sousa Woods.

When Charlie Rock rolled into the park, Melquan let him wait before he somberly appeared. He had to make sure Charlie Rock wasn't being followed.

"You lookin' stressed out nephew. You look like a beaten man," Charlie Rock said. "You can't keep sweatin' da details."

"I feel like I'm beaten, Unk. To tell you the truth, I don't know if it was me that killed the little girl. But Unk, I really feel fucked over it. I feel so terrible, I can't even sleep, Unk. I wanna call her people. You know…? Apologize. Think they'll accept it, Unk?"

"Anything can be forgiven, nephew. But not that… There's nothing you can do to bring that little girl back. Her father wants blood, nephew. He wants both parties responsible for his daughter's death, dead!" Charlie Rock solemnly stated.

Melquan's attention was drawn in by the seriousness of Charlie Rock's voice. He immediately stared at the man in the wheelchair. It dawned on him that he had no wins, the world was against him. Charlie Rock's words of wisdom became priceless and Melquan listened.

"Yo nephew, there's so much gunplay in the game now. Your generation has taken shit to the extreme. This game was never intended to be that way. Ain't none of this shit worth dyin' or killin' for. You do what you got to do to survive. You get in and get out. That's how it used to be."

Melquan continued listening to Charlie Rock. It was clear that he was feeling the weight of the wise man's lessons. A silence fell between the two men.

"Have you found out anything about Nashawn?" Melquan asked.

"He still runnin' and duckin' like you. But I gotta number for him from one of them lil' broads he fuck with."

"Did you bring it?" Melquan asked with hope.

"Yessir, got it right here fa ya, my nephew," Charlie Rock said, reaching into his pocket and retrieving a small piece of paper. "The first number up there is Nashawn's. And you already know who the other one belongs to…" Charlie Rock continued, handing the piece of paper to Melquan.

Melquan stared at the numbers, and his burden already felt like they were being lifted. He glanced at Charlie Rock with hope in his eyes and said, "Tell me Unk, you think I got a good shot at makin' this work?"

Charlie Rock paused for a couple beats before giving an answer. Melquan was anxiously awaiting his answer.

"I'm a keep it real with ya nephew. I don't know, but it's worth a shot. Any position is better than the one you're in."

"A'ight," Melquan sighed. "It is what it is. Good lookin', Unk."

"No problem my nephew, you been always good to me and treated me with much respect. Watch yourself, nephew. Stay low," Charlie Rock said.

They embraced, and Melquan dropped a few hundred dollar bills on the older man.

"One," Melquan said, walking away.

Nothing can ignite a neighborhood's sense of community than the lost of innocent lives. Over the past few months, the body count had been steadily rising in the northeast Bronx. It took the reckless killing of a thirteen year girl named Maria, to galvanize not only the residents, but community activists and politicians. They came from all angles, those with genuine interest in helping the neighborhood, and those pushing their own agenda.

In a noisy session outside and inside, they met with the precinct commander, clamoring for help in the Edenwald community center.

"Captain, you mean to tell me that your police precinct is right across the street from the projects. Yet you and your men cannot provide adequate protection for our community?" an activist asked.

"Well I…" the captain started say but the activist interrupted.

"Is it because it's a poor community? I mean, a thirteen year old girl, on her way home from school was gunned down a few days ago. Yet there no arrests have been made. What is going on with our police protection? This wouldn't happen in any other neighborhood but a minority one. Everyday there is more and more killings and nothing is being done by our friendly neighborhood cops."

"We're working hard to protect and serve…" the captain started to say, and again he was rudely interrupted by another activist.

"There have been just too many killings in Edenwald projects lately. And nothing seems to be getting done. Captain, I'm here to say that the community will no longer tolerate the Keystone Cops attitude of your men. We demand action now!"

There was round of applause greeting the activist. Residents endorsing the sentiments shouted encouragements to the speaker. The captain stood with a cynical look on his face. He did not speak until after the applause had died down.

"Sir, I'll have you know that I have detectives at this very moment combing the housing projects for potential witnesses. We must get cooperation from the citizens of the community who have information regarding any of the shootings. But it is a difficult process because of how your community feels about informants. I know like you know that someone saw something. We're hoping and waiting for a concerned citizen to stand up, and be willing to testify in a court of law."

A chorus of boos enveloped the room. Their displeasure was directed at the reference to the informant's role in a court of law. The police captain continued.

"We have one individual in custody and have interest in certain individuals. Due to the nature of the ongoing investigation, I cannot, at this time, disclose anything about the investigation. But trust me we're doing the best under the current circumstances."

"The problem is we can't trust the police, captain. You don't have such a great record working with the community," the activist shouted.

"Well there's a problem in that area I'll agree," the captain said.

"But Edenwald has been largely ignored by all. The community has been not only been overlooked but also under policed by the powers that be for decades. It's time we take matters in our hands" the activist said.

"It's time we take matters in our own hands!" a resident yelled.

The meeting ended in an uproar, but the politicians and activists were able to gather the hundred or so residents together. They led them in a protest demonstration, marching through the streets, chanting, "Down with dope… Up with hope! Drug dealer, drug dealer you can't hide. You just committing… Genocide…"

They marched through the projects and it culminated across the street from the 47th Precinct.

There they burned candles for shooting victims. Some carried photos of Maria, and others held up signs of protest.

"Up with hope down with dope…" the crowd sang.

# World's Getting Darker

Chapter Twenty-Nine

For days after his daughter's funeral Jose Torres Sr. wept inside his apartment. Under a great amount of duress, he had bouts of depression, and was forced to take a leave of absence from his job. He fought the urge to lay the blame of her death on his son. Even though he knew Jose Jr had been at fault. Sitting alone in his room, his cell phone rang. Jose answered the call without checking the number.

"Hello…?"

"Yes, hello may I speak to Jose…?"

"This Jose speaking… Who is this?"

There was a long pause and Jose glanced at his cellphone to see if he had lost transmission.

"Hello, hello I don't have all day… Who's this?"

"Look you don't know me right? My name is Melquan. I'm one of the guys possibly responsible for possibly causing your daughter's death."

Jose Torres glanced at the cellphone grimacing. He put the tray down and walked away from the other mourners. His blood was boiling when he went back on the call.

"You got some fuckin' cojones calling my fucking cellphone muthafucka. How'd you's get my number fuckin scumbag! You know my daughter was alive and smilin' the other day, muthafucka?"

"Look Jose, I'm apologizing that's why I called. If I could take that day back I would. I'd gladly trade places with your daughter. I didn't mean to cause her harm…"

"You listen up muthafucka, I don't give a fuck whether you meant it or not. My daughter is dead. And gone with her is all my hopes and dreams for her. I'll never get to see her graduate from high school. I'll never be able give her away in marriage. And all because of two stupid ass niggas with bad aim…?"

"Like I said man, I'm apologizing for all that…"

"Apologizing…? You muthafuckin' nigga don't even bother wastin' your breath… Let God forgive you cause I never will muthafucka! The day I see you, I'll try my best to bury your ass! You piece of shit," Jose spat, ending the call.

Angered Jose acted on a thought that ran through his mind earlier. He picked up his phone and began dialing, every thug he knew. He wasn't going to take this sitting down, not at all.

Melquan wore dark shades and a baseball cap inside the

criminal court building on 161st. He had his reservations about meeting Nashawn in this setting, after all he was a wanted man, but what choice did he have. After riding the escalator to the main floor he got off and immediately spotted Nashawn.

"I came here to talk. Not to argue or anything like that," Melquan said. "We both don't need to draw attention to ourselves."

"So speak, nigga."

Melquan began, "Look, this ain't about us, Nashawn. A lil' girl was shot by one of us that day—"

"Word…?" Nashawn sarcastically replied.

"Word up, we got bigger fish to fry instead of gettin' at each other. We gotta get our story straight before da cops snatch us up," Melquan said.

"I don't know what you talkin' bout. I ain't do shit," Nashawn smiled.

"Nashawn, right now I see you buggin' da fuck out. This ain't da time to catch amnesia, nigga. We gotta come together on this one or we both are done, finished, over…"

"My nigga, listen up. That day ya ass shootin' all reckless at me, ya shot da lil' girl, and miss me. Po-po wants ya ass not mine! Ya da shooter now, nigga! Not me. Don't get it twisted. Da way I see this, you in lots of trouble, Melquan!"

"So what you sayin', you gonna snitch on me?"

"Nah, nigga it's called co-operatin'," Nashawn sardonically smiled.

"You might as well turn yourself in then…"

"For what, nigga? I ain't a done a damn thing! I'll see po-po when I see them. Not before…"

"You fuckin' rat bastard!" Melquan hissed, walking away. He opened the door and shouted. "You da fuckin' police, I should a kill ya snitchin' ass when I had the fuckin' chance! Next time I see you, I will kill ya! They'll find ya ass when they smell ya!"

That night, six men sipped liquor, and spoke in hushed tones, gathered in the far bedroom of Jose apartment.

"I think that I can speak for all the fathers here in saying that Jose we support you one hundred percent in any way we can," one of the man said. "Your daughter could easily have been mine. Or his, his or his…"

"I'm ready to do this shit!" another said, chugging his whiskey. He took another swallow and continued. "These young boys are fucking out of control! Okay? We spread word out there for everybody to shut down shop today outta respect for Maria. And what, they still out there, slinging that shit as usual!"

"Don't worry. We gonna take care of those lil' niggas right now!" another said, producing a big gun. "Their ass is grass… Tonight shit's gonna hit the fan! We gonna mow the lawn and send 'em a message!"

"Thanks, to you's gentlemen for coming through. Tonight we're going to shoot first and ask questions last," Jose said, raising his liquor glass. "I got no time to figure out who did what, whoever is out there in the horseshoe drive, that's who's gonna get burned up. Are you's ready? We gonna make that damn horseshoe really hot tonight."

It was getting dark in the horseshoe when the group of men entered from all angles bearing automatic weapons. Suddenly the men opened fire, and the place was lit up like Christmas night.

Drug dealers scattered, running through the projects. Some were gunned down right there and others escaped. By the time the shooting was over, not a living soul was moving in the horseshoe drive of Edenwald. The place that used to be an open-air illicit drug mall, bustling with business had been completely shut down.

# The Past... The Present... The Future...

Chapter Thirty

That evening, the police were deployed in great numbers. All the task forces were united in a joint effort to search for and arrest Melquan. Residents were questioned and frisking young kids became part of the daily routine. Police had reintensified their efforts in the apprehension and arrest of Melquan.

Residents were under tight scrutiny and were agitated as cops crawled all over their business. The police were everywhere, in the halls, in the stairwells and around the project grounds.

Melquan was watching from the rooftop of the projects one night, when his cellphone rang loudly in the darkness. Melquan checked the caller ID and it was unknown. He put the phone away, but answered the call after the phone started ringing again.

"Melquan, what's up, my man?"

"Who da fuck is this?"

"It's Tommy, your friendly neighborhood detective, Melquan. You know what? You're a hard man to get a hold of."

"Yeah, what da fuck you doin' callin' me?"

"I wanted to tell you that you might as well turn yourself in, just so we can talk. We got your boy, Nashawn, and he doesn't speak too highly of you. Matter of fact, he fingered you to be the shooter of that poor little girl who was killed in the horseshoe. He said you did it over some type of drug feud. I know you don't want to take that rap, do you?"

Melquan speechlessly stared at the cellphone. His grip got tighter and he put the cellphone closer to his ear.

"Hello… You still there…?" The detective asked. "Do yourself a favor and come in. The longer you stay on the run, the worse it gets for you. You turn yourself and I promise, I'll get you a nice deal. I personally know the DA prosecuting this case. We can get this murder charge reduced to manslaughter. You'll serve a year or two and you're back on the block again. Melquan you have a clean record. I can get you a sweetheart-deal, and you don't have to worry, but you've got to turn yourself in first."

"A'ight, you might have gotten Nashawn with all that bullshit, but you ain't about to play me. You won't get me! I don't give a fuck what da lyin' nigga Nashawn said, he only a bitch ass and a snitch. And you can tell the DA that I ain't interested in none of his deals. Fuck all y'all!"

Melquan let the phone drop from the rooftop, and the instrument smashed in pieces against the pavement down below. The fugitive escaped using the rooftop.

The following day, Melquan cautiously crept to a public phone and made another call.

"Hello Precious, it's me, Melquan," he said. "I need you…"

Precious was happy to hear the call. It was the one she was expecting, and thought would never come. Melquan needed her. The idea hummed in her head, tickled her heart. She was very happy, making her way out the room. Later, Precious watched by a person sitting in a car, exited the Sousa woods.

She was carrying a duffel bag filled with money and clothing. The car pulled up, and Precious hopped in, smiling. She planted a kiss on Melquan's unshaven cheek and they drove away toward Interstate 95, heading south.

About an hour into their ride down the Turnpike, Melquan and Precious heard the sound of siren. A New Jersey State trooper's car accelerated behind them. Melquan's heart sunk to the bottom of his stomach.

His eyes darted from the rearview to the side mirrors, Precious held her breath. A young, black man on the run, Melquan maintained his speed. They breathe a collective sigh of relief when the State trooper flew by, and pulled over another motorist.

The couple was silent the rest of the ride. Each of them submerged deep in their own thoughts. Now that she had Melquan to herself, Precious was contemplating how different her life would be. Melquan's mind raced with thoughts of doing his thing when he reached Baltimore.

# HARDWHITE

SHANNON HOLMES

ANTHONY WHYTE

WHERE
**HIP-HOP**
**LITERATURE**
BEGINS...

**AUGUSTUS**
**PUBLISHING**

Augustus Publishing was created to unify minds with entertaining, hard-hitting tales from a hood near you. Hip Hop literature interprets contemporary times and connects to readers through shared language, culture and artistic expression. From street tales and erotica to coming-of age sagas, our stories are endearing, filled with drama, imagination and laced with a Hip Hop steez.

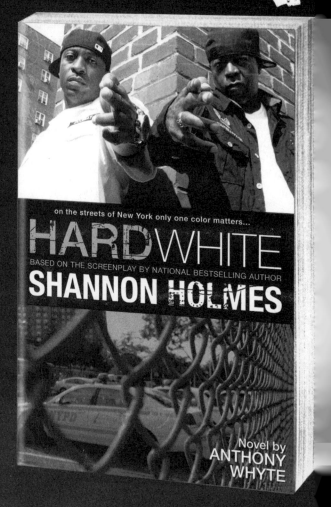

on the streets of New York only one color matters...

# HARDWHITE

BASED ON THE SCREENPLAY BY NATIONAL BESTSELLING AUTHOR

## SHANNON HOLMES

Novel by
ANTHONY
WHYTE

**Hard White:** On the street of New York only on color matters
Novel By Anthony Whyte Based on the screenplay by Shannon Holmes

The streets are pitch black...A different shade of darkness has drifted to the North Bronx
hood known as Edenwald. Sleepless nights, there is no escaping dishonesty, disrespect,
ignorance, hostility, treachery, violence, karma... Hard White metered out to the residents
quan and Precious have big dreams but must overcome much in order to manifest theirs.
the novel is a story of triumph and tribulations of two people's journey to make it despit
Nail biting drama you won't ever forget...Once you pick it up you can't put it down.  Deftly
Anthony Whyte based on the screenplay by Shannon Holmes, the story comes at you fas
offering an insight to what it takes to get off the streets. It shows a woman's unWlimited l
man. Precious is a rider and will do it all again for her man, Melquan... His love for the s
be bloodily severed. Her love for him will melt the coldest heart...Together their lives har
ously over the crucible of Hard White. Read the novel and see why they make the perf

### When Love Turns To Hate
By Sharron Doylee

Petie is back regulating from down south. He rides with a new ruthless partner, and they're all about making fast money. The partners mercilessly go after a shady associate who is caught in an FBI sting and threatens their road to riches. Petie and his two sons have grown apart. Renee, their mother, has to make a big decision when one of her sons wild-out. Desperately, she tries to keep her world from crumbling while holding onto what's left of her family. Venus fights for life after suffering a brutal physical attack. Share goes to great lengths to make sure her best friend's attacker stays ruined forever. Crazy entertaining and teeming with betrayal, corruption, and murder, *When Love Turns To Hate* is mixed with romance gone awry. The drama will leave you panting for more.

**Street Chic**
By Anthony Whyte

A new case comes across the desk of detective Sheryl Street, from the Dade county larceny squad in Miami. Pursuing the investigation she discovers that it threatens to unfold some details of her life she thought was left buried in the Washington Heights area of New York City. Her duties as detective pits her against a family that had emotionally destabilized her. Street ran away from a world she wanted nothing to do with. The murder of a friend brings her back as law and order. Surely as night time follows daylight, Street's forced into a resolve she cannot walk away from. Loyalty is tested when a deadly choice has to be made. When you read this dark and twisted novel you'll find out if allegiance to her family wins Street over. A most interesting moral conundrum exists in the dramatic tension that is Street Chic.

$14.95 / / 9780982541500

## SMUT central
By Brandon McCalla

Markus Johnson, so mysterious he barely knows who he is. An infant left at the doorstep of an orphanage. After fleeing his refuge, he was taken in by a couple with a perverse appetite for sexual indiscretions, only to become a star in the porn industry... Dr. Nancy Adler, a shrink who gained a peculiar patient, unlike any she has ever encountered. A young African American man who faints upon sight of a woman he has never met, having flashbacks of a past he never knew existed. A past that contradicts the few things he knows about himself... Sex and lust tangled in a web so disgustingly tantalizing and demented. Something evil, something demonic... Something beyond the far reaches of a porn stars mind, peculiar to a well established shrink, leaving an old NYPD detective on the verge of solving a case that has been a dead end for years... all triggered by desires for a mysterious woman...

$14.95 / / 9780982541586

## Dead And Stinkin'
By Stephen Hewett

Stephen Hewett Collection brings you love as crime. Timeless folklores of adventure, heroes and heroines suffering for love. Can deep unconditional love overcome any obstacles? What is ghetto love? One time loyal friends turned merciless enemies. Humorous and powerful Dead and Stinkin' is tragic and twisted folktales from author Stephen Hewett. The Stephen Hewett Collection comes alive with 3 intensely gripping short stories of undying love, coupled with modern day lies, deceit and treachery.

$14.95 / / 9780982541555

### Power of the P
By James Hendricks

Erotica at its gritty best, Power of the P is the seductive story of an entrepreneur who wields his powerful status in unimaginable — and sometimes unethical — ways. This exotic ride through the underworld of sex and prostitution in the hood explores how sex is leveraged to gain advantage over friends and rivals alike, and how sometimes the white collar world and the streets aren't as different as we thought they were.

$14.95 / / 9780982541579

### America's Soul
By Erick S Gray

Soul has just finished his 18-month sentence for a parole violation. Still in love with his son's mother, America, he wants nothing more than for them to become a family and move on from his past. But while Soul was in prison, America's music career started blowing up and she became entangled in a rocky relationship with a new man, Kendall. Kendall is determined to keep his woman by his side, and America finds herself caught in a tug of war between the two men. Soul turns his attention to battling the street life that landed him in jail — setting up a drug program to rid the community of its tortuous meth problem — but will Soul's efforts cross his former best friend, the murderous drug kingpin Omega?

$14.95 / / 9780982541548

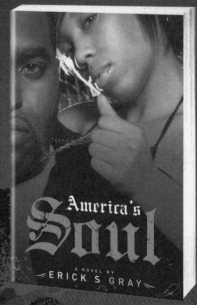

# GHETTO GIRLS IV

*Young Luv*

ESSENCE BESTSELLING AUTH
**ANTHONY WHYT**

**Ghetto Girls IV Young Luv**
$14.95 // 9780979281662

**Ghetto Girls**
$14.95 // 0975945319

**Ghetto Girls Too**
$14.95 // 0975945300

**Ghetto Girls 3 Soo H**
$14.95 // 0975945351

THE BEST OF THE STREET CHRONICLES TODAY, THE **GHETTO GIRLS SERIES** IS A WONDERFULLY HYPNOTIC ADVENTURE THAT DELVES INTO THE CONVOLUTED MINDS OF CRIMINALS AND THE DARK WORLD OF POLICE CORRUPTION. YET, THERE IS SOMETHING THRILLING AND SURPRISINGLY TENDER ABOUT THIS ONGOING YOUNG-ADULT SAGA FILLED WITH MAD FLAVA.

### Love and a Gangsta
author // **ERICK S GRAY**

This explosive sequel to **Crave All Lose All**. Soul and America were together ten years 'til Soul's incarceration for drugs. Faithfully, she waited four years for his return. Once home they find life ain't so easy anymore. America believes in holding her man down and expects Soul to be as committed. His lust for fast money rears its ugly head at the same time America's music career takes off. From shootouts, to hustling and thugging life, Soul and his man, Omega, have done it. Omega is on the come-up in the drug-game of South Jamaica, Queens. Using ties to a Mexican drug cartel, Omega has Queens in his grip. His older brother, Rahmel, was Soul's cellmate in an upstate prison. Rahmel, a man of God, tries to counsel Soul. Omega introduces New York to crystal meth. Misery loves company and on the road to the riches and spoils of the game, Omega wants the only man he can trust, Soul, with him. Love between Soul and America is tested by an unforgivable greed that leads quickly to deception and murder.

**$14.95 // 9780979281648**

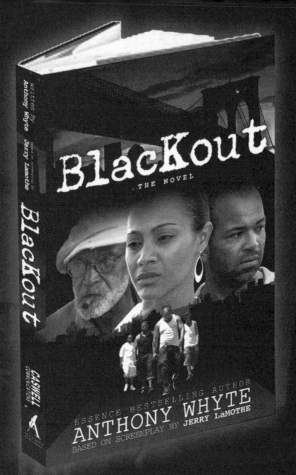

# The lights went out and the mayhem began.

It's gritty in the city but hotter in Brooklyn where a small community in east Flatbush must come to grips with its greatest threat, self-destruction. August 14 and 15, 2003, the eastern section of the United States is crippled by a major shortage of electrical power, the worst in US history. Blackout, the spellbinding novel is based on the epic motion picture, directed by Jerry Lamothe. A thoroughly riveting story with delectable details of families caught in a harsh 48 hours of random violent acts, exploding in deadly conflict. There's a message in everything... even the bullet. The author vividly places characters on the stage of life and like pieces on a chessboard, expertly moves them to a tumultuous end. Voila! Checkmate, a literary triumph. Blackout is a masterpiece. This heart-stopping, page-turning drama is moving fast. Blackout is destined to become an American classic.

# BASED ON SCREENPLAY BY JERRY LaMOTHE

## Inspired by true events

US $14.95  CAN $20.95
ISBN 978-0-9820653-0-3

**CASWELL**
COMMUNICATIONS

# A POWERFUL UNFORGIVING STORY

## CREATED BY HIP HOP LITERATURE'S BESTSELLING AUTHORS

THIS THREE-VOLUME KILLER STORY FEATURING FOREWORDS FROM
**SHANNON HOLMES, K'WAN & TREASURE BLUE**

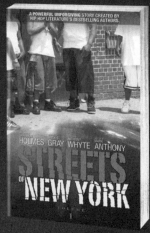 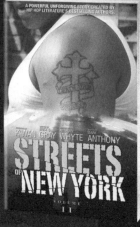 

**Streets of New York vol. 1**
$14.95 // 9780979281679

**Streets of New York vol. 2**
$14.95 // 9780979281662

**Streets of New York vol. 3**
$14.95 // 9780979281662

AN EXCITING, ENCHANTING... A FUNNY, THRILLING AND EXHILARATING
RIDE THROUGH THE ROUGH NEIGHBORHOODS OF THE GRITTY CITY. THE MOST FUN YOU
CAN LEGALLY HAVE WITHOUT ACTUALLY LIVING ON THE STREETS OF NEW YORK. READ
THE STORY FROM HIP HOP LITERATURE TOP AUTHORS:

# ERICK S. GRAY, MARK ANTHONY & ANTHONY WHYTE

## Lipstick Diaries Part 2
### A Provocative Look into the Female Perspective
Foreword by **WAHIDA CLARK**

Lipstick Diaries II is the second coming together of some of the most
unique, talented female writers of Hip Hop Literature. Featuring a
feast of short stories from today's top authors. **Genieva Borne, Came
Endy, Brooke Green, Kineisha Gayle, the queen of hip hop lit; Carol
McGill, Vanessa Martir, Princess Madison, Keisha Seignious**, and a
blistering foreword served up by the queen of thug love; Ms. **Wahida
Clark**. Lipstick Diaries II pulls no punches, there are no bars hold
leaves no metaphor unturned. The anthology delivers a knockout wit
stories of pain and passion, love and virtue, profit and gain, ... all told
with flair from the women's perspective. Lipstick Diaries II is a
must-read for all.

**$14.95** // 9780979281655

Hated by many, loved by few,
yet respected by all...

A **SHANNON HOLMES** FILM

# EDENWALD PROJECTS

DVD
VIDEO

The **Edenwald projects documentary** chronicles life inside the second biggest Housing project in New York City. Come journey into this urban maze, of 40 brownish-red brick buildings, a place where outsiders dare to venture. For some residents it's a danger zone for others a safe haven simply put home. Witness a mother's worst nightmare materialize. Explore some of the biggest misconceptions about the projects both dispelled and confirmed.

Understand why Edenwald projects is a place where poverty, hopelessness and ignorance could set in at any moment to create a murderous climate. See for yourself why Edenwald is a place that seldom offers happy endings, success stories are few and far between. Why on any given day here could be your last.